Praise for the novels of Delores Fossen

"This is a feel good, heartwarming story of love, family and happy endings for all."
  —*Harlequin Junkie* on *Christmas at Colts Creek*

"An entertaining and satisfying read...that I can highly recommend." —*Books & Spoons* on *Wild Nights in Texas*

"The plot delivers just the right amount of emotional punch and happily ever after."
  —*Publishers Weekly* on *Lone Star Christmas*

"Delores Fossen takes you on a wild Texas ride with a hot cowboy."
  —B.J. Daniels, *New York Times* bestselling author

"Clear off space on your keeper shelf, Fossen has arrived."
  —Lori Wilde, *New York Times* bestselling author

"This is classic Delores Fossen and a great read."
  —*Harlequin Junkie* on *His Brand of Justice*

"This book is a great start to the series. Looks like there's plenty of good reading ahead."
  —*Harlequin Junkie* on *Tangled Up in Texas*

"An amazing, breathtaking and vastly entertaining family saga, filled with twists and unexpected turns. Cowboy fiction at its best." —*Books & Spoons* on *The Last Rodeo*

DELORES FOSSEN

HEART LIKE A COWBOY

CANARY STREET PRESS

CANARY
STREET
PRESS™

Recycling programs
for this product may
not exist in your area.

ISBN-13: 978-1-335-00948-7

Heart Like a Cowboy

Canary Street Press
22 Adelaide St. West, 41st Floor
Toronto, Ontario M5H 4E3, Canada
CanaryStPress.com

Printed in U.S.A.

HEART
LIKE A COWBOY

CHAPTER ONE

THAT WHOLE DEAL about bad news coming in threes? Well, it was a crock. Lieutenant Colonel Egan Donnelly now had proof of it.

First, there'd been the unexpected visitor, AKA the messenger, who'd started the whole bad-news ball rolling. That'd teach him to open his frickin' door before he'd even finished his frickin' coffee.

Then, there was the so-called celebration that would stir up the worst of his past and serve it up to him on a silver platter. Or rather on a disposable paper plate, anyway.

Then, a letter from his ex, which he figured was never a good sign. Who the heck actually wanted to hear from their cheating ex? Not him, that was for sure.

Those were the three things—count them: one, two, three—that was supposed to have been the final tally of bad crap even if for only a day, but apparently the creator of that old saying had no credibility whatsoever. Then again, Egan had known firsthand that bad news didn't have limited quantities.

Or expiration dates.

Now he was faced with ironclad confirmation that

those other three things were piddly-ass drops in the proverbial bucket compared to bad-news number four.

And now, everything in his world was crashing and burning.

Again.

Thirty Minutes Earlier

IN THE DREAM, Lieutenant Colonel Egan Donnelly saved his best friend's life. In the dream, the explosion didn't happen. It didn't blast through the scorched, airless night. Didn't tear apart the transport vehicle.

Didn't leave blood on the bleached sand.

Didn't kill.

In the dream, Egan was the hero that so many people proclaimed he was. He made just the right decisions to save everyone, including Jack. *Especially Jack.*

Egan didn't fight tooth and nail to come out of this dream—unlike the ones that were basically a blow-by-blow account of what had actually happened that god-awful night nearly three years ago. Those dreams were pits of the darkest level of hell where everything spun and bashed, stomping him down deeper and deeper into the real nightmare. Those dreams he fought.

Had to.

Because Egan had learned the hard way if he let those dreams play out, then it was a damn hard struggle to come back from them. Heck, he was still trying to come back from them.

Despite wanting to linger in this particular dream

where he got to play hero, it didn't happen, thanks to his phone dinging with a text. He frowned, noticing that it was barely six in the morning. Texts at this hour usually were not good. Considering that all three of his siblings were on active duty, *not good* could be really bad.

He saw his father's name on the screen, and the worry instantly tightened Egan's gut. His dad had just turned sixty so while he wasn't in the "one foot in the grave" stage, he wasn't the proverbial spring chicken, either. Added to that, his dad still ran the day-to-day operation of Saddlebrook, the family's ranch in Emerald Creek, Texas. The ranch that'd been in the Donnelly family for over a hundred years and had grown and grown and grown with each succeeding generation. All that growth required hours of upkeep and work.

Found this when I was going through some old photo albums, his dad had texted.

What the heck? That gut tightness eased up, some, when Egan saw it was a slightly off-center image taken in front of the main barn on the ranch. His dad had obviously used his phone to take a picture of the old photo. Emphasis on *old*.

It was a shot that his grandmother, Effie, had snapped thirty years ago on Egan's eighth birthday. His brother, Cal, would have been six. His sister, Remi, a two-year-old toddler, and his other brother, Blue, was just four. Stairsteps, people called them, since they'd all been born just two years apart.

In the photo, his dad, looking lean, fit and young,

was in the center, flanked by Egan and Remi on the right, and Cal and Blue on the left. Remi and Blue were both grinning big toothy grins. Cal and Egan weren't. Probably because they'd been old enough to understand that life as they'd known it was over.

Their lives hadn't exactly gone to hell in a hand-basket, but this particular shot had been taken only a couple of weeks after their mother had died from cancer. A long agonizing death that had left their dad the widower of four young kids. Still, his dad was eking out a smile in the picture, and he'd managed to gather all four of them in his outstretched arms.

Bittersweet times.

That's when their mom's mom, Grammy Effie, had come to Saddlebrook for what was supposed to have been a couple of months, until his dad got his footing. Effie was still living on the ranch thirty years later and had obviously put down roots as deep as his father's.

Egan was wondering what had prompted his dad to go digging through old family albums when his phone dinged again. It was another text from his dad, another photo. It was an image that Egan also knew well, and he mentally referred to it as the start of phase two of his life.

The first phase had been with a loving mother that sadly he now couldn't even remember. That had ended with her death. Phase two had begun when his dad had gotten remarried four years later to a young fresh-faced Captain Audrey Granger, who'd then been stationed at the very base in San Antonio where Egan was now. It was an hour's commute to the ranch that Audrey had diligently made.

For a while, anyway.

In this shot, his dad and new bride dressed in blue were in the center, and both were flashing giddy smiles. Ditto for Remi and Blue. Again, no smiles for Cal and Egan since they'd been ten and twelve respectively and were no doubt holding back on the glee to see how life with their stepmom would all play out.

It hadn't played out especially well.

But then, it also hadn't hit anywhere near the "hell in a handbasket" mark, either.

If there'd been a family photo taken just two years later, though, Audrey probably wouldn't have been in it. By then, she'd been in Germany. Or maybe England. Instead of an hour commute, she'd come "home" to the ranch a couple of times a year. Then, as her career had blossomed, the visits had gotten further and further apart. These days, Brigadier General Audrey Donnelly only came home on Christmas. If that.

Egan sent his dad a thumbs-up emoji to let him know he'd seen the pictures, and he was considering an actual reply to ask if all was well, but his alarm went off. He got up, mentally going through his schedule for the day. As the commander of the Fighter Training Squadron at Randolph AFB, Texas, there'd be the usual paperwork, going over some stats for the pilots in training, and then in the afternoon, he'd get to do one of the things he loved most.

Fly.

Of course, it would be under the guise of a training mission in the T-38C Talon jet, not the F-16 that Egan used to pilot, but it would still give him that hit of adrenaline. Still give him the reminder of why he'd first joined the Navy and then had transferred to the Air Force so he could continue to stay in the cockpit.

Egan showered, put on his flight suit, read through his emails on his phone and was about halfway through his first cup of coffee when his doorbell rang. He had the same reaction to it as he had the earlier text. A punch of dread that something was wrong. It wasn't even seven o'clock yet and hardly the time for visitors. Especially since he lived in base housing and therefore wasn't on the traditional beaten path for friends or family to just drop by.

Frowning, he went to the door. And Egan frowned some more when he looked through the peephole at the visitor on his porch. A woman with pulled back dark blond hair and vivid green eyes. At first glance, he thought it was his ex-wife, Colleen, someone he definitely didn't want to see, but this was a slightly younger, taller version of the woman who'd left him for another man.

Alana Davidson, Colleen's sister.

"Yes, I know it's early," Alana sighed and said loud enough for him to hear while she looked directly at the peephole. "Sorry about that."

Wondering what the heck this was all about, he opened the door and got an immediate blast of heat. Texas in June started out hot as hell and got even hotter. Today was apparently no exception. He also got another immediate blast of concern because there was nothing about Alana's expression that indicated this was a social visit.

Then again, Alana and he never had social visits. Never.

Just too much old baggage, old wounds and old everything else between them. Ironic, since she'd been married to his best friend. Now, she was his dead best friend's widow and bore that strong resemblance to his cheating ex-wife who'd left him just days before Jack's death.

Egan was no doubt an unwelcome sight for her, too. He was the man who'd not only failed to keep her husband alive, but he was also the reason Jack had been in that transport vehicle in the first place.

So, yeah, old baggage galore.

"Sorry," Alana repeated, looking up at him. Not looking at him for long, though. Like their avoidance of social visits, they didn't do a lot of eye contact, either. "But I have an appointment at the base hospital in an hour, and I wanted to catch you before you went into work."

"The hospital?" he automatically questioned.

She waved it off, clearly picking up on his concern that something might be medically wrong with her. "I'm consulting with a colleague on a chief master sergeant who's being medically retired and moving to Emerald Creek. I'll be working with the chief to come up with some lifestyle changes."

Alana made that seem like her norm, and maybe it was. She was a dietitian, and because as Jack's widow she still had a military ID card so she wouldn't have had any trouble getting onto the base. Added to that, Emerald Creek was a haven for retirees and veterans since it was so close to three large military installations. There were almost as many combat boots as cowboy boots in Emerald Creek.

"How'd you know where I live?" he asked.

"I got your address from your grandmother." She glanced over her shoulder at the street of houses. "I occasionally have consults here, but it's the first time I've been to this part of the base."

Yeah, his particular house wasn't near the hospital, commissary or base exchange store where Alana would be more apt to go. Added to that, Jack had never been stationed here, which meant Alana had never lived here, either.

"Full disclosure," she said the moment he shut the door. "You aren't going to like any of what I have to say."

Now it was Egan who sighed and braced himself for Alana to finally do something he'd expected her to do for three years. Scream and yell at him for allowing Jack to die. But there was no raised voice or obvious surge of anger. Instead, she took out a piece of paper from her sizeable handbag and thrust it at him.

"It's a mock-up of a flyer that Jack's mom intends to have printed up and sent to everyone in her known universe," Alana explained.

At first glance, he saw that the edges of the flyer had little pictures of barbecue grills, fireworks, the

American flag and military insignia. Egan intended to just scan it to get the gist of what it was about, but the scanning came to a stumbling slow crawl as he tried to take in what he was reading.

"Join us for a Life Celebration for Major Jack Connor Davidson, July Fourth, at the Emerald Creek City Park. It'll be an afternoon of food, festivities and remembrance as a celebratory memorial painting for Jack will be unveiled by our own Top Gun hometown hero, Lieutenant Colonel Egan Donnelly."

Well, hell. Both sentences were full-on gut punches and thick gobs of emotional baggage. Memorial. Life celebration. Remembrances. The icing on that gob was the last part.

Top Gun hometown hero.

Egan was, indeed, a former Top Gun. He'd won the competition a dozen years ago when he'd been a navy lieutenant flying F-16s. The hometown part was accurate, too, since he'd been born and raised in Emerald Creek, but that *hero* was the biggest of big-assed lies.

"I can't go," Egan heard himself say once he'd managed to clear the lump in his throat.

She nodded as if that were the exact answer she'd expected. "I'm guessing you'll be on duty?"

He'd make damn sure he was, but wasn't it ironic that the memorial celebration would fall on the one weekend of the month he usually went home to help his dad on the family ranch? Maybe Jack's mom knew that, or maybe the woman just believed that such an event would be a good fit for the Fourth of July.

It wasn't.

Barbecue, hot dogs, beer and such didn't go well with the crapload of memories something like that would stir. He didn't need a memorial or a life celebration to remember Jack. Egan remembered him daily, hourly even, and after three years, the grief and guilt hadn't lost any steam.

"I'll let Tilly know you can't be there," Alana said, referring to Jack's mother. "She's mentioned contacting your stepmom to see if she could be there for the unveiling."

"Good luck with that," he muttered, and Alana's sound of agreement confirmed that she understood it was a long shot.

What would likely end up happening was that his brother Cal would get roped into doing the "honors." He'd known Jack, and Cal's need to do the right thing would have him stepping in.

"The last time I ran into Tilly, she didn't want to discuss anything involving Jack's death," Egan recalled.

Alana nodded. "That's still true. Nothing about how he died, et cetera. She only wants to chat about the things he did when he was alive."

"So, why do a *memorial* painting?" Egan wanted to know.

"I'm not sure, but it's possible the painting will be another life celebration deal that she'll want hung in some prominent part of town like city hall or the library. In other words, maybe the painting will have nothing to do with Jack even being in the military.

Tilly was proud of him," she quickly added. "But she's never fully wrapped her mind around losing him."

That made sense. The one time he'd tried to talk to her about Jack's death, she'd shut him down. As if not talking about his death would somehow breathe some life back into him.

"There's one more thing," Alana went on, and this time she took a pale yellow envelope from her purse and handed it to him. "It's a letter from Colleen."

Egan had already reached for it but yanked back his hand as if the envelope were a coiled rattler ready to sink its fangs into his flesh. The mention of his ex-wife tended to do that. Memories of Colleen didn't fall into the "hell on steroids" category like Jack's. More like the "don't let the door hit your cheating ass" category. Colleen had obviously liked that direction just fine since she hadn't spoken a word to him since the divorce.

He glanced at the envelope, scowled. "A letter? Is it some kind of twelve-step deal about making amends or something?" he asked.

Alana shook her head. "No, I think it's a living will of sorts."

That erased his scowl. "Is Colleen dying?"

"Not that I know of, but she apparently decided she wanted to make her last wishes known. She sent letters for me, our aunt and your dad. I have his if you want to give it to him."

Egan reached out again to stop her from retrieving it, and Alana used the opportunity to put the letter for him in his hand. "I don't want this," he insisted.

"Totally understand. I read mine," she admitted. "Along with spelling out her end-of-life wishes—cremation, no funeral, no headstone—she wants us to have some sister time, like a vacation or something."

Egan had no idea how much contact Alana and Colleen had with each other these days, but it was possible when Colleen had walked out on him, she'd also walked out on Alana. He thought he detected some animosity in Alana's tone and expression.

He went straight to the trash can in the adjoining kitchen and tossed the envelope on top of the oozing heap of the sticky chicken rice bowl that had been at least a week past its prime when he'd dumped it the night before.

"I'm not interested in wife time with her," he muttered, knowing he sounded bitter and hating that he still was.

Unlike what he was still going through with Jack, though, his grief and anger with Colleen had trickled down to almost nothing. *Almost*. He now just considered her a mistake and was glad she was out of his life. Some days, he could even hope that she was happy with the Mr. Wonderful artist that she'd left him for.

When he turned back to Alana, he saw she had watched the letter trashing, and she was now combing those jeweled green eyes over his face as if trying to suss out what was going on in his head. Egan decided to diffuse that with a question that fell into the polite small talk that would have happened had this been a normal visit.

"Uh, how are you doing?" he asked. On the surface, that didn't seem to be a safe area of conversation since it could lead to that screaming rant over his huge part in her husband's death. But Egan realized he would welcome the rant.

Because he deserved it.

Alana took a deep breath. "Well, despite nearly everyone in town deciding I should live out the rest of my life as a widow, I've started dating again."

That got his attention. Not because he hadn't known about the town's feelings. And not because he believed she shouldn't have a second chance at romance. But Egan had thought she didn't want such a chance, that she was still as buried in the past as he was. Apparently not.

"I'm only doing virtual dating for now," she went on, not sounding especially thrilled with that. "Last week, I had a virtual date with a guy who has six goats and eleven chickens in his one-bedroom apartment in Houston."

Egan didn't especially want to smile, but he did, anyway. "Sounds like a prize catch. You'd never have to buy eggs again. Or fertilizer."

She shrugged. "He was a prize compared to the one I had the week before. Within the first minute of conversation, he wanted to know the circumference of my nipples." Alana stopped, her eyes widening as if she hadn't expected to share that.

Egan smiled again, but this one was forced. He

hadn't wanted Alana to think he was shocked or of-
fended, though he was indeed shocked. He'd never
considered nipple size one way or another.

He'd especially never considered anything about
Alana's nipples.

And he hated that was now in his head. That kind
of stuff could mess with things that already had a
shaky status quo.

"Dating at thirty-five isn't as much a 'fish in the
sea' situation as it is more of a, uh, well, swamp,"
Alana explained. "Think scaly critters, slithery, that
sort of thing, with the potential and hope that some
actual fish lingering about will eventually come out
of hiding."

That didn't sound appealing at all, but then he
hadn't had to hit any of the dating sites. He could
thank the eternal string of matchmakers for that.
Unlike the widowed Alana, apparently everyone
thought a divorced guy in his thirties shouldn't be
solo. Especially a guy who'd had his "heart broken"
when his wife had walked out on him right before
his best friend had been killed.

"How about you?" she asked, clearly aiming for
a change of subject and her own shot at small talk.
"Have you jumped into dating waters?"

He shook his head. "Too busy."

She broke their unwritten rule by locking her gaze
with his for a second or two. "Yeah. Busy," she repeated. And it sounded as if that were code for a
whole bunch of things. For instance, wounded. Damaged. Guarded. Guilty.

All of the above applied to him.

It was hard for Egan to think about his happiness when he'd robbed Jack of his. *Busy*, though, was a much safer term for it.

"Well, I gotta go," Alana said when the silence turned awkward, as it always did between them. "I'll let Tilly know you won't be at the life celebration so she can find someone else to do the unveiling."

Egan frowned when a thought occurred to him. "She won't ask you to do it, will she?" Because he couldn't imagine that it'd be any easier for Alana than it would be for him.

"No." Another sigh went with that. "Tilly still has me firmly in the 'grieving widow' category, which apparently will preclude me from lifting a veil on a painting and doing other things such as dating or appearing too happy when I'm in public."

He wanted to ask, *Aren't you still a grieving widow?* But that would go well beyond small talk. It could lead to an actual conversation that would drag feelings and emotions to the surface. No way did he want to deal with that.

Obviously, Alana wasn't on board for such a chat, either, because she headed for the door, giving him a forced smile and a quick glance before she left and went to her car. Egan watched her, doling out his own forced smile and what had to be a stupid-looking wave.

Since he didn't want to stand around and think about this visit, Colleen's trashed letter—or Alana's nipples—he grabbed his flight cap and keys so he could go to his truck. He barely made it a step, though, before his phone dinged with another text.

Great. Another photo trip down memory lane.

But it wasn't.

It was his father's name on the screen, but there was no picture. Only six words that sent Egan's heart to his knees.

Get to Emerald Creek Hospital now.

CHAPTER TWO

ON THE DRIVE back from the base, Alana used the recorder on her phone to dictate her observations from the consultation she'd just had. Notes that included things like fully loaded bacon cheeseburgers and "seven hundred calories a pop" Dairy Queen Peanut Buster Parfaits.

Her stomach growled.

Being a dietitian/nutritionist didn't make her have a magical resistance for such foods or give her cravings for all things good for the body, but her growling tummy wasn't going to get its way on this.

Not today, anyway.

But she frowned because now she was craving a blasted Peanut Buster Parfait.

Alana forced herself to tune back into dictating her notes, which sadly meant mentioning other foods that the retiring chief master sergeant was going to have to cut back on. Honey-barbecued ribs, slabs of cherry cheesecake and deluxe hot fudge sundaes that, according to the base dietitian, were on the sergeant's menu multiple times a week.

She'd have to figure out a way to convince the chief that those particular meal choices didn't play nice with his potentially deadly hypertension, sky-high cholesterol and Type 2 diabetes. She would give him the gentle lecture, dotted with some lighthearted foodie humor, so that he wouldn't tuck tail and run when she laid out that there had to be some serious changes if he wanted to live past the age of forty-five.

Ironic, since that *serious changes* part sort of applied to her, too. Not the food selections, though, but rather for her late husband. She loved Jack. God, she loved him. She had married him, made plans to have a family with him, and he'd died in an IED explosion twelve thousand, four hundred and thirty-six miles from home. From her.

It had taken months and months just for Jack's death to really sink in. Even longer for her to grasp that what she felt about his life and death wasn't going away. That nasty mix of so many emotions. The love glopped together with, well, the rest of it.

The worst of it.

She had no doubts, none, that Egan was metaphorically chowing down on that particular gloppy dish as well. She had seen it in his face earlier today, and it was as strong and raw as it had been three years ago when they'd stood over Jack's grave in the pouring rain while his coffin had been lowered into the ground.

Once, before the emotional glop, Egan and she would have greeted each other with real smiles. Real warmth. Real everything since they'd both loved Jack. But the realness was gone, replaced by...

She wasn't sure exactly what.

Definitely some awkwardness. Then, there was some girded loins and walking on eggshells. There was that "never going to heal" wound in his eyes that she was certain was mirrored in hers. On those rare occasions when they saw each other, that was the norm now.

Too bad nipple circumference was also in the proverbial mix.

She groaned, cursing herself for blurting that out. It was the sort of thing to joke about with girl pals and close siblings. Not with her dead husband's best friend.

Alana took the final turn to Emerald Creek just as her phone rang, and she groaned again when she saw the caller. Tilly, Jack's mom. She answered it, of course, on speaker. Well, she answered it after she took a deep breath. Girded loins and yes, even some walking on eggshells were standard operating procedure for Tilly, too, because her former mother-in-law was a reminder of Jack.

"Tilly," she greeted, trying to make her voice seem as if she weren't dreading this call.

"Well, did you talk to Egan?" Tilly immediately asked.

"I did, and unfortunately, he has to work the day of the life celebration. He won't be able to attend."

The sound that Tilly made was of disappointment, and it came through loud and clear. "Oh, I'm so sorry." She paused a moment. "Maybe I can try to call his stepmom and see if she can arrange to get him the day off."

"No," Alana couldn't say fast enough.

Then, she had to come up with something else that wouldn't spell out that Egan likely didn't *have* to work but would choose to do that so he wouldn't have to put himself through what was essentially a sad, horrible trip down memory lane.

"Audrey's not in Egan's chain of command," Alana tried. "And besides, he wouldn't want that kind of special treatment. It wouldn't play well with the morale in his squadron."

Alana couldn't swear on a Bible any part of that was the gospel truth, but she thought that was probably how Egan would feel. She was already on the hot seat for this life celebration, no way around that. She'd be front and center in attendance so that everyone could get a gander at the hero's widow. However, she couldn't blame Egan for wanting to spare himself.

Tilly made another sound, this time of mild agreement over the "chain of command and morale" argument. "All right, then I'll just talk to Egan myself and see if I can convince him to rearrange his schedule. Or maybe I'll ask him for the dates he's available and change the life celebration to whatever works for him. I want him to do it since he'll have a lot of funny stories to tell about when Jack and he were kids."

Alana nearly tried to talk her out of that as well, but she decided to let Egan deal with it. He could probably do a better job of saying no than she could. "He'll be at work now so you'll likely have to wait until tonight to call him."

"Will do," Tilly agreed. She paused again. "Uh, how did your visit go with him?"

"Okay," Alana settled for saying. Sheesh, she couldn't get more wishy-washy than that.

"It's been a while since you've seen Egan so I suspect you two did some catching up on what's going on in your lives?" Tilly pressed.

"Some." All right, so wishy-washy was going up a notch, after all. "Egan seems busy," she added. *And bitter-ish*, Alana mentally tacked on to that when she remembered him tossing Colleen's letter. Heck, she was bitter-ish about the letter, too. "He asked how I've been, and I told him about the virtual dating."

Silence for a couple of moments from Tilly. "How's that going?" asked in the same tone of someone questioning a toddler who'd just made an unwise choice to eat an entire sleeve of Oreos.

"Badly," Alana admitted, and she made darn sure not to blurt out anything to do with nipples.

"Obviously, that means you're not ready to move on," Tilly promptly concluded.

That was highly possible, but Alana was afraid that might always be the truth. That she might never be ready, that moving on could never happen. And that she'd live the next fifty years as Jack's widow. Not exactly comforting thoughts. Especially since the first three years as his widow had taken her to hell and back.

Repeatedly.

"Possibly," Alana answered, and she was thankful when she took the turn into the hospital parking lot. "I'm back in Emerald Creek now and need to get some work done, but please let me know how your conversation goes with Egan."

Tilly assured her that she would, and they ended the call. Alana pushed aside the dread of another chat with Jack's mom, and she parked so she could head into her office that was located inside the hospital where there was a small wing of clinics.

Of course, *small* was the operative word to pretty much everything in Emerald Creek. Unless it applied to ranches and acres of pastures, that is. But no one would argue that the hospital itself, and therefore her office, was anything but small.

Gathering up her purse and phone, Alana went through the ER entrance since it was the shorter route to her office. She didn't have any clients coming in for another two hours, and that would give her time to finish up her file on the chief master sergeant so she could then set up their first appointment. However, that plan immediately went south when she spotted the elderly woman sitting in one of the chairs in the waiting area of the emergency room.

Effie McKinsey, Egan's grandmother.

Alana got an immediate punch of dread and gave the woman the once-over to see if she was hurt and waiting for medical attention. No visible injuries, but based on her hunched shoulders and drawn expression, something was clearly wrong.

Alana shifted her purse to her shoulder and walked toward her. That's when she spotted Egan, too, on the other side of the room by the nurses' station. He was still in his flight suit that he'd been wearing nearly two hours earlier, and he had his phone pressed to his ear while he talked. And paced. Alana couldn't hear what he was saying, but like his Grammy Effie, everything about his body language confirmed her "something was wrong" theory.

"What happened?" Alana asked the woman, and her first thoughts flew in a bad direction. That maybe one of Egan's siblings had been hurt. Or worse.

Mercy, please don't let it be that.

One by one, the images of his brothers and sister spun through Alana's head. All of them in uniform. All of them in high-risk, often dangerous positions what with Cal and Blue being fighter pilots and Remi being in special ops. Losing one of them would crush Egan to the bone. Again. Alana wasn't sure his bones could stand any more crushing.

Effie managed to steel up her expression a little, and she patted the chair next to her, indicating for Alana to sit. She did.

"It's Derek, Egan's dad," Effie said. "I found him on the floor in his office at the ranch. He'd fallen or something and wasn't conscious." Her voice trembled, and Alana automatically put an arm around her. That's when she saw something else.

Blood smears on the front of the woman's shirt.

Alana nearly fired off a bunch of questions to ask what'd happened and what Derek's condition was, but she held back, giving Effie the time the woman clearly needed to do more of that steeling up.

"Derek's head was bleeding. I guess he hit it when

he fell. Anyway, his cell phone was on the floor next to him," Effie went on, "so I called 911 right away. Then, I sent a text to Egan to tell him to get here."

That must have happened shortly after Alana had left his house. Too bad she hadn't stayed a little longer, and then she could have taken him to Emerald Creek. She couldn't imagine that he'd been in the right frame of mind to get behind the wheel, especially since she'd already hit him with the bad news about the life celebration and Colleen's letter.

Effie drew in a long breath. "Egan's calling his brothers and sister while we're waiting for the doctor to tell us what happened." Her voice cracked, and she pressed her trembling fingers to her mouth for a moment before her weary eyes met Alana's. "You work here. Maybe if you ask, they'll tell you what happened to Derek."

Alana nodded, stood, though she wasn't holding out any hope of getting that kind of intel. Yes, she worked there, but normally emergency medical personnel kept info close to the vest until they had confirmation of the problem. Even then, they'd want the attending doctor to tell the family first.

Alana glanced at Egan who was still on the phone, still pacing, so she gave him a wide berth and made her way to the nurses' station. Of course, she knew the nurse on duty, Dalton Reeves. It was that small-town thing again where there wasn't anything close to six degrees of separation or even three. It was usually just one, and in this case, Dalton and she had been in the same classes from pre-K all the way through to their senior year.

"I don't know anything about Mr. Donnelly," Dalton said right off the bat, obviously well aware of what she'd been about to ask.

Alana recalled that one degree of separation hadn't exactly created a friendship between Dalton and her, but he hadn't snapped out his response. It's semi-sharp tone seemed to be generated by frustration. Yet another effect of a small town since after all, Dalton knew Egan and his father as well. Added to that, she'd heard Dalton was a darn good nurse so he'd probably want to be able to dole out something to help the family. Or in her case, the former wife of a former friend of the family.

Dalton sighed, leaned in and lowered his voice. "Mr. Donnelly was unconscious when they brought him in. Dr. Abrams is with him in ICU."

Despite the skimpy account, that was somewhat of a relief. Dr. Abe Abrams—yes, his parents had actually given him that name—was one of the most experienced doctors on staff. Derek was in good hands. Hopefully, hands that would fix whatever the heck was wrong with him.

Alana didn't press Dalton to speculate as to what was wrong or a prognosis, but she'd worked around medical staff long enough to know that many things could cause a sixty-something-year-old man to fall and lose consciousness. Of course, none of those causes was especially good, but maybe it would turn out to be an easy fix, like medication to relieve a quick drop in blood pressure or glucose to increase too low blood sugar.

She turned to step away from the nurses' station to go back to Effie, and Alana practically ran smack dab into Egan.

"Anything?" Egan demanded, managing to sound both like a commander in charge and a worried son at the same time when he aimed that question at Dalton.

Dalton shook his head. "Dr. Abrams will be out to talk to you as soon as humanly possible."

Judging from the combo huff-sigh that Egan made, it wasn't the first time he'd gotten that response from Dalton. Still, Dalton didn't balk. "I'll see if I can find out anything," the nurse finally muttered. "Take a seat, and if I get anything, I'll let you know."

Alana took Egan by the arm to get him moving back toward his grandmother. A super slow walk since she wanted her own updates.

"Were you able to get in touch with your siblings?" she asked.

"Cal and Blue, yes. Remi can't be reached so I had to leave a message with her commander."

Alana rifled back through the talk she'd heard about the heroic Donnelly siblings and recalled that Cal was stationed in South Carolina, and Blue was in California. Remi was an Air Force combat Rescue Officer, CRO, as Jack had been, and last Alana had heard, she was on deployment somewhere in the Middle East.

"What can I do to help?" she asked.

He opened his mouth, closed it and shook his

head. His gaze fell on his grandmother. "She might need some water or something."

Alana would have gladly offered that to Effie if the ER doors hadn't opened, and two women hadn't come rushing in. The Betterton sisters, Jane and Annie, who were Effie's longtime friends, and the ranch's equally longtime cook, Maybell Warner. They'd obviously heard about Derek being at the hospital because they rushed toward Effie, pulling her into their arms.

Egan must have decided to give them some time to help settle Effie because he stopped while Alana and he were a good fifteen feet away.

"I knew something was wrong," Egan muttered. "He sent me two old pictures early this morning."

It took Alana a moment to shift gears and realize he was talking about his father. "What kind of pictures?"

"Of when I was a kid. One was of that birthday right after my mom died."

She knew about that one. Or rather she knew about the occasion. Alana had only been five and hadn't been invited to the get-together, but Jack had gone, and years later, after Jack's death, Tilly had shared photos of it with Alana.

"Dad sent me another picture taken of all of us right after he married Audrey," Egan added.

That got her attention. "Does Audrey know your dad's in the hospital?"

"I left a message with her assistant's assistant. There might be a third assistant in that job title," he muttered not with the bitter-ish tone he'd had for Colleen's letter. This was more of an annoyance at a time when he just couldn't deal with anything that didn't relate directly to his father's condition.

"I could try to contact Audrey if you want," Alana offered. "I might be able to talk my way through the line of assistants."

Egan quickly waved that off and muttered some more profanity under his breath. "The point is I should have known something was wrong when he texted those pictures. He's never done anything like that before. *Never*. And I thought…" He paused, did more cursing. "Well, I thought maybe he was depressed or something."

That got her attention, too. "Has your dad shown any signs of depression before?"

"No." Another pause. "Maybe," Egan amended. "How the hell would I even know? I mean, I got stationed here in Texas so I'd be closer to him, and I see him less than twelve hours a month. I come out to the ranch, fix whatever the hell I can fix, have dinner with him, and the next morning, I get up early and head back to the base so I can start the cycle all over again."

Alana figured no words of comfort would fix this, and she was fully prepared to let Egan go on and on. That's why she stunned herself when she blurted out, "One point two inches."

That stopped him, and after he noticeably blinked, Egan stared at her.

"That's the circumference of my right nipple," she

supplied. "Which is on the small side, FYI. I was curious and measured after I ended my virtual date."

He just kept staring, but Alana saw some of the raging guilt and worry ease up a bit. Egan released one long breath that seemed to have been pent-up for the past hour or so. But he didn't respond. Didn't have time. Because at that exact moment, Dr. Abrams came walking into the waiting room, and Dalton was right behind him.

Effie and her companions stood, all hurrying toward the doctor and joining Egan at his side.

"It's not good," Dr. Abrams said right off. "Derek had a massive heart attack, and he was put in ICU. We're still trying to stabilize him. Trying," he emphasized. "Derek's not out of the woods yet."

That stunned them to silence. Everyone but Effie, that is.

"Will he…" Effie started but had to stop. "Will Derek be okay?"

"We'll know soon," the doctor answered. "All of you just sit tight, and the moment I have answers, I'll come back out."

That was it, no more from Dr. Abrams. He just turned and left. None of them stopped him, of course. Right now, he needed to be with Derek while Egan and Effie tried to deal with that *it's not good*.

Distraction talk about nipples wasn't going to fix this, but since Egan didn't look very steady on his feet, Alana led him to a chair and had him sit. Effie's friends did the same for her on the row of seats behind them.

"I'll get some water," Dalton offered. "Anyone want any coffee?"

They all conveyed a no through headshakes, murmurs and waves of their hands. None of them would want the water, either, but that didn't stop Dalton from going to the small fridge in the nurses' station and coming back with bottles for all of them.

Egan took the bottle offered to him but didn't open it. "Shit," he ground out. Groaning, he put his hand to one side of his head, the bottle to the other, and he pressed hard. "This is my fault."

Alana didn't bother to argue with him even though she seriously doubted he'd been the cause of his father's heart attack. Lots of factors could go into that. She knew because she often worked with recovering heart attack patients to help them adjust their diet if that had, indeed, been a contributing factor.

"I don't think I can do this again," Egan said, his voice a hoarse whisper.

She didn't believe he was actually talking to her, but Alana heard the bone-deep emotion in each word. And knew he wasn't just talking about his dad. This was about watching his mom die.

And Jack, of course.

It was always about Jack.

About the what-ifs and what might have been if they could go back in time and change what had happened. Change one little thing that would have allowed Jack to live.

Egan had never come out and confirmed that he felt that raw, bitter guilt. The guilt that came in smothering, soul-crushing waves. Over and over again. Still, she recognized the signs of that kind of guilt because she had firsthand knowledge of it. Added to that, Alana knew something that he didn't.

Egan wasn't the reason Jack was dead.

She was.

CHAPTER THREE

THE EMOTIONS WERE crashing into Egan like out of control bumper cars, and three words kept repeating in his head.

Massive heart attack.

Egan had never personally known anyone who'd had a heart attack, but he knew that Grammy Effie's husband had died from one years ago, even before Egan had been born. Since that grandfather had been on Egan's mom's side of the family, then what his dad was dealing with wasn't genetic. And Egan had no idea why that thought was swirling around with all the others.

"Why don't we all go to my office?" he heard Alana suggest. "It's small, but there's a sofa that'll be more comfortable than these chairs."

Egan shook his head. "I want to be here when the doctor comes back."

Alana laid her hand on his shoulder. "I can let Dalton know where we'll be, and it's the same distance from my office to ICU as it is from here."

Egan was about to do another headshake, but the ER doors swished open again, and he saw several people hurrying in. Hank Gonzales, Betty Garner and Louis Cantrell. Friends and acquaintances of his dad. That's when it hit Egan that others would come.

Lots and lots of others.

And while Egan was appreciative of the care and concern they'd all be doling out, he just wasn't steady enough to deal with that right now.

He stood, and that must have been the only cue Alana needed because she hurried to Dalton to let him know where they'd be. Effie stood, too, and she greeted the newcomers. Egan managed a quick greeting as well. Barely managed it, and he hoped he didn't have to do more until he'd tried to wrap his head around what the hell had just happened to his dad.

"I'll join you in a minute or two," Effie told them when Alana began to lead Egan out of the waiting room.

Egan stopped, holding his ground and assessing the situation since he didn't want Effie bogged down with anything that was going to make this more stressful for her. But Effie gave him a quick reassuring glance and mouthed, "Go."

He still hesitated until he realized that Effie seemed to be steady enough. In fact, it appeared she was actually glad the worriers and well-wishers were there. Maybe because they gave her a kind of distraction. But Egan didn't want any of that. He needed to face this head-on, needed to figure out what he was dealing with and see if he could fix it.

Three years ago, before Jack had died, Egan wouldn't have added that "if he could" to the mental mix of what he had to do. He'd believed he was capable of fixing any and everything. Obviously, he'd been wrong. And that cockiness had led to Jack's death. Probably to Colleen leaving him, too, since he obviously hadn't fixed whatever the heck had been wrong in his marriage.

He followed Alana out of the waiting room and to the hall that led to the clinics. Her office was the first one, and after fishing through her bag to retrieve her keys, she opened the door.

She'd been right about two things. It was small and there was a sofa, which did look more comfortable than any chair in the waiting room. After seeing it, though, Egan figured the comfort would be wasted on him. But at least in here he wouldn't have to maintain a military bearing. Well, not fully.

It quickly occurred to Egan, though, that he might have traded the frying pan for the fire since he now found himself alone with Alana. Great. He'd avoided her for years, and now he'd seen her twice in the same day.

He stepped into the office, glancing at her desk— also small—and then looked at the posters on the walls. Not medical charts or pastoral paintings. These were basically framed memes.

I have removed all the bad food from my house, one read. *It was delicious.*

Another was, *You are what you eat so don't be cheap, easy or fake.*

If only sarcasm burned calories was scripted out on the third.

"I try to make nutrition fun," Alana explained when

she followed his gaze. "I mean, most people aren't happy when they come in here. They've usually been referred to me by their doctors. Or else they're miserable and just need help. Every now and then I'll get the super fit, no sugar, no fat eater who wants me to do a tune-up to see if there's a tweak I can make to their already tweaked choices."

Maybe she'd said some of that to make him smile or at least help him relax, but it didn't work. Not completely, anyway. However, he did recall all the jokes Jack had made about Alana's less than stellar eating habits.

"A chili cheese fries addict," Egan murmured. "That's what Jack said."

"Still am," she readily admitted, "but I had to cut back. I gained double the usual freshman fifteen when I was in college. That's when I changed my major from English literature to nutrition. Now, I'm lucky enough to have the townsfolk be my dietary conscience anytime I eat out."

She put *lucky* in air quotes, causing Egan to raise an eyebrow.

Alana had a sip of her water before she explained. "You're the town's hero so people watch you for heroic stuff." Egan nearly stopped her to say he wasn't a hero, but she continued before he could do that. "Dropping minimal f-bombs, not getting into trouble, being polite, helping little old ladies cross the street and such. Added to that you're a Top Gun and a cowboy who still holds the record for a perfect score at bronc riding at the town's fair."

"I'm not a hero," he finally managed to say. "I drop plenty of f-bombs. And I've never helped any old ladies across the street."

She shrugged. "If it walks like a duck, quacks like a duck…" Alana waved away the rest of that. "For me, there's no hero aura. Yes, people give me some leeway because I'm Jack's widow, but they watch what I eat. A plate of chili cheese fries will earn me some 'behind the hand' whispers. I heard a horrified gasp once when I ordered a banana split." She pointed her bottle at him as if proving her point. "I'll bet no one's even whispered about the size of your butt because of a banana split."

Egan had to admit that had never happened to him, and he was sorry Alana had to deal with such things. She'd glossed over the leeway part of being Jack's widow, but he was betting she was having to deal with that, too. He was surprised she hadn't given up on eating out. And no wonder she was trying her hand at virtual dating.

That notion, and the whispers about her butt size, lingered in his mind a moment before reality came back with a vengeance. He mentally saw the blood on Effie's shirt and replayed what the doctor had told them. All of that smeared together, slinging him to one crappy conclusion. Right now, there was nothing he could do to help his dad. Right now, his dad's fate was out of his hands.

Not very heroic, he thought with bitterness that tightened his mouth.

Squeezing his eyes shut, he sank down onto the

sofa and stayed that way for a couple of moments. When he opened his eyes, though, he got a jolt when he spotted the photo of Jack and him on the wall of bookshelves behind Alana's desk. In the shot, Jack and he had their arms slung over each other's shoulders, and they were grinning around cigars clamped in their mouths.

The frame was probably custom-made since the engraving around the silver frame was one of Jack's favorite sayings. *Damn the torpedoes. Full speed ahead.* Jack's motto of sorts.

And a phrase that ate away at Egan like acid.

Like the photos his father had texted him earlier, Egan knew exactly when this one had been taken. Twelve years ago at Naval Air Station Fallon, Nevada, where minutes earlier Egan had won the Top Gun competition. Egan was in his flight suit, of course, and Jack was in BDUs and his hard-earned maroon beret that signified his special ops status as a Combat Rescue Officer. Jack had flown up just for the celebration. As he was prone to do. Even though they no longer lived in Emerald Creek, they'd made the effort to be there for each other whenever it was wanted or needed.

Ironically, that's what had gotten Jack killed.

Another irony was that before that fatal encounter, Egan had been there for Jack and vice versa more than he had been for his own dad. It was the reason Egan was drowning in guilt right now.

"If I'd gone home more often, I might have seen that my dad was sick," Egan muttered.

"Maybe not," Alana was quick to say. "Sometimes, a heart attack can hit out of the blue."

Egan wasn't buying that for a second. There'd likely been signs, and if he'd been there, he would have at least stood a chance of seeing them.

When he didn't open his water, Alana did that, handed him back the bottle and then sat behind her desk. Egan was thankful for that because it put some distance between them. Despite everything else going on with his dad, the rules still applied as far as Egan was concerned. The less contact with Alana, the better. Less contact held the hope of fewer bad memories. Right now, he couldn't handle any more bad memories.

"There was blood on Grammy Effie's shirt," he said, the words just tumbling out before he even knew he was going to say them. "I don't even think she noticed it, but it probably came from my dad."

"Probably," Alana agreed. "If he hit his head, even a slight cut would have bled. That doesn't mean the injury is serious, though. If it had been, Dr. Abrams would have likely mentioned it."

The doctor wouldn't have if he'd thought Egan and Effie already had too much to handle. Or maybe in the grand scheme of things, a head injury was secondary to a massive heart attack.

Even though Alana wasn't a doctor or nurse, Egan would have asked her if she had any idea what was going on right now in the ICU with his dad, but her phone rang. She didn't exactly drop an f-bomb, but she did grimace more than a little.

"Tilly," she said, taking the call.

Alana didn't put her phone on speaker so Egan couldn't hear specifically what Tilly was saying, but he did catch a word here and there.

Derek. Hospital. Bad.

"Yes, it's true about Derek being admitted to the hospital," Alana said to Tilly. "I'm with Egan now while he waits for news."

Egan caught another word. *Way.* He also caught the sudden frantic look in Alana's eyes.

"No need for you to come here," Alana told the woman. "I can text you when we know something." But judging from Alana's huff, she was talking to the air because Jack's mom had already ended the call.

Egan groaned. No way did he want to have to deal with seeing Jack's mother today.

Alana put her phone away and nodded as if she'd known that would be his reaction. "Odds are Tilly will get sidetracked once she's in the ER, but if she makes it here to my office, I'll take her down to vending under the guise of everyone needing coffee and candy bars to keep them going. The vending machines always jam so it'll take a while to churn out enough Snickers, honeybuns and bad coffee."

Egan muttered an automatic thanks just as her phone rang again. Alana's reaction was even stronger this time, and she clearly wasn't looking forward to the call. She took it, anyway.

"Aunt Loralee," Alana greeted after a really long sigh.

He understood Alana's sighing reaction. Her aunt Loralee, who was the principal at the elementary school, had raised Colleen and her after their parents basically ditched them in Emerald Creek when they'd been kids. Their aunt had been good enough to take them in and give them a decent life, but to label her overprotective was like saying Texas could get a tad bit warm in August. Egan figured at times the smothering could feel like actual smothering, especially since he'd heard Loralee considered Alana permanently heartbroken and fragile because of losing Jack.

"Yes, it's true that Derek Donnelly's in the hospital," Alana said, responding to her aunt. "But there's no need for you to come since the ER waiting room is filling up fast," she quickly added. "I'm with Egan, and as soon as we hear anything from the doctor, I'll let you know."

Silence. No audible murmurings from Loralee, no response from Alana. For a long time. And Egan knew he was the reason for it. Unlike everyone else in town, Loralee did not think of Egan as a hero, and she blamed him for Jack's death. He deserved that in spades.

Loralee was also fully convinced Egan was at fault for Colleen cheating and ultimately divorcing him and leaving town. Apparently, if he'd been a more attentive husband instead of gallivanting around in fighter jets—and yes, Loralee had used the word *gallivanting*—Colleen wouldn't have looked elsewhere.

"Aunt Loralee?" Alana finally said to prompt her aunt to respond.

If there was indeed a response, Egan didn't hear

it because his own phone rang, and he saw the name on the screen. His stepmother.

"Audrey," Egan greeted when he answered, and he got the usual pang of awkwardness at addressing a general officer by her given name. It didn't matter that this particular general officer was also married to his dad.

"Egan," she stated. Yeah, she definitely sounded more like a general than a stepmom. "I got your message. What happened? How's your father?"

He went with a quick briefing, trying to keep the emotion out of it. Of course, that was impossible. The emotion was there. "He had a massive heart attack, and his condition is still to be determined. He's in ICU."

Audrey muttered something he didn't catch. "Has Derek asked for me?"

"I'm not sure," Egan had to admit. "I was at the base when it happened, and by the time I got to the Emerald Creek Hospital, he was already in ICU. I haven't been able to see him or speak to him."

"All right," Audrey said, as if that info had caused her to reach some kind of conclusion. "I'll make some calls and see what I can find out. If this is as serious as it sounds, I'll see if I can arrange a visit. It won't be today because I'm at Ramstein, Germany, but I'll try to get there soon."

He hadn't missed her *I'll see* and *I'll try*. Definitely not firm commitments to hurry to her husband's hospital bed. She ended the call, leaving Egan to wonder if Audrey would try *to arrange a visit* because she still loved his dad or because it would look bad to her peers and subordinates if she, an Air Force general, didn't show up to be with her critically ill husband.

And maybe her motive didn't even matter.

His dad had chosen to stay married to Audrey for over twenty-five years, and if the woman could help his dad in any kind of way, then Egan was all for that.

He wasn't sure how long he sat there staring at his phone, but when he looked up, Alana had finished her conversation with her aunt and was looking at him. She quickly glanced away, of course, pretending to be interested in a paper on her desk. No, not a paper he realized when he spotted the envelope next to it. A pale yellow envelope that was identical to the one Alana had given him earlier at his place.

A letter from Colleen.

That reminder likely would have given him a good jolt of anger or at least annoyance that his ex was trying to contact him, but there was a tap at the door a split second before it opened. Dr. Abrams came in.

Egan practically jumped to his feet and saw that Effie was with the doctor. No one else, though, which meant Abrams had maybe thought it was best not to have an audience for what he was about to say. Alana must have picked up on that, too, because she quickly muttered something about going for a cup of coffee and left, after giving Effie's hand a gentle squeeze. Egan moved to circle his arm around his grandmother, pulling her close to him.

Dr. Abrams shut the door behind Alana and then met Egan's gaze. "Your dad's alive." And while that gave Egan a whole boatload of relief, that was all the doctor said for what felt like an eternity. "We've stabilized him and are still in the process of assessing the damage."

"Damage," Egan repeated under his breath. Oh, yeah, a fresh gut punch of emotion came.

Abrams nodded, gathered his breath. "A massive heart attack or elevation myocardial infarction means a large portion of the heart muscle has been affected. In your dad's case, it happened because of a complete blockage in one of the coronary arteries that supplies blood."

"Can you fix that?" Egan immediately asked.

"A heart surgeon is on his way to Emerald Creek now, and he'll be doing the procedure. That should fix the immediate problem of restricted blood flow, and then we can have a better assessment of the damage." The doctor paused, glanced at both Effie and Egan. "There is damage," he spelled out, "and that's almost certainly going to mean some serious changes in your dad's life."

"What kind of changes?" Effie wanted to know.

Egan wanted to know the same thing, and judging from the doctor's bleak expression, what he was about to say wouldn't be good.

"Derek is going to need to be in the hospital for a while, and even after he's discharged, he'll likely have a long recovery," the doctor spelled out. "Egan, I don't know how much leave you've got saved up, but take it all. Your dad's going to need you here with him for a long time."

CHAPTER FOUR

ALANA WATCHED AS newly retired Chief Master Sergeant Clifton Wright looked over the lifestyle changes she'd mapped out for him. Changes she'd come up with after her consultation on the base three days earlier.

The chief was frowning, of course, and if she could have been a fly on the wall of his house, she would have likely heard him cursing her. Still, it was a fairly generous plan, considering that he was in bad enough health to have spurred an earlier retirement than he had anticipated.

"You want me to eat only half of everything I order or cook from my favorite foods list?" he asked, as if requesting some kind of clarification. "And then have an apple or some other kind of raw fruit or vegetable."

"Yes," she verified. "That's for starters."

She didn't always offer such a deal to her clients, but after talking with the chief, Alana had known he wouldn't stick to a "cold turkey" approach to sugar and fat. Or even to plain cold turkey. This was going to be a process, and the best chance of succeeding would be for him to take baby steps. Or rather baby-ish ones. Especially since he'd said the only fruit or veggie he'd touch was an occasional apple, preferably coated with caramel, or butter-sautéed onions on his hamburgers.

"Of course, I'd prefer you save those foods like the chicken fried steak for special treats on equally special occasions," Alana went on, "but since I'm clearly not a size zero, I obviously indulge a few of my own cravings. The idea is to not overindulge and skew lab results into sketchy ranges that make your doctor scowl."

"Only half?" he repeated, still looking for that clarification that she'd already clarified.

"Half for now," she insisted. "In a month, at our next appointment, I'll want you to move to quarter portions of the indulgent foods and treats. Then, if your lab work is still producing scowls, we'll discuss some other diet changes."

The chief frowned and stood. "I heard you ordered a banana split deluxe from The Sweet Tooth," he said like a challenge as he named the town's ice-cream and candy shop.

Alana sighed. Some gossip never died and was fueled big time by that lack of degrees' separation. He didn't give her a chance to explain that she probably wouldn't have ordered the treat if she had his lab levels. Or if she'd known it was going to haunt her for eternity, but Chief Wright added another mutter that he would "try it her way for now," and walked out.

She made a note to do a follow-up call with him in a week, but the truth was, she'd know more or less how the chief was progressing with the inevitable gossip she'd hear. After all, the gossip longevity didn't only apply to her. Whether she wanted it or not, and she didn't, she'd eventually hear what the town's newcomer was ordering from the various eateries.

The chief's dietary choices wouldn't be the only gossip, though.

Nope.

Over the past three days, she'd heard plenty about Derek, Egan and their family. Derek was recovering *somewhat slowly* after his heart procedure and the two cracked ribs and head injury he'd received when he'd fallen during his heart attack. She'd gotten that info directly from one of the nurses. Other spatterings of tidbits hadn't come from such ironclad sources, but she figured they were reliable enough.

Multiple people had told her that Egan had taken a month's leave and had temporarily moved back home so he could run the ranch and be near his dad. His brothers had come for quick visits, too, and would both be returning during the month. Remi had gotten the bad news about her dad and would be coming home as soon as she possibly could.

There'd been talk about Audrey, too, but the gabbers hadn't treated her as harshly as one might imagine. That was because of her status as a general, which gave her a higher calling than being a dutiful wife by her husband's bedside. Egan got some of those higher calling concessions, too, but his hero status kicked in, and everybody just knew he would step up to help his dad and family.

At the thought of Egan, Alana, well, thought of him. Not the hero part per se, but she knew he had to be worried sick about his dad. In the old days, when Jack had still been alive, she would have hurried to Egan, asking and reasking if there was anything she could do to help until he assigned her some task that might indeed help. But this wasn't the old days, Jack wasn't alive, and Alana knew her presence was much more likely to add to Egan's troubles than it was to give him any kind of comfort. That's why she would try her level best to stay away from him.

Not thinking about him, though, was out.

He'd been a constant on her mind, and in the moments when Alana didn't try to mentally fudge the truth, she admitted that her thinking wasn't solely related to his current situation. When she'd visited him at his base house to deliver the letter and tell him about Tilly's plans, she hadn't expected to feel anything but awkwardness for the man who'd been her husband's best friend.

She hadn't expected the tingle.

That tiny trickle of heat that reminded her that she'd been looking at the face and body of a hot guy. Of course, since she wasn't blind, she'd always known that Egan was hot, what with that young Elvis black hair and stunner blue eyes. Egan and his brothers were all hot, all desirable.

Alana, though, had never been on that particular train of desire until her gaze locked with Egan's. A lock where it seemed as if a dozen things passed between them. Maybe an entire conversation that they'd never be able to have aloud. That's when the tingle had come, and talk about the most inappropriate timing in the history of such things. She'd been there to talk about his ex-wife and a memorial for her late husband, not to tingle over a man who shouldn't stir such things in her.

Truth be told, it still didn't seem completely right to feel that way about any guy, but it was especially true about Egan. So, wide berths and avoidance would continue even though she suspected he could very well be just one corridor away if he was visiting his father.

She jolted when there was a quick knock at her door, and for one heart-jittering moment, she thought it might be Egan. But it wasn't. The door opened, and her aunt Loralee stuck her head in the room.

"Just checking to make sure you weren't with a patient," Loralee said, stepping inside. "There's a big fellow just up the hall reading some papers and complaining about you."

Alana nodded, not surprised by that, and she tamped down the heart jittering while automatically checking the time of her next appointment. Not for another hour, but she wouldn't let Aunt Loralee know that or she'd settle in for the entire sixty minutes. Alana would need to work in lunch and go over the client's record before the hour was up.

"I thought I'd stop in and check on you since I was just up the street at Harlow's," her aunt explained, referring to the beauty salon. The mention explained why Loralee smelled of the hairspray that kept her graying curly hair anchored firmly in place. Even monsoon winds wouldn't ruffle those locks.

Loralee took a plain brown paper bag from her purse and glanced around as if checking to make sure they were alone. "It's a blueberry scone. I baked them fresh this morning."

"Thanks." Alana smiled and didn't question her aunt's furtive look or concealed packaging for the treat. No need since Loralee would have heard all about the banana split and any other such goodies.

"Figured you could use a little pick-me-up." Loralee sat, eyeing her the way a doctor would look at a trauma patient.

"I'm not stressed out because of Egan," Alana volunteered, figuring that she knew where this was going.

The sound her aunt made conveyed that she wasn't buying that. Perhaps because there was a smidge of truth to it since the tingle Alana had felt for Egan was definitely a stressor.

"Have you talked to Tilly in the last day or so?" her aunt asked.

This wasn't a change of subject. Nope. Alana also knew where this was leading. "I called Tilly after I found out Derek's diagnosis, but I'm guessing she told you about me speaking to Egan in regards to the life celebration."

"She did," Loralee verified, "but Tilly totally understands that the timing isn't good to bring all of that up with Egan. I advised her to wait until Derek was out of the hospital, and then Tilly can talk to Egan directly. That'll get you out of the loop."

And there it was—her aunt's bottom-line reasoning. Loralee would have almost certainly preferred for Alana to have no contact at all with Egan. In part because she believed that her being around Egan would stir bad memories.

And it did.

But there was also the other side of this coin. That Loralee thought Egan was somehow responsible for Jack's death. One day, Alana was going to have to confess that she, not Egan, was the culprit for that, and if Loralee wanted to assign blame, then she had to look no further than her own niece.

"Speaking of the life celebration," Loralee went on. "I'm worried about it. Not for the obvious reasons of it being a sad, hard reminder for you but also because of the painting itself."

Alana frowned. "What do you mean?" She had no idea what the painting would look like because Tilly had guarded it at a top-secret level, wanting to keep it a surprise until the unveiling.

Loralee pulled up something on her phone and handed it to Alana. "That's the artist's web page," her aunt explained. "Just look at what he calls art."

Alana did look, and even though she didn't want to judge, her frown deepened some. The artist's name was Javier Cartier, and there were a half-dozen photos of his work on the page. All the paintings were composed of what appeared to be barbed wire, tiny concrete chunks, assorted trash and paint blobs. She picked out a partial Coke can in one and a crunched Pringles' can in another and tried to imagine how such things could come together to create a memorial painting. Then, she remembered who'd commissioned the work.

"Tilly would have given him specifics about what to paint," Alana said. No doubts about that. Tilly wouldn't have wanted any raised eyebrows over the tribute for her fallen son. She would have aimed for reactions of oohs, aahs and throwback memories to happier times.

"Let's hope," Loralee muttered. "If not, you'll have to steel yourself up not to gasp or anything since all eyes will turn to you to see your reaction when the painting is unveiled."

Alana wished that weren't true, but she knew that's exactly how the event would play out. She'd be expected to express both happiness and tears. And she would. It'd be impossible to get through something like that without yet more crying. But Alana was hoping this would be some kind of catharsis for the town. That Jack would finally, finally be laid to rest which in turn would lead to Tilly, Egan and her getting on with whatever their new normal turned out to be.

This new normal wouldn't be the end of the tears, that was for certain. Wouldn't be the end of the grief, either, but Alana was hoping beyond reason that it would allow her to move on without carting the wagonload of guilt with her.

"Speaking of Tilly, Jack and such," Loralee went on, "you didn't ask what your sister had written to me in her letter, but she talked about Jack and his mom. About how she regrets she hadn't been there to help you through your grief."

This was boggy ground, for sure. Alana had mixed feelings about Colleen. Yes, they were sisters, but Alana hadn't been a fan of Colleen's cheating and walking out on her husband. Especially since Egan had had to deal with that and get slammed with Jack's death just a couple of days later.

Still, Alana hadn't been an insider when it came to Colleen and Egan's marriage; she had no plans to disown Colleen for what she'd done. Alana just preferred not to have a lot of interaction with her since Colleen's actions were now part of the mix of what she felt over losing Jack.

"Did you give Egan the letter Colleen wrote to him?" Loralee asked. "Or did you just forward it to him?"

"I gave it to him in person three days ago when I went to the base to tell him about Tilly's plans." She paused a moment and came clean with the rest. "Egan tossed it unopened in the trash."

Loralee's mouth tightened in disapproval. "Figures. I doubt Egan's the forgiving sort." She continued before Alana could maybe point out that Colleen hadn't actually earned any forgiveness. "I just hope Egan doesn't upset Tilly. She's all excited because she thinks Egan will be doing the painting unveiling, after all. I mean, since he's in town and can't get out of it."

Her aunt was fishing to find out if she knew Egan's plans. Since she didn't, Alana just shrugged. That gesture seemed to be all that was needed to get Loralee to continue.

"Of course, I can understand why Egan would be hesitant to show up," Loralee continued. "Tilly doesn't know the details of how and why Jack died."

The last part was true. Tilly didn't know, and as far as Alana knew, neither did anyone else in town other than Egan, Loralee and her. And Loralee only knew a fraction of it because in the horrible hours after the notification, Alana had mentioned that Jack had been on a non-duty visit to see Egan. Her aunt had kept that detail to herself.

"Jack wouldn't have been in that awful place if it hadn't been for Egan," Loralee added.

No shrug from Alana this time. She couldn't sit still and just ignore her aunt's bashing of Egan. "If Jack hadn't been there, it's just as likely he would have been in an equally awful place or worse," Alana pointed out. "He was a Combat Rescue Officer, and he stood by their motto of *that others may live...to return home with honor.*"

Loralee would have almost certainly pointed out that Jack hadn't been on duty that night, that the visit to the area had been a personal one. To see Egan. But Alana cut that off by standing and checking her watch.

"I need to get a few things done before my next appointment," Alana said. She went to her aunt and kissed her cheek.

Like her feelings for Colleen, Loralee was a mixed bag of emotions, too, but Alana still loved the woman and was beyond thankful that she'd taken Colleen and her in after their parents had abandoned them.

Loralee gave a little huff but stood, too, and returned the cheek kiss. When she pulled back, she touched Alana's hair and gave a thin smile. "All right. No more talk of Egan. But before I go, please tell me you've given up on that virtual dating stuff."

Alana returned the huff, added an eye roll because this was old territory. On the plus side, unlike the rest of the town, her aunt believed she should move on and start seeing other men. She just didn't think it should happen virtually but rather with men Loralee herself had handpicked.

Men that her aunt considered safe so they wouldn't end up like Jack.

Alana agreed with some of that. It'd been hell worrying every night and day if her husband would be hurt or killed, but safe wasn't at the top of her list.

A tingle was, though.

Not necessarily a tingle caused by Egan, but Alana wanted that all-consuming feeling of giddy happiness where she could believe that all things were possible. If that came with someone safe, then it would be the perfect package, but Alana wasn't holding her breath.

She walked Loralee to the door, gave her another kiss and then headed in the opposite direction to prevent her aunt from launching into more of the dating chat. Loralee took the hint and went toward the exit. Alana ended up at the vending machines to see if elves had magically appeared and left anything other than the usual.

They hadn't.

And she mentally kicked herself for forgetting to

bring the tuna salad sandwich she'd left sitting in her fridge at home. She didn't want to hit the diner just up the street because at this hour, it'd be jammed. Ditto for the small hospital café. Besides, the selection there was usually nothing to excite her taste buds. Unfortunately, the pickings were slim in that area for the vending machines as well.

Alana started with a bottle of water and then shifted to the middle vending machine, knowing the one on the end would contain only coffee and someone's really bad interpretation of hot chocolate. Over half the selections were sold out, though, and after she ruled out anything chocolate- and sugar-based, that left her with trail mix. She had to battle the machine, thumping it a couple of times before it coughed out the little bag.

And four Milky Way bars.

Alana sighed. This had to be some kind of cosmic joke, and there were likely four riled customers who hadn't gotten the candy they'd paid for. She gathered up the stash, intending to leave the candy at the nurses' reception desk when she spotted Dr. Abrams making his way toward her.

"Is Mr. Donnelly okay?" she immediately asked.

He made a so-so motion with his hand. "He's making some progress. That's why I wanted to see you. Have you got a minute to talk some things over?"

"Of course." Balancing the water, candy and trail mix in her hands, she followed him when he started walking.

"I was just in with Derek, and we were discussing

some options," the doctor went on. "And your name came up." He glanced at her vending stash and smiled a little. "Am I cutting into your lunch?"

"Not exactly. Vending machine hiccup." Alana looked for a place to ditch the candy, but there wasn't an available table, chair or windowsill in the hall so she just kept moving. "How'd my name come up? Is there something I can do to help?"

"That's what I'm hoping," he said, clearly answering her last question but not the first.

He opened the door to Mr. Donnelly's room, and when Alana stepped in, she saw Egan standing by his father's bedside. Egan's head whipped up, his gaze zooming to hers, but she didn't notice any "I'm happy to see you" glint in his eyes. There was a slight tightening of his shoulders, though.

"Alana," Mr. Donnelly said from his bed.

Oh, mercy. She had never seen him like this. Just the opposite. Normally, he looked like the tough, rugged rancher that he was with a side order of intimidation that came from being a tough, rugged, *powerful* rancher. And one of the richest men in the county.

She'd always heard that he was a fair man. Unless you crossed him, that is. Or if you messed with his family in any way. Then, Derek Donnelly was known to wield that power and smash you like a bug.

But that powerful facade was gone.

He was pale, so pale, and he looked as if one touch would shatter him into a million tiny pieces. The heart attack had clearly taken its toll on him, and judging from his appearance, he was far from a full recovery.

For a horrible moment, she thought maybe Dr. Abrams had brought her here so that Derek could say goodbye to her. But that didn't make sense. Derek had been fairly close to Jack but not her.

"Did Alana agree to do it?" Derek asked the doctor.

"Not yet," Abrams said. "But I thought it'd be best if I brought her here to discuss it."

"Agree to what?" Alana wanted to know. "Discuss what?"

After glancing at Egan's face, she realized this was going to be something she wouldn't like. Or more accurately, something *Egan* wouldn't like. She got confirmation of that when Egan spoke.

"You can say no if you're too busy," he insisted.

She glanced at the doctor and Egan's dad to see which one would go ahead and finish filling her in. Abrams took the lead.

"It's possible, *possible*," Dr. Abrams emphasized, "that Derek will be able to go home in a week or so. When he does, he's going to need help making some changes to his diet and lifestyle."

The relief came, washing over Alana. This wasn't a deathbed farewell. It was part of her job, what she'd done for other patients like Mr. Donnelly.

But the relief vanished just as quickly as it'd come.

Because whatever this was, all she had to do was look at Egan's face again and realize it was a lot more than merely a job.

"Dr. Abrams wants you to go to the ranch to work with Dad," Egan finally spelled out.

"I know you usually take appointments in your office," the doctor added while Derek kept his weary eyes fixed on Alana, "but I was wondering if you'd be able to go to the ranch every day for the next month or so. That way, Egan and you can maybe help Derek get back on his feet. I'm really hoping you don't say no," he tacked on to that.

Alana couldn't say anything, but she darn sure couldn't refuse. So she nodded, knowing this was going to put her on a collision course with Egan. Judging from his expression, he was well aware of all the colliding that would be going on.

CHAPTER FIVE

IN THE DREAM, Egan didn't save Jack. Everything moved like sludge, a slow crawling pace. Frame by frame. So that he couldn't miss a single second of the nightmare.

He saw Jack's smile, that cocky grin that was often on his face. Then, there was the blast. Also slow as Jack's grin vanished. As the sound roared through the transport vehicle.

Egan had the sensation of being weightless. Of being propelled through the air. It hadn't lasted, though. He'd landed hard in the sand, which had managed to be both hard and soft. It sucked him down into a dry, gritty bog while he fought for breath and reason. While he fought to understand what the hell was happening.

And then he saw it.

The mangled heap of what had been the vehicle. Even over the roaring in his ears, he'd heard the fire eating its way through it. What he hadn't heard, though, were any sounds of life. He hadn't heard Jack because while the sand had cushioned Egan, Jack had been trapped inside the vehicle and hadn't survived the impact. Jack was dead.

Egan woke, snapping to a sitting position, and

for a second or two he'd expected to be in that hot drowning sand or in pain from the broken bones and injuries. He wasn't. But the adrenaline was slamming through him as if this were the real deal and not the recurring nightmare.

His breath came out too fast, in short gasps, and the muscles vised in his chest, making it almost impossible to drag in any air. He was well on his way to either hyperventilating or a full-blown panic attack. Those weren't as frequent as the nightmares that sometimes triggered them, but Egan was no stranger to either of them.

As the counselor he'd seen had told him to do, he tried to anchor himself, to name the things he could see in his bedroom at the ranch. The king-sized bed. The sitting area with a comfortable reading chair and a desk. The Turkish rug with its muted shades of calm blue on the hardwood floor.

This hadn't been his childhood room. That one was just up the hall where he'd lived out all but the first two years of his life. And the last three. Apparently, he'd spent the first two in the nursery next to his parents' bedroom before being moved into a "big boy room" once Cal had been born.

After Colleen and he had divorced, Egan had moved rooms again, taking over one of the guest suites in the sprawling house. It wasn't that he had a lot of memories of her there since they hadn't married until long after he'd moved out and started his military career. But they had had sex in that room, shared the bed from time to time, and he hadn't wanted to risk anything interfering with the possibility of his getting a good night's sleep.

He had enough to mess with his head without adding Colleen to the mix.

His grandmother, though, had taken it upon herself to bring in some of the things from his childhood. Not all at once, but pieces that she'd added over the years. The quilt she'd made for him was on the bed and had been since he'd turned twenty. Framed family photos were on the desk. None were of Jack and especially none of Jack and him together with Alana. That would have brought on the memories, which would have created a perfect storm for the nightmare.

Still doing some anchoring attempts, he glanced around at the reminders in here of his teenage years. Trophies he'd won in local competitions for bronc riding. They were on the shelf above the desk, mixed with ones he'd won for football. Mixed, too, with some early military photos and awards that he'd gotten while in ROTC.

Every time Egan slept in this room, he made a mental note to pack up all the stuff and ask Effie to quit her moving efforts so he wouldn't wake up to reminders of the person he'd once been. It definitely didn't help with his mood. Ironically, though, some of the items, like the bronc-riding trophies, helped with the panic, and he could feel himself leveling out some.

He recalled that Alana had mentioned the bronc riding, and she'd verbally tossed that into the mix to try to prove to him that he was considered heroic. It didn't take heroism to climb onto the back of a bronc that was surely going to try to throw you and perhaps maim you in the process. It took the love of the ride and the adrenaline and a massive amount of stupidity.

Perhaps that's why it helped level him. Because he knew it was his real self on display in the photo. No heroism, just stupidity combined with luck that had given him a win.

Egan checked the time again and knew there was no way he could risk trying to go back to sleep. Not with the threat of the nightmare still boiling just beneath the surface. Besides, it was nearly seven o'clock, and his alarm would be going off soon, anyway. This would give him a slightly earlier start to the day, which would be a good thing since he wanted to check on some new horses that had been delivered the day before and then go to the hospital to see his dad.

It'd been a week since the nearly fatal heart attack. A week of trying to come to terms with the fact he'd nearly lost his dad. Egan knew a week wasn't nearly long enough to wrap his mind around that. He was basically taking things hour by hour, focusing on what he could do at the ranch versus what life would look like once his dad came home from the hospital in a day or two.

He got out of bed, heading to the en suite bathroom, something all nine of the bedrooms had at the main ranch house. He grabbed a shower and dressed. Not in his usual uniform, though, but rather in jeans, a shirt and cowboy boots.

It was another irony that these items, along with his Stetson, were anchors, too. Maybe because there was nothing about the clothes to remind him he was a lieutenant colonel with a crapload of bad memories about a fatal explosion in the desert.

Egan made his way to the kitchen, following the scent of fresh coffee, and wasn't surprised to see both Effie and Maybell at the stove, putting together some breakfast burritos, a specialty that he suspected they were making because they knew it was one of his favorites.

Since Egan occasionally did paperwork and tax info for the ranch, he knew that Maybell was in her mid-sixties, but she hadn't expressed a single word about retiring. It was the same for six or so of the ranch hands who were similar in age to Maybell. That was good as far as Egan was concerned. Not only because all of them were hard workers, but they had become part of the family, and that meant his dad and Effie would have support once things returned to normal.

If they returned to normal, he mentally amended.

"Morning," Maybell greeted, flashing him her usual smile. She was tall, nearly hitting the six-feet mark, and her hair was far more salt than pepper these days.

Effie also doled out a greeting and a smile while she sat down to eat her disassembled burrito with a fork. "Your dad called a bit ago," she said, getting Egan's attention as he was pouring his coffee. "He's fine," she quickly added when she no doubt saw the alarm in his eyes. "He just wanted someone to bring him a few more of those old photo albums he's been looking at."

Egan nodded, though, he wished his dad had wanted books, his laptop or heck, even some work. Not that he wanted him to work, but Egan also didn't think it was a good idea for his dad to keep poring over the past in those albums.

"I'll take one or two to him when I visit this morning." He paused. "He didn't ask for snacks or junk food, did he?"

"No," Effie said, sighing.

That sigh said loads. She was worried about his dad, too. And not just about his physical recovery. His dad had a fondness for snacks that in no way fell into the healthy category. The proof of that was in the pantry where he kept his caramel corn and double-fudge cookie stash.

Egan got himself a mug of coffee and took one of the burritos that Maybell offered. "I'll be back," he told them. "I just want to check on the horses."

Effie smiled again, and he didn't have to guess the reason for this one, either. He'd always loved the horses so it wasn't a chore. In fact, seeing them would almost certainly be the best part of his day, and he might as well take advantage of it while he was still here at the ranch.

He walked out through the back and down the porch steps while he mulled over that "here at the ranch" part. He'd already burned seven of his thirty days of leave, but he could ask for another week or so if things didn't improve. Once the leave ran out, though, he could end up commuting for a while which would make for hellish long days since he often worked a sixty-hour week at the base.

Still, it might be necessary.

Lots of things might be necessary to get through this.

Despite the lingering effect of the nightmare and the worry about his dad, he felt himself settle as he thought of his ancestors, of their boots that had walked over this very ground. Of what they must have been thinking when they looked out at the land and the livestock. The livestock breeds had changed over the past hundred years, but the core of the ranch had stayed the same. Saddlebrook raised the best bloodlines possible whether it was Angus cattle, cutting horses, rodeo bulls or the champion Andalusian horses.

Now he was walking in their footsteps. Literally. And in a way, this was his watch. Temporarily, that is, until his dad was back on his feet. But Egan couldn't escape the realization that this place, this legacy, was his responsibility.

No pressure there.

He spotted the ranch foreman, Jesse Whitlock, going into the main barn where he had his office. Derek had offered Jesse office space in the main house, but he had turned it down, insisting he preferred to be closer to the livestock and the other hands. Egan suspected Jesse had chosen that arrangement because he'd wanted to keep some boundaries and a private personal life since he wasn't exactly an open book.

Egan walked to the pasture fence, eating his breakfast while he watched the Andalusian mares chow down on the grass. It was like a picture that could go on a postcard. The dew on the emerald green grass. The soft gold colors of the rising sun cutting through the morning haze that gave everything, including the horses, a lazy, serene feel.

He could feel his heartbeat slow, could feel the tightness in his chest fade. The burrito helped with that, and the horses must have thought they'd get to sample the tasty treat because a pair of them started to mosey toward Egan. It didn't last because the sound of his phone ringing shot through the serenity and sent the slightly skittish mares darting away from him.

Cursing the interruption, Egan's profanity didn't last long when he noticed it was a FaceTime call from his sister. Setting his coffee on the ground, he took the call and saw Remi's face on the screen.

"Remi," he said, automatically shifting to a smile.

She smiled back, and he could see that she was in uniform. Complete with the maroon beret that signified her status as Special Forces. A rarity since there were only a handful of women in her career field. Egan was bursting with pride over her accomplishments, but he had to get in a brotherly dig.

"Who the heck chooses the color red for a uniform hat?" he came out and asked. "Isn't it like painting a bullseye on your head?"

"It's the same people who choose flimsy light-weight flight caps that can blow off and get sucked into the engine of a fighter jet," she quickly countered.

Satisfied that he'd given as good as he'd got, Egan smiled again. "Are you Stateside?"

"Can't say." She grinned. "Well, I could, but then I'd have to kill you." Her grin faded as fast as it'd come. Considering their present circumstances, the old joke had fallen hard and flat. "How's Dad?"

Egan didn't want to put any more worry in her eyes, but she'd see right through any attempts for him to pretty up the truth. "Weak. He looks as if he's aged a decade since the heart attack. He looks old," Egan added in a mutter. "But don't go on a guilt trip. He totally understands why you can't be here."

She sighed and stared at him with blue eyes that were a genetic copy of his own. It was about the only genetics they had in common. Unlike him and their brothers, Remi hadn't gotten the black hair but rather dark auburn, and she favored their mom and Effie while the brothers took after their dad.

"Is he officially out of the woods?" Remi pressed.

Again, Egan didn't pull any punches. "To be determined, but it appears he's making some progress. He's got a long way to go, Remi. A long way."

"Thanks for not lying. Cal said pretty much the same thing. Blue is Blue and living in a fantasy that this is a temporary glitch. I'm hoping for the temporary but bracing for the long haul. I'm just sorry I can't be there. Is Dad asking for me?"

"He's asked about you," Egan said, emphasizing the difference. "He knows you're on the job."

"And Audrey?" she added a moment later.

"No sign of her yet."

Remi didn't offer up an opinion on that. "Well, let Dad know that I'll get home as soon as I can." Off screen, he heard someone mutter that it was time to go, and he saw the immediate shift in her expression from concerned daughter to Captain Donnelly, Combat Rescue Officer.

"Stay safe," Egan and she said at the same time. It had become their usual way to sign off ever since Remi had been commissioned in the Air Force.

Egan ended the call, put away his phone and picked up his coffee. His plan was to finish his breakfast with the horses, do an hour or two of paperwork and then head to the hospital to visit his dad and bring him those photo albums. There was an immediate hitch in that plan, though, when he saw the car pull into the driveway. Or rather when he saw the driver after she parked and stepped out.

Alana.

He felt a whole bunch of that leveling out bite the dust, and he cursed his reaction. He couldn't keep doing this, not when Dr. Abrams had asked Alana if she'd be willing to come to the ranch daily to work with his dad. She'd agreed, but Egan hadn't expected that "daily" to start even before his dad was out of the hospital.

Alana started for the house, but then she spotted him and walked his way. Not good. And this wasn't about leveling and such. Nope. This was about the fit of that pink dress she was wearing. It wasn't particularly short or clingy, but the morning breeze was doing a darn good job of molding it against her body. All those curves.

He didn't want to think of Alana that way. Didn't want to be reminded she had curves. And great legs.

Or have any thoughts about her blasted nipple size.

No, he didn't want any of that so Egan had worked up what he was sure was a scowl by the time she reached him.

"I know," she said right off the bat. "It's awkward with me being here, and I'm sorry if just seeing me brings back anything bad for you."

It was the right thing to say. And the wrong thing. Because in that instant before, she hadn't caused him to think of anything from the past. Not Jack, not his guilt. Nope. He'd been trying to tamp down the blasted heat he felt when he saw an attractive woman coming his way. A woman he'd be stupid to think of as anything but his best friend's widow and his dad's dietitian.

"It's okay," he managed, though it was a whopper so big he was surprised his jeans hadn't spontaneously caught on fire. "You're just doing your job. And doing my dad a favor by making house calls."

That caused the tension in his face to ease up a bit. Only a bit, though. But when she met his gaze, everything amped up. Everything, including the stupid urges inside him to notice anything and everything about her body.

"Dad's not here, though," he went on, forcing himself to speak. "He's still in the hospital."

She nodded. "I'm going over recipes and a shopping list with Maybell and your grandmother. I called Maybell last night, and they thought this would be a good time for me to come out."

Egan wondered if that was because the early hour fit better with Maybell's schedule or if there was some matchmaking going on since both Maybell and his grandmother knew he'd be around at this hour. But he immediately rethought that. No matchmaking. Maybell and Grammy Effie would be focused on his dad's needs, and there was no way the two women would think it was a good idea for Alana and him to get together.

Would they?

He was working up another scowl at that possibility when Alana spoke, drawing his attention back to her. Not that his attention had strayed too far.

"A heads-up," Alana went on. "Maybell and your grandmother told me your dad doesn't have a lot of willpower when it comes to snacks, and they asked me to get rid of the worst of his temptations. I might have to clean out any goodies stashed in the fridge and pantry. So, if you've got something in there, you might want to move it elsewhere."

"I'm stash-less at the moment, but there'll be my dad's cookies and caramel popcorn in the pantry. His ice cream in the freezer, of course." And that brought Egan to something he'd been meaning to bring up with her. "My dad isn't overweight, and I don't think his eating habits are terrible, so I don't understand why he had a heart attack."

"His eating habits aren't terrible," Alana readily agreed. "In fact, plenty of people eat the way he does and never have a problem. But in your dad's case, he had a serious blockage along with coronary artery disease. Surgery gave him a temporary fix, but changing his diet could prevent future problems. Could," she repeated for emphasis. "Right now, Dr. Abrams just wants him to eat as healthy a diet as possible to see if it makes a difference."

Egan was all for anything that would do that—make a difference. And he immediately felt the pangs of selfishness. The sooner his dad got back to normal, the sooner he could, too, but Egan wasn't just wishing and hoping for that.

"I want that frail look off his face," Egan muttered, surprised that he'd said it aloud.

Alana's nod was quick. So was the sound of agreement that followed. "He's scared, Egan. Really scared. It's a normal reaction, but knowing it's normal to feel that way doesn't lessen the fear."

Because his thoughts were a mess right now, with Alana part of that messy mix, he wondered if that applied to him. He didn't like to think of himself as afraid. Nobody did. Especially not a fighter pilot. But there was certainly some deep scary emotion from noticing that Alana was, well, a woman.

And there was the heat.

The timing for it totally sucked, but the wind shifted, carrying her scent straight to his nose, which in turn went straight to every other part of him. Hell's bells. This had to stop.

"Look, I'm just going to say this. Not for your benefit but for mine," he insisted. "It's Jack, not me, who's the town's real hero, and it would be disrespectful of me to think of you in any way other than his wife."

There. He'd spelled it out, but Alana didn't jump in with any nods or sounds of agreement. Just the opposite. Something went through her eyes. A fire. But unless he was totally misreading the signals, that fire had nothing to do with any thoughts whatsoever of how Egan felt about her.

"Disrespectful," she snarled. And yeah, it was definitely a snarl. "Real hero. His wife." She snarled those repeated phases, too.

Alana closed her mouth, opened it, pointed her index finger at him and then turned and marched away. After only a few seconds, she marched right back, and the finger aimed his way again.

"Let me tell you something about disrespect, heroism and being Jack Davidson's wife." Alana's voice had moved from a snarl to a snap that she spoke through clenched teeth. "Jack cheated on me."

It was as if Alana was speaking a foreign language. The words just didn't make sense, and that's why it took a while for them to sink in. Egan managed to shake his head, ready to launch into a denial, but Alana cut him off.

"That's not conjecture or a wild accusation," she insisted. "He cheated on me, and when I confronted him about it during a phone conversation, he admitted it was true."

Well, hell. Egan was wishing for that "foreign language" effect again, but it wasn't there. That came through loud and clear, and he couldn't think of a single reason why Alana, or Jack, would have lied about something like that.

Alana did more marching away, returning just as quickly, and he could see the struggle she was having to rein in her temper. He also saw the exact moment the temper burned itself out, leaving the pain, sadness and grief to wash over her.

It was washing over him, too.

"Did you know he'd cheated?" Alana came out and asked. "And don't you dare lie for him."

Egan shook his head. "I didn't know."

He held back on asking, *Who was she?* He didn't want to know, but he did rifle back through his memory to try to recall if Jack had ever mentioned anything about another woman. He hadn't.

Egan fully intended to respond to that with… something. He just didn't know what.

"I saw some unusual charges on his credit card bill," Alana continued a moment later. "I wasn't snooping," she added, "but I noticed that his automatic payment on it had expired so I logged into his account and looked at the bill, intending to pay it and then let him know about it." She paused, swallowed hard. "I saw charges for a hotel in London. Restaurants and taxis. All out of the ordinary expenses for him especially since I didn't even know he'd been in London."

Alana stopped, put her arms on the top of the corral fence and looked out at the horses. She stayed that way for a long time.

"I called him, figuring he could explain the charges," she finally went on. "But instead he made a full confession that he had, indeed, been with another woman. He gave me the spiel that he hadn't meant for it to happen, that it was just someone he knew and that they'd both been going through a hard time. I hit the roof. Full-scale yelling and ranting. Calling him every name in the book. Lots of f-bombs."

She turned, looking at him, and he saw the tears in her eyes. Shit, shit, shit. He'd spent three years building up a barricade between Alana and his emotions, and those tears sent that barricade crashing down.

Part of him wanted to pull her into his arms to try to comfort her. Another part of him wanted to defend Jack. And curse him at the same time. But Egan didn't do any of that. Instead, he came out with a response that could best be described as underwhelming and shitty.

"All Jack ever talked about was you," Egan managed. "He loved you," he added, hoping that would help.

It didn't. The fire in her eyes didn't ignite again, but more of that pain and grief did.

"But he didn't love me enough to stay faithful," she muttered. "And a few hours later, he died, no doubt still hearing the last words I said to him."

"Last words," Egan said, not making it a question, but Alana answered it as one, anyway.

"I told him *go to hell, you cheating son of a bitch*." Her voice was barely a whisper, and she repeated the rest of it from over her shoulder as she walked away from him. *"Go straight to hell, Jack Davidson."*

CHAPTER SIX

ALANA DIDN'T OFTEN allow herself to wallow in the past because she'd learned the hard way that wallowing just sucked her down lower and lower. When memories of Jack, his cheating and her last words to him came slamming into her like an entire fleet of semitrucks, she usually tried to throw herself into work. Or did some online retail therapy. Heck, even virtual dating.

She wasn't doing any of those things now.

Nope. She had rescheduled her de-stashing appointment with Effie and Maybell. Had rescheduled all her other appointments today as well, and was sitting on the sofa in her house with all the blinds closed. Instead of a proper lunch, she was eating rocky road ice cream straight from the half-gallon carton with a spoon she normally reserved for serving mashed potatoes and such. One of those little teaspoons just hadn't seemed indulgent enough for her mood.

The TV was on and streaming the second movie of a *Jurassic Park* marathon. They weren't what anyone would call comfort movies, but Alana figured there wasn't much hope in any movie being able to console her so she'd allowed Netflix to choose with its Surprise Me option.

While the dinosaurs chased people and roared enough to shake the TV, Alana just let the tears come. Again, that was normally something she tried to keep in check only because crying jags required long recoveries, but everything inside her was whirling in a tight ball of that insatiable guilt and regret.

She'd already played the what-if stuff. What if she'd never looked at the credit card bill? What if she'd waited until Jack was home to talk to him about it? What if she'd sent him an email, which he likely wouldn't have seen for a day or two? What if? What if? What if?

Without the phone call and Jack's confession of an affair, without her screaming obscenities at him, he might not have felt the need to go see his old pal, Egan. Jack might have stayed put at whatever military site or station where he'd been waiting to respond to whatever mission came up. Heck, he might have even stayed with the woman he'd been cheating with.

Yes, even that would have been preferable to him being dead.

Mercy, this hurt. Reliving the what-ifs and replaying everything that'd happened from the time of her phone call rant to the military officers showing up at her door early the next morning to notify her of Jack's death.

She could replay the notification, too, the slowly spoken words of the colonel from the local base who'd never met Jack but had had the misfortune of being the bearer of such heart-crushing news. He'd brought a minister and a nurse with him, and the pair had kept their attention pinned on her, no doubt ready to jump in if either of their services were required.

But there'd been no such requirements.

Because Alana hadn't been able to speak, scream, pass out or have any other extreme outward reaction. No words had come. Only the silent tears.

Ironically, Colleen had been with her for that because she'd dropped by to check on her since Alana hadn't responded to any of Loralee's or her texts. By then, Alana had known about Colleen leaving Egan. She hadn't, however, known that her sister had been having an affair as well, and in those moments before the dreaded knock at her door, Alana had been about to launch into spilling all about her cheating husband. But she hadn't gotten the chance. The notification had stopped her words.

And her world.

After that, everything was a sickening, throbbing ache that left her, rightfully so, an emotional mess.

Alana hated, hated, hated that she couldn't just be pissed off at a cheating husband. That he wasn't alive for them to hash it out face-to-face and for them to find some kind of resolution that wouldn't make her feel as if she were being eaten alive. Their marriage almost certainly wouldn't have survived since she would have never been able to trust him again. But if Jack were alive, then she would just be a cynical divorcée with trust issues and not a screwed-up widow who didn't deserve the pity that so many people doled out to her.

Her phone rang, and she scowled at the interruption. And then frowned when she saw her sister's name on the screen. It was rare for Colleen to call her, and the timing was eerie since she'd just been thinking about her.

Alana instantly got a bad thought, that maybe Egan had called Colleen and asked her to check on her. After all, he was the only person who'd witnessed her recent meltdown.

But she couldn't imagine Egan doing something like that.

If he were genuinely worried about her, he would have either checked on her himself or braved a call to Loralee to do that. Loralee and he weren't buds by any stretch of the imagination, but it would take more of an imagination stretch for there to be a scenario where he'd call his ex-wife.

Even though she didn't want to talk to anyone, Alana took the call in case this was some kind of emergency, but she put it on speaker so she could continue to eat the rocky road.

"Alana," her sister greeted, and then Colleen stopped, no doubt because at that exact moment, a T. rex and a velociraptor got into a deafening confrontation. Colleen continued after a moment, but Alana missed a good chunk of what she said before Alana muted the TV. "…okay?" Colleen finished up.

"Sorry," Alana muttered. "Just watching a movie."

Colleen stayed silent, probably because she was

wondering why the heck Alana was doing that on a workday. "Uh, is everything okay?" she asked, which was likely a repeat of what she'd said earlier.

"Okay enough," Alana lied. "I just needed a little downtime. Is everything okay with you?" After all, it was a workday for Colleen, too, and since her sister was a lawyer for a nonprofit in Dallas, she would have probably been at her office.

"Yes, I'm fine." There was nothing in her voice to indicate otherwise, either, and the concern Alana had had just seconds before vanished. "I'm calling because I heard about the life celebration for Jack."

Alana couldn't bite back the groan in time, but it was muffled since her mouth was full of ice cream. "Yes," Alana answered, swallowing. "Tilly's arranging it."

And that made her wonder if Egan had figured out a way to decline doing master of ceremonies duties at the unveiling.

"Loralee told me about it," Colleen confirmed and then paused again. "I was, uh, wondering if you thought it'd be all right if I came."

Now it was Alana's turn to pause except hers turned into a big-time hesitation when she tried to grasp the request. Over the past three years, Colleen had mostly met Loralee anywhere but in Emerald Creek for their get-togethers. She'd come back to town a time or two to visit their aunt, but her sister had basically done a sneak in and out, knowing that she would get multiple stink eyes and even scowls from those who considered Egan the wronged hometown hero and Colleen the breaker of the hero's heart.

"I wouldn't be up front and center," Colleen went on. "I'd hang back just to watch and well, be there."

Alana nearly blurted out, *Be there for whom?* But Jack had been Colleen's brother-in-law, and they had gotten along well. Still, if Jack had gotten the chance to learn about what Colleen had done to Egan, that "getting along" would have ended pronto. Jack would have taken Egan's side.

Did that mean Egan would do the same for Jack?

Maybe. Brothers-in-arms and all that. It could mean that Egan would get past something his bestie had done even though he could never forgive his ex-wife for doing the same thing.

"Aunt Loralee said Egan probably wouldn't be there," Colleen went on, "or rather she said, he'd find a way out of it," she amended. "So, I thought it would be okay especially since people will be focused on you and the painting."

Alana sighed. She definitely didn't want the focus. Heck, she didn't want the life celebration, period, but her sister was wrong if she thought no one would notice her even if she stayed back.

"Even if Egan isn't there, his friends and supporters will be," Alana spelled out for her.

"I know, I know," Colleen said almost like a whine. "And I also know I'll deserve any raised eyebrows or whispers I get about what happened between Egan and me. But it's been three years, and I want to be able to visit Aunt Loralee and you more often. For that to happen, people have to get used to seeing me again."

"Whatever memories are better than elephants', that's what people around here have. I still get flak about a banana split I ordered two years ago." Alana left it at that, but the bottom line here was that Colleen would get flak for a lifetime.

Would Jack have, too?

Maybe. But it wouldn't have had the venom that folks aimed at Colleen. Jack could be forgiven because he had been all the things Egan was. Excuses would likely have been made about him being under so much pressure with his job that he'd caved and made a mistake.

Colleen hadn't gotten such concessions. Not from the town. Not from Egan.

"I was hoping you'd think it would be all right," Colleen concluded. "I guess the right thing to do would be for me to run the idea past Tilly."

Alana wanted to groan again, but instead she took another bite of ice cream to give her a moment to think of how this would play out. Tilly wouldn't want anything to spoil this big day she was planning. A day about Jack. And Colleen would be a serious distraction/gossip magnet, no doubt about that. So Tilly would tell Colleen—in the politest way possible, of course—to visit the memorial painting a day or two after the unveiling.

Alana felt a little cowardly for dumping that conversation on Tilly, but she didn't have the bandwidth right now to deal with it.

"Yes, talk to Tilly," Alana encouraged, and she welcomed the little dinging sound of the incoming call because it meant she could dole out a quick goodbye to her sister.

Alana soon regretted that, though.

She hit the answer button before she realized that it was a FaceTime call from her latest virtual date, a guy calling himself Lucky, which was probably wishful thinking on his part since he was after all on a virtual dating site.

After a glance, she was guessing he might not be actual date material for her since he appeared to be only in his early twenties. He had a gamer vibe going on with a PlayStation 5 T-shirt, bulky headphones now draped around his neck and a look in his eyes that conveyed it'd been a while since he'd seen a real human on a screen. She thought she saw specks of Cheetos on his chin.

"Sorry," Alana immediately said, and she cut off adding anything about why she'd hit Accept Call. Instead, she frowned when she looked at the time— 2:00 p.m. She did have a virtual date scheduled today, something she'd forgotten to cancel, but that wasn't supposed to happen for another five hours. "You're early," she blurted out.

"Yep. I play *Assassin's Creed* with a group of guys, and we're on our break. Figured I'd see if I could catch you while I was free." He frowned, studied her. "Um, are you free?"

"Not exactly. I'm in the middle of…something," she settled for saying. No way did she want to get into her meltdown or the cause for it. Especially since this "date" would be going nowhere. "You said on your profile that you were thirty-four."

"Oh, that." He grinned, as if there was something to grin about. "I changed it when I saw your profile pic. Figured you wouldn't accept a date request if you knew I was twenty."

"No, I wouldn't have," she admitted.

"See," he said, as if proving a point. "This way, we meet and see how it goes. That wouldn't have happened if I hadn't changed my age." He studied her again. "You don't look much like your profile pic. Was that like a fake or something you downloaded 'cause it kinda looked like Scarlett Jo. You know, Johansson. She's hot and kick-ass. But you sort of look like maybe her older sister or something."

She sighed because it was true. In the picture, she'd fixed her hair and put on makeup. She also hadn't been crying for hours.

"You didn't catch me at my best moment," she muttered.

"No problem." He seemed to perk up at the thought that somewhere underneath her sad face, there would indeed be a beautiful Scarlett. "I'll just call back in at seven, and we can go from there."

Alana was about to spell out there'd not be any going from anywhere and she didn't want a call back or another virtual date ever, but the knock at her door stopped her.

"Excuse me a second," she told Lucky, and she got

up and crept—yes, crept—to the door to look out and see who dared to intrude on her pity party.

It was Egan.

Specifically, Egan the cowboy, in his jeans and black Stetson. He wasn't the absolute last person she'd expected to show up, but he wasn't anywhere in the top five hundred possibilities, either. It wasn't hard to figure out, though, why he was there on her porch. Not with his expression practically screaming that he didn't want to be there but was too much of a good guy to leave things as they had.

Alana considered ignoring him, but she scratched that option when Lucky seemed to shout, "You still there? You're sure you're okay?"

No way could Egan have missed that what with the thin door of her house, and if she didn't respond, he might think she was harming herself or something. She didn't want to see him but didn't want him calling 911 on her, either.

Cradling the ice cream in the crook of her arm, Alana opened the door, ready to give him a spiel about her being just fine and dandy. Egan started his own spiel first, though.

"I won't keep you. I just wanted to check on you," he said in a way that made her think he'd rehearsed it. He looked at the tub of ice cream and what was likely smears of rocky road on her mouth. "I won't ask you if you're okay."

"Who is that?" Lucky wanted to know.

It wasn't an easy question because it required her to think of what label to put on Egan. Friend didn't seem right. Dead husband's best friend wasn't the way to go, either. Since it was causing her even more mental overload, Alana went with the easy solution. She ended the call and turned off her phone so that he wouldn't be able to call her right back.

"Did I interrupt something?" Egan asked, tipping his head to the phone.

"No." And once again, she fell short with possible answers since she didn't especially want to get into anything about Lucky, the lying gamer. "Nothing important, just an ill-timed virtual date," she added in a mutter.

Of course, ending that call now freed her up to talk to Egan, something else that would stretch her bandwidth, but she thought Egan might be the lesser of the two evils right now.

Egan made a sound that could have meant anything, and energy was practically radiating off him. Apparently, he'd done some "lesser of two evils" kind of thinking and had opted for a visit rather than trying to put their last encounter out of his mind.

"You've been crying," he grumbled. Then, he groaned. "I'm sorry."

It was such a "good guy" sort of thing to say. "It's not your fault," she grumbled right back.

His mouth tightened, and he slid off his Stetson and shook his head. "That's what I came here to tell you. It's not your fault that Jack died. It's mine."

Again, a "good guy" sort of thing to say, and it caused her to sigh and step back. The heat pouring in from the open door would soon cause the ice cream to melt, but she didn't think heat stroke should play into his "good guy" actions. Besides, she also didn't want any of her neighbors to get a peek at her because that in turn would generate "poor, pitiful widow" looks and murmurs for heaven knew how long.

She motioned for Egan to come in, shut the door and set the ice cream down on the coffee table. He glanced around as if seeing the place for the first time, and she realized that was exactly what he was doing since he'd never been here. This wasn't the place she'd shared with Jack. Alana had moved from there shortly after his funeral and bought this small cottage on the far edge of town.

Egan's attention landed on the TV where the dinosaurs and humans were finishing up the big finale scene with lots of CGI teeth, chomping jaws and muted sounds of terror. His attention shifted to the massive pile of tissues on the end table and sofa. Then, he looked at her again, no doubt piecing together what had gone on in her life for the past seven hours.

"I just took a little time for myself," she settled for saying. "And while I appreciate you checking on me, it really wasn't necessary."

He gave her a serious "I beg to differ" look. "I was worried about you. I swear, I didn't know about Jack having an affair. And I didn't know about the argument you had with him." He paused. "Have you talked to a grief counselor about all of this?"

"Yes," she admitted. "Have you?"

"Yeah," he verified.

When he didn't add more other than a long weary breath, Alana contributed what had been the counselor's mantra for their dozen or so visits. "She told me it wasn't my fault, that my screaming rant probably hadn't contributed to Jack being killed. That was BS, of course. What about you? What did your counselor tell you?"

The weariness and the length of the breathing fired up a notch. "That it wasn't my fault, that there was nothing I could have done to stop that IED. But in my case, that was real bullshit. I could have done something by not asking Jack to drop by to see me. If I hadn't asked, he would have been twenty miles away and safe."

Twenty miles. She hadn't known that. In fact, other than the location, Alana didn't know a lot of the details about Jack's last moments on earth. Only what the colonel doing the notification had told her, and that had been just the basics. Jack's date, time, location and cause of death along with an estimation of when his body would be returned to the States. She hadn't pressed for more, hadn't been able to do that because any and everything only reminded her of the blasted argument.

She hadn't missed Egan's *real bullshit* and knew what it meant. That he was minimizing any part she might have had in Jack's death while putting the blame squarely on his shoulders. Which were toned and wide.

Something she wished she hadn't noticed.

"One day, when we're drunk or something, maybe you can tell me how Jack spent the last hour or so of his life," she muttered.

He lifted one of his toned wide shoulders, but it wasn't a casual gesture. Far from it. She saw the pain in his eyes. The ache in every inch of his body. Even if that last hour or so with Jack had been all happy, it would still stir up the horrible memory since anything happy would have blown up with the IED.

"Maybe," Egan finally said, and she didn't know if he'd hedged for her sake. Or his. Maybe both since no matter what Egan recalled, it would bring on a fresh round of grief.

Perhaps it was that prospect of grief that had Egan staying silent for a long time before doing another glance around at the TV and ice cream. They were her failed attempts at digging her fingernails in to stop herself from taking a total plunge into that hell place inside her head.

"So, did this virtual date own goats, chickens or ask about things that shouldn't be asked?" he wanted to know.

Of course, this was a diversion attempt, one meant to draw her on to a different subject where tit-for-tat jokes might be possible. Where for a couple of moments, she might not think of why she had just consumed two thousand calories of ice cream and watched a snarky Jeff Goldblum evade dinosaurs. Even though Alana was sure his attempt would fail big-time, she went along with it, anyway.

"No, but he gave me a backhanded compliment by

saying I looked like Scarlett Johansson's older sister or *something*. I suspect by *something*, he meant more of *The Creature from the Black Lagoon*."

"Never," Egan said, but it looked as if he immediately wanted to take back the words. Maybe because they had been too personal and an insider revelation that he didn't believe her capable of bearing such a resemblance to a swamp monster.

Despite everything, that made her smile a little. "Thanks. *Or something*," she added in a tongue-in-cheek mutter.

He smiled a little, too, and then just as quickly throttled back on it. "Look, I know things aren't... comfortable between us, but if you want to talk, I'll listen. No alcohol, food or dinosaurs required."

It was a generous offer, and Alana didn't point out that it only cemented his "hero/all-around good cowboy" image. But she did go ahead and bring up one big sticking point to such a talk.

"Earlier, we were upset because there's this... whatever it is stirring between us," she said. Such a frank discussion was treading on boggy ground, but at the moment it felt as if staying silent would be even boggier. "It could lead to some honesty that might be hard for you to handle."

He stared at her, reminding her that in addition to "good guy" stuff, he was also "hot cowboy" stuff. That was a big reason for the stirrings. Hot was hot no matter how much baggage it came with.

"The offer stands," he said with his jaw muscles

at war with each other. "If you want or need to talk, call me."

He slid back on his Stetson, giving her a view of his backside as he strolled out the door and into the sunset. Well, the sun and the heat, anyway. And even without the romantic sunset, he still managed to look amazing.

She frowned. This was why her head was so messed up. One minute she was grieving and guilting over her dead husband, and the next minute she was lusting over a hot cowboy who probably had a good streak that went all the way to the bone. One minute, she was wondering about Jack's last hours, and another she was wondering what it felt like to kiss Egan.

Oh, yeah. Clearly identifiable reasons for a messed-up head.

She shut the door and cursed when she saw the screen of her phone light up. At first, she thought it might be the lying "barely legal" Lucky, but it was Tilly. Alana didn't especially want to talk to her, but this was probably about how she'd told Colleen not to attend the life celebration. Because no way would Tilly actually want her there to steal any thunder from Jack. A brief conversation, emphasis on *brief*, might cleanse her emotional palate of Egan.

Or not.

She answered the call while she watched Egan climb into his big pickup truck, a maneuver that caused his jeans to mold against his superior butt. She nixed the notion of what it would feel like to kiss

Egan and went with wondering if he looked as good out of those jeans as in them.

"This, this, this," she grumbled. It was what you got when you hadn't had sex in three years and logical thoughts had a very short shelf life in her mind.

"This what?" Tilly asked.

That was a reminder of her former mother-in-law being on the line, and Alana was so thankful she hadn't blurted out Egan's name. But his name got spoken, anyway. By Tilly.

"I just talked to Colleen," Tilly let her know when Alana didn't respond. "I told her I didn't think Egan would be at the life celebration because of being so torn up about his dad and all. He is still torn up, right?"

There seemed to be some unspoken questions tacked on to that one. A fishing expedition to see just how much Alana did know about Egan's state of mind. It was possible that one of the ranch hands had witnessed their emotional encounter at the pasture fence this morning and already started some gossip about it. Then again, maybe Tilly was just aware that Alana had been hired to work with Derek and therefore might wind up seeing Egan as well.

"Egan's torn up," Alana confirmed. It wasn't exactly a bombshell since anyone who'd caught a glimpse of him in the past week would have seen the worry all over his face.

"That's what I figured," Tilly concluded. "And it's why I told Colleen that it'll be all right for her to come to the life celebration."

While that stunned Alana to silence, Tilly let out a little sound of glee.

"It'll be so good to have Colleen there," Tilly went on. "It'll be just like old times."

CHAPTER SEVEN

EGAN GLANCED OVER the notes he'd just made at his father's desk and then handed them to the ranch foreman, Jesse Whitlock. It was a schedule of sorts, starting with today's date. When his dad would be coming home from the hospital.

Phase one of their new normal.

In a couple of hours, his dad would finally be released, with a whole bunch of medical orders and instructions, that is. Egan would drive him home and make sure that his dad understood the orders and instructions weren't suggestions but rather hard-and-fast rules he'd have to obey.

Unless his dad had gone through some kind of serious mood change in the past twenty-four hours, though, he wouldn't balk about those rules. Wouldn't balk about much of anything other than maybe how tired he was. It was one of the reasons Egan wanted to push a little.

All right, maybe push a lot.

If Egan laid down a bunch of rules, the old Derek might resurface. The Derek who had a mile-wide stubborn streak and the fierce independence that'd been the legacy of his ancestors who'd built Saddlebrook from the ground up. The Derek who hadn't made a habit of threats, but when he had used that particular tool in his arsenal, it could have caused the one on the receiving end to piss his or her pants. That wasn't the literal image Egan was going for, but he wanted to see some fire in his dad's eyes again.

Below the note of his father's return, Egan had put the dates of his leave. He had three more weeks because he'd already used nine days of the thirty since the heart attack. Egan had added a question mark after his leave dates, and then listed out more dates and question marks for Cal's and Blue's visits. There were gaps, serious ones, where neither Egan nor one of his brothers would be at the ranch, and that's why he'd asked Jesse to come into the office.

Jesse looked over the notes, his forehead bunching up some, maybe because of the uncertainty of what he was reading. After all, this was phase one of his new normal, too. From what Egan had seen, Jesse and his dad had worked out the ranching duties with Derek handling most of the paperwork and the livestock purchases and sales, which included livestock shows and lots of meetings. Jesse, along with training some of the horses, handled the work schedule for the hands and did the hiring and firing.

"Any chance you'll be able to extend your leave?" Jesse asked.

Egan lifted one shoulder. "It's possible, but that would only buy us another two weeks at most. I need you to look at that schedule and tell me if we should temporarily hire someone else. Maybe someone who can hit the stock shows and deal with some of the meetings."

Jesse shrugged, too. "You think Derek will be okay with hiring someone?"

"No," Egan said without hesitation.

But that was wishful thinking. He didn't want his father to be okay with him hiring anyone to semi take his place, but it was possible his dad had the same disinterest in that as he had everything else. Except those photo albums, of course.

"I've had conversations with his doctor and heart surgeon," Egan explained, "and they want him to take off at least a couple of months and then slowly ease back into work."

Jesse stayed quiet a moment, obviously mulling that over. "Then, rather than piss off Derek by bringing in someone new, even temporarily, how about I cover some of the meetings and livestock shows? Maybe you can deal with the rest by working remotely from the base?"

Egan nodded, figuring that was the way this would play out. That also wouldn't give his dad the option of permanent retirement because someone had been hired to fill his boots. Or rather the toe of one of his boots, anyway.

Of course, working remotely from the base meant that Egan would have to squeeze in the ranch stuff along with the other things he had on his commander's plate. It wouldn't be easy. In fact, it'd be damn hard, but he was already carrying too much guilt over Jack's death, and he didn't want any additional guilt that he hadn't done everything possible for his dad.

"Remi's not on the schedule," Jesse muttered.

Egan glanced up to take note of Jesse's expression, but he couldn't read the man's usual poker face. Still, he figured there were some emotions stirring beneath the surface since Remi and Jesse had hooked up a time or two when they'd been teenagers and Jesse had just been starting out as ranch hand. Egan didn't know how his sister and Jesse had left things since Remi wasn't much of a blabbermouth about her personal life, either.

"No, Remi's not on the schedule," Egan answered. "She's not due for leave for months and is on deployment somewhere." Even with his high security clearance, Egan didn't know where exactly. He rarely did know where she was. "She's going to try to get here soon, but there are no guarantees."

Jesse's poker face stayed in place, but Egan did see his attention shift to the window. "Alana just drove up."

Egan got up and went to the window, immediately realizing that the gesture was nowhere near close to a "poker face" reaction. After all, he'd known Alana would be coming since she'd texted him that she was meeting Maybell in the kitchen at eight this morning. And here she was. Stepping out of her car and looking, well, like someone who was snagging way too much of Egan's attention.

Hell.

He'd dreamed about her. Not a good dream, either,

since it had involved kissing her. It was hard enough to keep his mind off her during the day without doing some dream making out.

Jesse made a low sound, which barely qualified as a sound, but with it and a quick glance at Egan and Alana, the man seemed to take in the big picture. Thankfully, Jesse didn't remark on it.

"Anything other than this?" Jesse asked, holding up the paper with the schedule riddled with question marks.

When Egan shook his head and added a muttered thanks, the man headed out. Egan did some mental heading out, too, by forcing himself away from the window. That became easier to do once Alana had gone inside and was no longer in sight.

Cursing himself and that brainless part of him behind the zipper of his jeans, Egan sat back down at the desk to go through the stack of mail. There was plenty of it to occupy his attention and get his mind off Alana. Or so he thought. But the first thing he opened was a flyer that Tilly had sent to his dad, and there was a note enclosed.

I really hope you can be there, Tilly had written.

There was more, but Egan stopped himself from reading it since it was personal and not business. He set it aside, creating a new stack of mail he'd take to his dad, and he went on to the next letter. There was no return address so he opened it.

And got an emotional blast of a different kind.

Because it was a family photo, similar to the ones

his dad had sent Egan right before he'd had a heart attack. This one had a huge difference, though.

It was a shot of Egan's mom with him and his three siblings.

This one had been taken at Remi's first birthday party, which had been around the time his mom found out she had cancer. There were no signs of the disease, though, on her face. Just a beaming smile as she watched her baby girl dig her chubby little hands into the small cake that was on the tray of her high chair. A much larger cake with a single lit candle was on the table, and in the shot, Egan, Cal and Blue were all eyeing it with intense anticipation that they would soon chow down on the sugary treat.

His dad was in the shot, too, standing just behind his mom, and like her, Remi was the center of attention. Just as she should have been. Everyone was smiling, or at least looking hopeful. There were no hints that soon the world in this photo would cease to exist.

Egan frowned and felt the flick of grief. It wasn't the same sea of it that had been there for the first couple of years after his mom's death, but it was there. Always there.

Unlike the flyer, there was no note with the photo, but he turned it over and saw that something had been written on the back. *Thought you might like this one for your family albums. Tammy.*

Egan instantly recalled the woman who'd once worked at the ranch as sort of a jack-of-all-trades. Sometimes, she did housekeeping and cooking.

Other times, she babysat. She would have no doubt been at Remi's party and had taken the photos.

He debated what to do with it. Yeah, it was a happy family shot all right and worthy of framing, but it might spur a fresh round of grief for his dad. And because it might not sit well with Audrey, either.

Egan suspected that's why there were no photos of his dad and mom together here in the office or in any of the living areas of the house. In fact, here in the office, pictures were in short supply, period. There was one of Egan and his siblings taken when Egan had become an officer in the Navy. A stiff pose where it appeared everyone but Egan wanted to be somewhere else. That was it.

Unlike next door.

That room had been his mom's crafting "studio" where she'd quilted, done stained glass, knitted and seemingly done a dozen other things in what had to have been very little spare time. After all, she'd had four kids, helped her husband run the ranch and even dabbled in barrel racing for charity fund drives at the local rodeos and fairs.

His mom had died in that room, too.

She'd been hospitalized for weeks before her death, and then when she had gotten the news that time was running out for her, she had decided to come home for her final days. Egan had been eight and therefore old enough to sneak around and hear some of the conversations that had taken place back then. Conversations that had stuck with him even after the passing of three decades. His mom had wanted to die at home but not in the bedroom she'd shared with his dad. She hadn't wanted him to have to deal with the memories of her death on a daily basis just by walking into it.

Ironic since his dad had ended up moving rooms when he'd married Audrey and presumably not wanted to bring his new wife to the suite he'd shared with his first wife. Still, his mom had been thinking about her husband when she'd chosen to live out her last moments in the craft studio. Her space, surrounded by dozens of family photos and some of her finished and unfinished projects.

Egan didn't go into that room. To the best of his knowledge, none of his siblings did. Which meant his mom had had it right about not wanting to die in a spot they'd have to see or walk through daily. Still, he knew it was there, and sometimes, that was a comfort.

Sometimes, just thinking about her was still unbearable.

Since his dad might be having one of those days, where he couldn't think about the woman he'd loved and lost, Egan didn't add the photo to the stash he'd take up to Derek. Instead, he made a note to send Tammy a thank-you note, and he'd set the picture aside for when his dad was further along in his recovery.

Shoving aside the thoughts of the photo, the craft room, his mom and everything else that wasn't work-related, Egan continued to make his way through the mail. He sorted through at least a dozen invoices for supplies and such when he came to a manila envelope addressed to him. When he opened it, he did some more cursing.

Because the blasted letter from Colleen was inside. It was now splotched with garbage stains, and there was a sticky note attached to it.

"This must have accidentally fallen off the counter and into the trash," his housekeeper had written. "Thought it might be important."

Crap. He didn't want to deal with reminders of his ex on top of everything else, but this was partly his fault. He should have shoved the letter deeper into the trash. Or poured ketchup on it to completely cover it. He didn't have any ketchup available right now, but he did the next best thing. He tore it in half and put it at the bottom of the wastepaper basket next to the desk.

If his dad had had a shredder, he would have used that, but Derek could be old school and a pack rat when it came to that sort of thing. He saved paper copies, which was the reason his filing cabinets were jammed to the hilt.

Egan was ready to dive back into more mail when his phone dinged with a text from Maybell.

I'm running late at the grocery store. Could you meet Alana in the kitchen? the cook asked.

To the best of his knowledge, Maybell had never run late in the entire time she'd worked at the ranch so this might be yet another attempt at matchmaking. Then again, there was a lot going on this morning so it was possible Maybell's shopping time had gone way over its usual because of the items she'd have to be getting for Derek's new diet.

Both wanting to see Alana and wanting to avoid her, Egan grumbled his way from his dad's office and toward the kitchen. He passed one of the house-keepers, Reba Neumann, along the way, and like Maybell, she was a long-time employee.

"I let Alana in," Reba let him know, and carrying a stack of folded towels, she headed toward the stairs.

Egan took a deep breath, stepped into the kitchen. But he didn't see Alana. It didn't take him long to hear her, though, and he followed the sounds of some shuffling around to the pantry. Then, he saw her, all right.

Or rather he saw her backside.

She had a huge canvas bag in one hand and had leaned down to gather items off the bottom shelf. She probably didn't realize that (a) anyone would be behind her watching and that (b) her position caused her pale green dress to ride up so he could see her thighs and nearly all the way to her panties. If she was wearing them, that is. He forced his brain not to consider that she might be commando.

He cleared his throat to let his presence be known, and she nearly smacked her head on one of the higher shelves when she spun around to face him. The peep show was over, but Egan got a show of a different kind when he looked at her face.

No tears today. Or bits of ice cream on her mouth. She looked rested and…amazing. He gave up trying not to notice that about her, and for a moment, he let himself savor the little kick of heat.

"I'm just putting the final touches in place for

your dad's homecoming," she said, lifting the bag. "Maybell's getting the new groceries, but I'm replacing a few of the items like brownie-stuffed chocolate chip cookies and marshmallow ice-cream topping with healthier options so he won't be tempted."

He saw those items in her canvas bag and noticed that there were different brands now on the pantry shelf.

"I've laid out some recipe cards for Maybell," Alana went on, sounding all business as she stepped around him and went to the kitchen counter where, yep, there were recipe cards. "And I've had some talks with your dad about sticking to his new food plan. He was very, uh, compliant, but if he has any questions, or if he's tempted to completely toss the diet, he can think of me as a foodie sponsor and call or text me."

She stopped her spiel and huffed.

"I dreamed about you," she said, no longer sounding all business. "I don't want to dream about you. Except now that I've had the dream, I do want that since it was a good one. Do you know what I mean?"

Sadly, he did. And he nearly blurted out, *Was the dream about kissing?* Because the kissing dream he'd had about her was damn sure sticking with him.

"I understand," he admitted.

That admission should have gotten him moving back away from her. It should have made him recommit to keeping Alana hands off. But Egan stayed firmly in place and wondered what cure he was going to need to make himself immune to what would certainly be an emotional train wreck if that kiss happened. Because a kiss would lead to other things.

Like hot naked sex.

Probably incredible sex. Which in turn would lead to hot, raw guilt. There. He'd mentally spelled it out, and while it didn't cool him down one little bit, it at least got him moving. Well, that and the alarm he'd set to remind him it was time to leave for the hospital to pick up his dad.

According to Dr. Abrams, he was expecting Derek to be released at ten o'clock, which was still well over an hour and a half from now, but Egan had wanted to get there early. Effie must have felt the same way since she'd already had one of the hands drive her there.

Egan tore his gaze from her face to the canvas bag. "Uh, you need any help with…anything before I leave for the hospital?"

She sighed as if the answer were obvious. Alana likely needed help dumping a proverbial cold shower on this lust just as much as he did, but she didn't voice that. She merely seemed to conjure up a smile and shook her head.

"No, I've got it," she assured him. "Go ahead and bring your dad home."

Before the moment could turn awkward, or hotter than it already was, he grabbed his keys and Stetson from the pegs by the door and headed out to his truck.

The ranch was two miles outside of town, but as usual there wasn't much traffic on the country road.

Added to that, it was usually a drive Egan liked to make because he could often spot the ranch's horses or Angus cattle in the east pastures that he passed on the way. Today didn't disappoint. The Angus were milling around one of the ponds that dotted the ranch grounds.

Egan reached the hospital in just a couple of minutes, parked and went in, heading down the hall that was familiar to him now since he'd visited his dad at least twice a day. This morning, the door to his room was slightly ajar so Egan poked in his head, figuring his dad would already be dressed and waiting to be released.

He was.

But he wasn't alone. And he wasn't with Effie, either. She was nowhere in sight.

Egan practically snapped to attention when he saw the woman in uniform sitting at the foot of the bed next to his dad. Audrey.

"Oh, hello, Egan," Audrey said, getting to her feet. She gave him what he thought of as a general's smile. Reserved and with no teeth showing. "Derek and I are just catching up while we wait on his release paperwork."

"Audrey," he greeted back, wondering if his expression was one of a lieutenant colonel addressing a higher-ranking officer. Probably.

Egan shifted his attention to his dad to see how he was handling this visit, and noticed he wasn't exactly smiling, but he also wasn't sporting the gloomy expression he had been since the heart attack. His dad was obviously happy, or rather happy-ish at least, to have Audrey there. Which, of course, only confused Egan. He couldn't imagine being happy with an occasional spouse, but his dad seemed to be just fine with it.

"Audrey and I were going over some of the diet changes on my agenda," his dad explained.

Egan thought there was more to it than that. There seemed to be some heat in the air. Or maybe he was just projecting because of the heated situation he'd just left with Alana. Maybe, though, he was picking up on actual attraction that was still there between Audrey and his dad.

"Alana's at the house now setting the stage for your diet changes," Egan told him.

"Alana," Audrey repeated, her gray eyes brightening a little. "That's the cute blonde who used to moon over you?"

Egan frowned. "She mooned over Jack."

"Later she did, after you showed no interest in her," Audrey was quick to point out.

Egan had shown no interest in Alana because Jack had told Egan he had plans to ask her out. That had made Alana off-limits. Too bad those off-limit lines were now blurring.

"Alana married Jack," Egan added, though he was positive Audrey remembered that. Even if Audrey hadn't been around for the wedding, she would have recalled Jack's spouse when she learned of his death.

At the mention of Jack's name, Audrey studied him as if he were a specimen under a lab slide. Probably checking to see if he had a raging case of PTSD. That's the label Audrey would likely put on it, anyway, but it was a particular label that Egan despised since it was way too vague for him personally. His baggage was guilt and grief, a whole boatload of it, and if Audrey gave him the once-over another three years from now, Egan was certain those two things would still be there.

"Where's Grammy Effie?" he asked to cut through the silence.

"She went to vending to get some coffee," his dad explained, checking the time. "She's been gone a while so I guess she wanted to give Audrey and me a little time."

"I only just got here about a half hour ago," Audrey tacked on to that. She, too, checked the time on the phone that she had gripped in her hand. A phone that dinged, causing her to frown. "Sorry, but I have to take this. I won't be long," she assured them, and she stepped out of the room, closing the door behind her.

His dad gave him the once-over, too, but it didn't feel as scrutinizing as Audrey's had been. "You know that thing people put on social media about their relationship status?" his dad asked.

Egan definitely hadn't been expecting the question. Until it dawned on him where this was going. "You mean, it's complicated?"

"That's the one." His dad aimed his index finger at him to indicate Bingo. "Well, that's how it is between Audrey and me, and I can see you're worried about it. Worried that her being here will stress me out at a time when I'm not supposed to be stressing."

Egan hadn't been expecting this conversation, either, but he welcomed it. "Will her being here stress you?" he pressed.

"No." His answer was quick and sounded resolved enough. "Just the opposite. I'm glad to see her. Glad she could get away long enough to come home."

Home. That was a term that Egan applied to the ranch and Emerald Creek, but he wondered if Audrey had ever felt that way about it.

"Like I said, it's complicated," his dad went on. "After your mom died, Audrey helped pull me out of a deep depression. Of course, you kids helped, too, but there was a lot of worry for all of you since I wasn't sure if you could deal with losing your mom. I didn't have to worry about Audrey. She was always so sure of herself, and that meant all I had to do was love her."

Egan could understand that. Partly, anyway. But that kind of relationship agreement felt like only part of a package. Half of a letter. Definitely not the whole shebang that most couples wanted or had when they said their I dos.

"That's what I want for all my kids," his dad went on. "Someone who'll love you and pull you out of the dark."

Well, when he put it that way, some of that "half package" theory faded a bit. But Egan still didn't think he could do what his father was doing.

The door opened, capping off the conversation

when a smiling Audrey came in with Dr. Abrams who was pushing a wheelchair.

"I just need to do a quick check of your dad's vitals," Dr. Abrams said, "and then he'll be good to go."

"I thought I'd ride back with Audrey," his dad quickly interjected, aiming his remark at Egan, "and you'd be able to take Effie back."

After what his dad had just told him, Egan couldn't fault him for wanting to spend time with the woman he loved, but it did sting a little. The sting was short-lived, though. After all, he hadn't been the dutiful, diligent son. It'd taken a massive heart attack to get Egan to spend more than his usual "less than twelve hours" a month at the ranch and with his dad.

"I'll find Effie," Egan let them know, and he headed out in search of the vending machines.

He didn't have to go that far, though, because he spotted Effie just up in the hall. She was having a conversation with a couple of the nurses, and one of them handed her a flyer before she stepped away and started toward him.

"Derek's ready to go home?" she asked.

He nodded. "Dad's riding with Audrey, and you're with me."

Effie's sigh was short and barely noticeable, but it confirmed to Egan that she, too, was worried if this visit would take its toll on his dad. Effie sighed again when she looked at the paper one of the nurses had given her, and then she passed it to him.

Egan had seen this before. It was the flyer for Jack's life celebration, but it had been amended. Instead of saying *a memorial painting for Jack will be unveiled by our own Top Gun hometown hero, Lieutenant Colonel Egan Donnelly*, it simply read *there'll be an unveiling of a life celebration painting, dedicated to Jack.*

And that gave him another slug of guilt.

Hell. Even after everything had gone down the way it did when Jack died, Jack would have wanted Egan to be there for this. Jack would have expected it, and while Egan never wanted a life celebration or anything dedicated to him, if their positions were reversed, he would have wanted Jack to attend.

"This has to be about Jack," he muttered.

"Yes," Effie agreed, as if she were well aware of what was going through his head. However, Egan couldn't say the same for her when Effie blurted out, "You should go with Alana to the celebration."

He frowned and gave Effie a flat look. "You think Alana should have a date to her late husband's memorial service?"

She huffed, gave his arm an admonishing poke. "Not a date. Just some friendly support."

A couple of days ago, Egan had suspected matchmaking. And sort of dismissed it. He wasn't dismissing it now. There was, indeed, some matchmaking going on with both Effie and Maybell. Maybe his dad, too. That could have been why he'd told Egan to find someone to love and pull him out of the darkness.

"Alana's sad," Effie went on, taking the flyer back from Egan when he handed it to her, "you're sad so you might as well—"

"Be sad together?" he finished for her.

"I was going to say cheer each other up." She leaned in, lowered her voice to a whisper. "Loralee is so worried about Alana because she hasn't been with a man since Jack died."

No way did he want to know that.

No way.

But there it was. In his head. Spurring on other parts of him that should in no way be spurred.

Egan nearly blurted out Alana was doing that virtual dating but, of course, that wouldn't necessarily lead to actual sex. And that was something else he didn't want about Alana in his head.

Thankfully, he got help pushing that aside because Audrey came out of his dad's room, and she held the door open for Dr. Abrams, who was maneuvering Derek out in a wheelchair. Audrey hurried away, muttering something about pulling her rental car around to the door, while the rest of them made their way toward the exit.

Derek glanced at the flyer that Effie still had clutched in her hand. "Reckon I'll be in shape enough to go to that?" he asked Dr. Abrams.

Egan silently groaned because instead of dealing with a punch of lust for Alana, he got another jab of guilt. If his dad wanted to go, then he should be there, too.

The doctor looked at the flyer, probably focusing on the date that was three weeks away. Ironically, on the last day of what would be Egan's month of leave. "Maybe. Let's see how you do at home, and we can talk about it at your next appointment. I do want you out and about, some, but an outdoor event might be too hot. And too soon."

While they continued to discuss it and wait for Audrey, Egan heard the dinging of a phone, but it wasn't his. It was Effie's, and she pulled out her cheaters to read it.

"It's from Reba," she relayed, looking at Egan. "She was taking out the trash in the office and saw a letter torn in half."

Egan groaned and would have dropped an f-bomb had his grandmother and dad not been right there. Hell's bells. What was it about that blasted letter that kept it from the garbage heap?

"Reba wants to know if you're sure about tearing it in half and tossing it?" Effie asked. "She means because it's from Colleen to you, and it doesn't look like it's been read."

Suddenly, Egan had the attention of Effie, the doctor, his dad and two nurses who'd just happened to have heard that comment when walking by. Egan decided what he was about to say was for everyone's ears, especially Colleen's since it might get back to her.

"Yes, I'm sure I want the letter torn up and trashed," he spelled out. "If I never see her or hear from her again, that's fine with me."

Egan decided to go ahead and tick another box off his "let's get something straight" list. He took out his phone and bit the bullet. Not with an actual call but with a text that he sent to Tilly.

I'll be at Jack's life celebration, he messaged, hoping like the devil that he didn't regret it. Even if he did, though, the regret would be a drop in the bucket compared to what he'd feel if he didn't go.

CHAPTER EIGHT

"As a general rule, I want you to try to avoid foods labeled with words like *surprise* and *better than sex*," Alana spelled out to Derek. "Ones with visible globs of fat on them, too, like that cheese ball with pork rinds for dipping and the twelve-layer lasagna."

She pointed to the lasagna and the cheese concoction that according to its maker had the unfortunate name of Yummy Tummy Ball. It sat on the kitchen counter with the other dozen or so casseroles, "heat and serve" dishes that mostly brimmed with gravy, cream sauces and cheese. They were side by side with decadent "better than sex" desserts that'd been brought over by well-meaning people.

And this was just today's haul.

Since Derek had come home from the hospital two days ago, there'd been a steady stream of folks dropping by the ranch with all sorts of things from Yummy Tummy Balls to potpies that would serve a dozen or more people, to desserts that would qualify as rare or occasional indulgences. Some had tried to stay in the healthy zone with salads and fruit trays, but those folks were clearly in the minority.

Behind them, Maybell was muttering her frustrations while arranging and rearranging stuff in the massive fridge to try to make room. Again. This, too, had been a daily, sometimes hourly deal for the poor woman, and there wasn't an easy solution in sight. Derek was clearly well respected in the community, and people wanted to help. This deluge of food was their way of showing respect and support, which meant it couldn't be refused or criticized. Not to the bringers' faces, anyway.

Derek was sitting in his wheelchair—a requirement that Audrey had insisted on, and one which Derek hadn't objected to. The motorized wheelchair was giving him an easy way to circle around the huge kitchen island and glance over the food choices. Choices he was clearly mulling over since Alana had told him he could have a small serving of one of the items to go along with the chicken breast stir-fry that Maybell had fixed using one of Alana's recipes.

Or maybe he was doing that.

But Alana thought that something else might be going on. That Derek was possibly just feigning interest in the food since he thought that was what was expected of him. He was doing that perhaps so they wouldn't be worried about him.

"Any of it, I guess," he finally muttered.

Maybell stared at him as if he'd just sprouted a second nose. "Any of it?" she questioned. "When it comes to food, you've usually got some strong opinions, like telling me you want your porterhouse cooked for exactly four minutes and twenty seconds on each side.

And how about only that fancy Irish butter on your baked potato?"

The woman stopped because it must have occurred to her that all those requests were signs of a person who knew exactly what he wanted to eat. Signs, too, of a person who actually wanted to eat, period.

"Barbecue spareribs," he finally settled on. Again, not with a whole lot of enthusiasm.

That was Maybell's cue to leave the fridge and come to the counter so she could dish up two of the spareribs from the double rack that had been brought over by the owner of a smokehouse.

"Is Audrey joining you for lunch?" Maybell asked, popping the two ribs into the air fryer to reheat them.

"No, she's upstairs, packing," Derek muttered. "She's leaving later today," he added to Alana. "She has to get back to Germany for some big briefings."

Alana studied Derek's face to see if the man was upset about his wife's departure, but he didn't seem to be. Well, not upset but maybe just more down than he had been during her short stay. Then again, from what Alana had heard, a two-day stay for Audrey was longer than her usual, and it was possible her duties didn't allow her to extend this visit despite the circumstances.

"You should have something to eat," Derek offered while he wheeled over to the breakfast area where Maybell had already dished up his food. "Obviously, there's plenty."

"I had a late breakfast but thanks. Though, that Yummy Tummy Ball is tempting," she joked.

Derek attempted a smile. Failed. "Then, have a glass of tea or something and sit for a minute or two." He looked up at her, their gazes connecting, and Alana knew this was more than an offer of tea. He had something on his mind.

Apparently, Maybell picked up on that, too, and the woman shut the fridge. "I'm going to call Jesse and ask him to come get some of this stuff to take to the bunkhouse. Somebody there will eat it."

Probably. Alana didn't know how many ranch hands lived in the bunkhouse, but even a couple of them could make a dent in this. Temporarily, anyway. Hopefully, people would soon feel as if they'd fulfilled their neighborly duties and back off.

Maybell poured that glass of tea for Alana, brought Derek his spareribs and headed out, to make that call and give Derek and her a little privacy. Alana mentally went through some possibilities that might be bothering Derek, and she hoped it wasn't the sex question.

As in when he would be ready for such things.

It was possible in light of Audrey's visit.

Clients usually asked that, but most posed those particular questions to their doctors, not her. Especially not her since most folks were well aware she hadn't been in a relationship since Jack. Still, she had gotten a sex query or two during the decade that she'd been a dietitian, and since she hadn't been qualified to answer, she'd bounced it back to the doctors.

She didn't push or prod him to continue. Alana

just sipped her tea and waited while Derek stabbed his fork into a piece of chicken from the stir-fry.

"I did something Egan's probably not going to like," Derek finally said.

Alana tried to keep a neutral expression, but that shot some concern through her. She prayed this wasn't about some kind of risk Derek had taken that would harm him or his recovery.

"What?" she asked with hope and caution.

"It's about that letter from your sister."

Her concern turned to puzzlement. "Egan threw that away at his house on the base."

Derek nodded. "And his cleaning lady there apparently found it and sent it to him here."

Alana groaned softly. Egan wouldn't have appreciated that.

"Anyway, two days ago, Egan tore the letter in half and put it in the trash can in my office," Derek went on. "Reba, the housekeeper, found it and called Egan about it. He told her to tear it up and trash it, that he never wanted to see or hear from Colleen again."

"Understandable," Alana muttered. "After all, Colleen walked out on him for another man."

"She did," Derek concurred. "And I get wanting to tear up an unread letter. Colleen sent me one, too, and my first response was to rip it to shreds," he tacked on to that after a short pause.

Alana certainly recalled a similar feeling with her own letter. "And me. Mine was just a request for some sister time. I think she's trying to mend fences or something since we haven't spoken much since Egan and she split."

Derek nodded again. "In the one she sent me, she apologized and said she figured what she'd done had hurt me, too, because of all the hurt it caused Egan." He shrugged. "I'm not ready to dole out any forgiveness, but I will say the mention of her name doesn't cause me to mutter things I shouldn't be muttering."

Alana supposed that was a start and probably what her sister had intended. "Did you tell Egan what Colleen had written to you?"

"No. Didn't figure he'd want to know." He paused. "But eventually he might want that. Might want to know what she wrote in the letter to him, too. So, that's why I had Reba save it. I'll keep it tucked away, and if Egan ever gets to the point where it's something he wants to read, I'll be able to give it to him."

Alana nearly said she doubted that day would come. But then she frowned. Because it might come, especially since he'd see Colleen at the life celebration. Tilly had texted her about that shortly after she'd gotten the word from Egan. So, yes, Egan would see his ex.

And that bothered Alana.

She wanted to believe that bother was because seeing Colleen might hurt Egan, but it might just be that first step to forgiveness, too. That would be a good thing—and this is where she felt petty and selfish—but she didn't want that forgiveness to lead to a reconciliation. The odds of that happening were slim to none, but Alana didn't want Egan and Colleen back together.

Because Alana was lusting after him herself.

Oh, yes. Petty and selfish, indeed, and it spelled out the problem with having the hots for her sister's ex. Added to that, it was stupid since Egan didn't want to do anything about that dreaded heat.

Derek and she both turned toward the sound of approaching footsteps, and a moment later, Audrey came in. She was wearing her uniform, which meant she'd likely be leaving soon. Alana decided it was time to do as Maybell had done and give them some privacy.

"If I don't get a chance to say goodbye before you leave," Alana told the woman, "it was good seeing you." Alana didn't tack on a *General Donnelly, Mrs. Donnelly* or Audrey's given name to that. None of those quite felt right.

"It was good to see you, too," Audrey replied, her attention already shifting to Derek.

"Mr. Donnelly, I'll see you tomorrow," Alana told him, feeling right about calling him that, and she headed out when Audrey snuggled onto the breakfast table bench next to her husband.

Alana had every intention of going straight to her car and driving to her office, especially since the forecast was predicting heavy rain in the next half hour, but she saw a sight that had her stopping in her tracks.

And drooling.

Egan was in the pasture just behind the house, and

he was astride an impressive-looking white horse. His shirt was open, billowing in the breeze from the upcoming storm, and that was giving her a view of his chest. Of course, he was toned, tanned and had a six-pack. Of course, he was perfect and could have added abs model to his résumé.

She watched, the drooling going up a notch, as he made a sleek maneuver with the horse. A fluid, graceful turn followed by the horse going into a gallop. Rider and horse seemed to glide across the pasture, seemingly racing against the gathering iron-gray clouds.

This was cowboy Egan, and he was just as impressive and memorable as Top Gun fighter pilot.

Egan put the horse through a couple more maneuvers, earning him a thumbs-up from the ranch foreman, Jesse, who was watching from the fence. When Egan finally reined in, Jesse and he had a brief conversation before the foreman walked away and Egan headed into the barn with the horse.

Alana had no plans to join Egan. Not until he turned, caught sight of her and motioned for her to come closer. She did, like a moth heading straight to a flame, and she tried her level best not to stare at his bare chest.

Tried and failed.

Thankfully, it helped when she joined him in the barn because then she was up close and could focus on his face, which was just as impressive as the rest of him. He was a little sweaty, not in a "bad smelly gym" sort of way. But in a "hot guy" way. Since that wasn't tamping down her pulse, she tried to focus on the barn instead.

Like the rest of the ranch, the barn was huge and much cleaner than she'd expected. There were stalls made of richly colored wood on each side, and the spacious floor in between the stalls was practically spotless. No hay strewn around, though there was a hayloft with a ladder made of that same wood leading up to it.

The temperature inside the barn was cooler and less humid than expected as well. Probably thanks to the industrial fans that'd been built into the walls. No doubt to keep the horses and give the ranch hands a place to escape the unrelenting summer heat.

"You were just with my dad?" Egan asked, his attention on the horse that he was now unsaddling.

"Yes." When that came out as sort of a croak, she cleared her throat and repeated it. "I was just going over the basics with him about avoiding foods with the words *surprise* or *better than*…" Good grief. She had actually gone there.

"Sex," he filled in for her. He glanced at her and hoisted the saddle and carried it to a rack outside one of the stalls. "I was in the kitchen when Sadie Mendoza dropped off a cake with such a name."

Egan hadn't smirked at her bringing that up or the dessert's name. His expression was serious, and she soon found out why.

"How's my dad actually doing?" Egan asked, and she heard the serious worry in his voice. This time it was more than a glance as he carried the wet saddle pad to yet another rack.

"Okay as far as I can tell," she decided. "If he's holding anything back from you, he's holding it back from me, too."

Well, except for that letter. Derek was, indeed, holding that back from Egan, but there was nothing else she knew of for sure. *For sure.* Alana had her suspicions, though, about his dad that she didn't want to voice. Such as possible depression? Fatigue-generated apathy? Fear that he was never actually going to recover?

What she had chosen to say didn't seem to ease any of Egan's worry, and while his unbuttoned shirt continued to give her a peep show, he finished dealing with the tack on the horse.

"Why, is there something specific you're concerned about?" Alana came out and asked when he didn't continue.

"Yeah," he verified. "He's keeping something from me. I can't tell what, but there's something."

Again, she thought of the letter and wondered if Egan was picking up on that. But that wasn't her secret to spill especially since it would likely lead to Egan going to his father and having words about it.

Well, maybe that would be Egan's reaction.

And that led her to something else. Not a secret, but she was wondering how Egan had taken the news about Colleen attending the life celebration. Certainly, Tilly or someone had told him by now.

Hadn't they?

As she watched Egan go to a sink mounted between two of the stalls and turn on the tap, it occurred to her that if he'd known, Egan probably would have called or texted her to rant. Especially since he'd agreed to do the unveiling of the memorial and would therefore be there.

Crud.

She was going to have to be the messenger again. First, the letter from Colleen, then the flyer and now this. Alana really wished the gossips would have done their usual jobs and gotten this out of the way. Since there was no easy way to do this, she just went with blurting it out.

"Tilly gave Colleen permission to come to Jack's life celebration." No croak this time. The words came out loud and clear.

Egan had just tossed handfuls of water on his face, but he stopped, turning his head to the side to look at her. The water dripped off him while he stared and stared and stared.

"What?" he demanded.

Alana didn't think the question was because he hadn't heard her. Nope, this was an anger reaction, and if anyone had a right to be pissed off about this, it was Egan.

"Colleen called Tilly, begged her to let her come and Tilly agreed," Alana spelled out.

She thought of Tilly's comment. *It'll be just like old times*. So, maybe it hadn't taken much begging on Colleen's part.

"This might be some kind of fantasy deal for Tilly," Alana reasoned. "You know, because when Jack was alive, you and Colleen were usually there at any get-together or celebration. Tilly might be trying to capture a bit of that."

Egan stood fully upright, the water continuing its journey down his face. To his neck and to his chest. Alana tried not to watch that journey, especially since this was not a fun conversation.

"*Capture the past* by inviting my ex-wife to a celebration that's already going to be a gut-wrencher," Egan stated, his voice flat. But that was the only place the flatness applied. The rest of him was, well, not exactly seething with anger, but it was close. "Well, shit."

Alana thought that was the perfect sentiment. "If it's any consolation, Colleen agreed to stay at the back of the crowd, and I can try to make sure she doesn't try to have any contact with you."

As expected, that didn't console him one bit. The "contact" would happen simply by Egan catching a glimpse of her and knowing she was there.

"I'm sorry," she felt compelled to tell him.

He opened his mouth as if he had plenty to say about that, plenty which would involve cursing, but just as fast, Egan seemed to change his mind, and he huffed. Then groaned.

"I just want to hear Colleen's name and not feel a damn thing except maybe indifference." Egan stopped again, and she saw something change in his eyes.

It seemed to be some kind of "lightbulb over the head" moment because the tension in his shoulders relaxed, and instead of another groan, his mouth moved into what was almost a smile. Alana wasn't sure what he was feeling, but she hoped it wasn't some kind of plot to try to get back at Colleen during the life celebration.

"Indifference," he repeated, as if testing the word. "I'm getting damn close to that."

Alana blinked and mentally replayed it. Then, she almost smiled, too. "How close?" she asked.

He looked at her with those bedroom eyes. "A hell of a lot closer than I was just a few days ago."

"So, you wouldn't mind if she sent you a letter or if you catch a glimpse of her at the life celebration?" It was definitely a question, and she had a reason for it. If the indifference still had roots in bitter anger, then she would have that chat with Colleen about staying out of Egan's path.

His look went level again. "I wouldn't go that far. Yeah, I'd still mind, but I don't think it'd have the sting it once did. About time," he added in a mutter.

She nearly said he deserved to hang on to his crap feelings for Colleen for the rest of his life. But she knew firsthand that wasn't the way to go. It'd be like eating hourly servings of Yummy Tummy Balls. Perhaps savory and possibly even yummy, but it'd get old fast. Too bad she couldn't quite get her mind wrapped around that because she was still feeling a whole boatload of anger at Jack. Not just about the affair but because he'd died before she could confront him face-to-face.

"You're smiling," she said at the same moment he said, "You're frowning."

There it was. Their current bottom line when it came to their tangled wad of emotions. But Alana didn't want to be the frowner here. She wanted to have something lift her spirits, to make her think of the here and now instead of the past.

Here and now got some fuel when she looked at Egan again.

Egan, with his shirt still unbuttoned. Egan, with his damp face and chest. Egan, looking at her as if he were thinking about a new bottom line for them.

Perhaps one that involved a kiss.

Egan didn't seem to have another lightbulb moment, but he was staring at her, maybe thinking the same thing. Maybe.

"How much of a mistake do you think it would be?" she muttered, hoping he could fill in the *it* blank with a kiss.

His smile faded but not in a bad kind of way. No scowl or grimace. Just the intensity of a man who was battling lust. Oh, yeah. The lust was definitely there. She might have been out of the relationship game for a while, but she could still detect heat when it was aimed at her.

"A big mistake," he assured her.

So, he'd not only filled in the blanks but the likely outcome as well. That's why it surprised her when he took a step toward her while he kept his gaze locked with hers.

Alana knew that outcome, too, but she still took a step toward him, itching to get her mouth on his and her hands on that incredible bare chest.

He moved, she moved, as if being manipulated by an unseen force. In this case, the force was plain old lust mixed with plain old need. Which suddenly didn't seem plain at all because it involved Egan.

They finally stopped just inches away from each other, and his gaze dropped to her mouth. Hers went to his. And she was within one hot breath of moving in to take that kiss.

But a sound stopped her.

A sort of whirring noise, followed by a blur of motion. Not coming from around them but above. Their heads whipped up, spearing the blur of motion coming from a rope zooming down from the hayloft. The motion quickly came into focus, and she saw the person wearing a familiar uniform.

The woman wearing it was familiar, too.

It was Remi, and she had on her Combat Rescue Officer's uniform. Familiar to Alana since Jack had worn a very similar version of it when he'd been on duty.

Remi grinned as she swung down superhero style from the rope and gave them both a long once-over. "My, my, my," she said. "And what exactly am I interrupting here?"

CHAPTER NINE

EGAN EXPERIENCED A quick hit of emotions. Joy at seeing his sister. Relief that she was home in one piece. And annoyance at her for her untimely arrival since it had put a halt to him kissing Alana.

Along with those three things, there was also some consolation since the interruption stopped him from doing something stupid. Then again, he was 100 percent certain that he would have gotten a lot of pleasure from the stupidity.

So, yeah, that mix of emotions was a soupy mess.

Remi's grin toned down some of the annoyance both at her and himself. So did the hard hug she gave him when she pulled him into her arms.

"Sorry, but I couldn't resist a grand entrance," she said, aiming the apology at both of them. "I rarely get to put that part of my training to use so when the opportunity arose, I went with it."

With her hands now locked on his forearms, his sister gave him a long look, maybe gauging to see what kind of toll these last eleven days had taken on him. There was a toll all right, a big-assed one, but he was hoping he was doing a big brother job of covering it up. Especially since he didn't want Remi taking any worry about him back to the job.

Too late, though.

Remi's right eyebrow rose as if she were already silently disputing his facade and then her grip melted off him as his sister turned to Alana. Remi pulled her into a hug as well.

"It's so good to see you," Remi greeted. "How are you?" However, before Alana could answer, she added, "Hope I didn't give you a jolt."

Maybe Remi was referring to just the surprise of her grand entrance. But she could have also meant the uniform. There was an image in Egan's head of a photo taken when Remi had finished her long grueling CRO training, one of the first women to accomplish it, and Jack and Egan had flown in to celebrate her achievement, with Jack wearing his own CRO uniform. Jack had had the honors of putting on Remi's maroon beret and giving her the first official welcome into the elite group.

"I'm fine," Alana assured her. "No jolt other than a moment when I thought maybe we were about to get hit by a falling hay bale." She checked the time on her phone. "I just remembered I had a recipe book in my car that I wanted to give Maybell. I should do that before the rain starts and give you two a chance to catch up."

Egan suspected that there could, indeed, be a recipe book, but it was just as likely that Alana wanted to skip out before Remi could quiz her about the near kiss that his sister had almost certainly witnessed.

Added to that, Alana would know how good it was for him to see Remi and do that *catching up*.

"Yeah, I heard you were helping Dad with a new diet," Remi remarked. "How's that going?"

"Good. Really good, actually. He's not cheating one bit. Now, we just need to convince people to stop bringing over food with names like…" Alana stopped, obviously deciding not to mention the Yummy Tummy Ball and Better than Sex cake. Probably because she'd learned her lesson with him. "…cheese-a-plooza pasta."

"Yum," Remi joked. "I hope you saved some of that for me."

"There's plenty," Alana assured her.

Alana gave Remi a parting hug, and then she glanced at Egan as if she might have automatically done the same to him. Which clearly would have been a mistake, what with the near kiss thing, because there was still some heat—yes, even now—waffling back and forth between them. Instead, she settled for a wave, a muttered goodbye, and headed out of the barn.

"How long have you been home?" Egan immediately asked Remi, hoping to dodge questions about Alana and him. "Have you seen Dad yet?"

"Less than fifteen minutes, and no, I haven't seen Dad yet. He's in the bedroom with Audrey, helping her pack." Remi put those last three words in air quotes.

Egan frowned. "Please don't tell me they're having sex."

Remi rolled her eyes. "Sex, sex, sex. Is that all

you can think about?" she teased. "I have no idea what they're doing, but I'm going to embrace Maybell's comment that packing is the only thing going on in that bedroom right now. I figured I'd give Audrey and him some goodbye time and then let him know I was here."

Egan had been doing his own version of giving Audrey and his dad alone time when he'd taken one of the new Andalusian mares for a ride. Of course, he hadn't expected the ride to end the way it had in the barn with Alana.

"Maybell told me you were likely in the front pasture riding or in the barn," Remi went on with her explanation. "So, I came out here, heard Alana and you talking and decided to use the exterior ladder to climb up to the loft and show off my rope swinging skillset."

"It's a useful skillset," he joked right back. "Might come in handy if you ever have to rescue someone in a barn with a hayloft and an available rope."

"You never know." When Egan took a brush and started to groom the horse he'd ridden, Remi grabbed a second brush and began to help. "So," Remi continued, stretching out the word a bit, "what exactly was going on between Alana and you when I swooped in?"

He hadn't expected to dodge this particular bullet, but he also had no intentions whatsoever of pouring out his heart about Alana to Remi. That was mainly because he didn't know what exactly was in his heart when it came to Alana. Right now, his feelings for her were all hot lust and worry that he'd screw up her life big-time if he didn't manage to get the lust under control.

"Alana was Jack's wife," he settled for saying.

"And I was once a teenager with braces, acne and a quarter-sized freckle on my right butt cheek," she countered with her usual sass. "Okay, the freckle is still there and the occasional acne, but the braces are off." She grinned to show him her teeth. "Want me to tell you what I saw?"

"No," Egan quickly answered.

But Remi just rolled over him. "I saw two people this close to kissing." She lifted her thumb and index fingers and closed the already narrow gap between them until the distance was miniscule. "I saw two people who would have almost certainly kissed if one of them hadn't gotten an unexpected visit from a 'pain in the ass' sister. Sorry," she muttered, "but in hindsight, I should have given Alana and you some *time to pack*." Again, she put air quotes on those last three words.

"No," he repeated, but this time there was no urgency or bite to it. "The interruption was good."

"Good?" she repeated in a tone to indicate otherwise. "Are either of you involved with someone else?"

Egan gave her a flat look since Remi already knew they weren't. If they had been, she would have heard some gossip about it from Effie's emails.

"No, because Alana and I wouldn't ever be able to be together in a romantic kind of way and not think about Jack," he spelled out for her.

No way would he admit, though, that Jack hadn't

been on his mind when he'd been within a breath of kissing Alana. Nope. The only thing he'd been thinking about was the kiss and sex.

"Oh, really?" Remi stretched that out, too, and she slipped her arm around his waist. "Want some advice?"

"No," he repeated before she even finished.

Just as he'd known, that didn't stop her. "I think Alana and you should become friends with benefits. I mean, it wouldn't be that hard since you're already more or less friends. And don't you dare repeat that part about her being Jack's wife or I'll give you multipage details of the first time I had sex. I'm no more hooked up with that guy than Alana still is with Jack."

Egan didn't want to hear a word about Remi having sex, but it wasn't the same. "You don't have a buttload of unresolved feelings and guilt for your first lover. Alana has that for Jack." He stopped, cursed, wondered just how much he should add to that, and Egan went with more. "Jack cheated on Alana."

He watched, waiting for Remi's stunned reaction, but it didn't come. Her sigh was weary as if that'd been something she'd expected. Egan sure as hell hadn't.

"Jack told you he cheated?" Remi asked.

He repeated the same word he'd already been using way too much in this conversation. "No."

She sighed again. "He wouldn't have. Even though you were the same age, Jack looked up to you, Egan. That whole 'hero worship' stuff can cause you to hold back on any seedier stuff you happen to be doing."

Egan frowned. "Is that a confession?"

And for one sick moment, he thought maybe Jack had cheated with Remi. That gave him a hard jolt of anger before Remi must have interpreted his expression and repeated his denial.

"Noooo," she said, stretching out the word. "Just a big fat no. Jack was like another big brother to me. Not that I needed another one since my cup already runneth over with three," she added in a tone that reeked of kid sister frustration. "But Jack appointed himself as the surrogate big brother whenever Cal, Blue or you weren't around."

Egan probably looked ready to face-plant with relief. Talk about adding another layer of baggage if Remi had been the one. Thank heaven she wasn't.

And it made sense about the "surrogate brother" part. Remi and Jack could have ended up on assignments together. Frequently. CROs typically were on deployment for four months out of every eighteen, and in between deployments, they went on shorter temporary duties to wherever they were needed. If they'd ended up working together, Jack would have almost certainly tried to look after her and keep her safe.

Of course, that was a reminder that he hadn't done the same for Jack.

"Anyway," Remi went on. "No affair with Jack. And no relationship for a long time. I just don't have time…"

Her words trailed off when there was movement at the open front door of the barn, and Jesse walked by.

He must have been in a hurry to get something done because he didn't even glance inside. Still, Remi reacted as if Jesse had been ready to come barging in, and she moved closer to the stalls so she was no longer in the line of sight of the door.

An interesting reaction since he'd never known Remi to dodge anyone or anything.

"Something about Jesse and you I should know?" Egan asked, only partly teasing since Remi and Jesse had in fact once had a thing for each other. Egan didn't know how far that "thing" had gone since Remi had left shortly thereafter for college.

"No," she insisted. "Nothing I want to tell you because there's nothing to tell." She paused. "It's just that's the first time I've seen him in a while."

Another interesting comment since Remi made trips home at least once or twice a year. Jesse didn't live at the ranch, but he was around plenty enough for Remi and him to have run into each other.

Well, unless Remi was avoiding him as she was right now.

"FYI, Jesse's not seeing anyone at the moment," Egan threw out there.

Remi frowned. "But he's less than a month out of a relationship with former cheerleader and current yoga instructor, Marla Henderson. That means he's a walking, talking rebound."

Egan wasn't so sure of that. Jesse and he weren't regular drinking buddies, but during his "one day a month" visits to the ranch, Egan had heard the talk about Jesse and Marla. It'd seemed to him that their relationship was much like what Remi had suggested for Alana and him. Friends with benefits or as Egan preferred to call it, strings-free sex.

Something he could never have with Alana.

Hell, everything about their relationship was strings and baggage, and sex would only add to that. He sighed. Because that sure as hell didn't make him want to kiss her any less.

"Besides, I broke Jesse's heart once," Remi muttered. "Best not to test those waters again."

"You broke his heart?" he asked. "When?"

But Remi waved that off and got back to brushing down the horse. "Let's conclude this particular portion of the conversation with me saying it would muddy too many waters to try to get involved with Jesse."

"Yet, you're encouraging me to have a fling with Alana," Egan enjoyed pointing out.

"You didn't break Alana's heart. Judging from what I saw, you were just about to kiss her for the very first time, and the heat was practically flying off you two like a handful of overheated Fourth of July sparklers."

Egan wanted to deny that. Man, did he. But he couldn't because he had a good idea of how Alana must have looked when they'd been on the verge of a lip-lock. Sparklers, indeed. That was a good description of it.

However, he had broken Alana's heart.

By not saving Jack. Now, because he'd failed, Alana was putting the blame for his death on her own shoulders where it damn sure didn't belong.

No way did Egan want to jump into those conversational waters, though, so it was obviously time for yet another change of subject. Thankfully, just catching up with Remi would take care of that.

"So, how is it, Captain Remi Donnelly, Air Force Combat Rescue Officer?" He used his free hand to tap her maroon beret. "Is it everything you thought it'd be?"

She nodded. "And more."

Hell. She'd no doubt meant that *and more* to sound light. Flip, even. But she didn't quite pull it off. He'd been around enough CROs to know they often went through hell and back, and because they were often sent in to rescue civilians and even children behind enemy lines, they saw shit that was too bad even for nightmares.

"It's what I've always wanted to do," she added, and it sounded as if she were giving herself a reminder and an assurance for him. "Blue, Cal and you always wanted to fly jets. It's that whole phallic deal of holding onto the throttle," she tacked on a little sisterly jab, adding that lightness. "Me? I've always wanted to rescue people."

Because of their mother.

Remi didn't have to spell that out, but he'd watched her grow up. He'd seen that constant need for her to get things out of harm's way. It'd started with the puppies and kittens on the ranch and progressed to horses and cattle. When she'd been ten or so, he'd found her about to be headbutted by a pissed off cow because Remi had been trying to untangle a briar from the cow's calf. Remi had been aware of the danger, too, but it hadn't stopped her from trying.

Later on, she'd ignored Effie's and his dad's murmurs about her aiming for such a high-risk career field. Probably even higher risk than anything Cal, Blue or he would encounter. The odds were low that they would face danger only a handful of times in their careers, but for Remi, repeated higher risk was part of her job description.

The silence settled between them until they'd finished brushing the mare, and Remi looked at him over the horse's back.

"Do you think Alana actually wants to know any of the details about Jack's cheating?" Remi asked.

He definitely hadn't been expecting the question, which, of course, led to other questions as well. "You know details?"

She nodded, sighed and tossed the brush onto one of the drying racks. "I was at a base in England for some briefings, and afterward a few of us ended up catching the train to London. It was a total fluke, but I ran into Jack when he was with the *other woman*."

Part of him wanted to shut this down. Another part of him needed answers. "Did you know her?"

"I did," Remi said at the tail end of another sigh. "She was an intel officer stationed at the base where the briefings were being held. I'd met her before that, though, at another briefing in Germany."

So Remi knew the woman's name. Egan didn't want to know that. But there was something else, something that might comfort Alana if it ever came up. Well, it would be a comfort if the cheating was a one-off.

"Did Jack and this woman seem tight?" he pressed.

And he hated like the devil that Remi didn't immediately respond in the negative. Just the opposite. She paused and scrubbed her hand over her face.

"I talked to the woman after Jack excused himself to go take a call," Remi finally continued. "Not exactly a friendly chat. More of a WTF are you doing, don't you know he's married? She did know and expressed the usual whining stuff about her being in a really bad place personally. I knew about the bad stuff, a death in the family, and judging from what she said, the bad caused things between Jack and her to just happen." She rolled her eyes. "As if sex had been accidental."

Egan figured that hadn't been a pleasant chat for Remi or the woman. "Did you talk to Jack, too?"

She shook her head. "Didn't get a chance since he had to leave right after he finished his call, but according to Miss Things Just Happened, she was in love with Jack. She hadn't intended for that, either, but she just couldn't stop her feelings."

"And did he feel the same way about this woman he was seeing? Was Jack in love with her, too?" Egan asked, hoping Remi wouldn't do another of those long hesitations.

She didn't, but that was because she didn't get the chance. A gasp stopped them in their tracks.

Egan's gaze whipped to the sound, and he saw Alana standing in the doorway of the barn. He couldn't be sure exactly what she'd heard, but obviously, it'd been enough to cause the color to drain from her face.

"Alana," he said, moving toward her.

But she threw up her hand in a stop gesture. Her fingers were trembling. So was her mouth. And that let him know she'd heard plenty.

"Sorry," she muttered, and she repeated it as she turned away and bolted toward her car.

"Shit," Remi cursed, adding a groan. She moved as if she were about to go after Alana, but Egan did his own version of a stop.

"I'll go," he insisted.

And Egan started running.

CHAPTER TEN

DESPITE EGAN TAKING off like a bat out of hell and in-sisting he'd be the one to go after Alana, Remi went after both of them.

Alana already had a head start, though, a lengthy one, and she was fast, probably motivated by her own "bat out of hell" need to get away from there and not have to face them. Remi could only watch as she jumped into her car and sped away, leaving Egan cursing while he was still trying to catch up with her.

Egan didn't give up, thank goodness. Remi saw the lieutenant colonel in him kick in, and he moved straight to a quickly improvised plan B. He went to one of the ranch trucks parked in the side driveway of the house, probably deciding on it rather than his own vehicle simply because it was closer and the keys would already be in it. The moment he started the engine, he floored the accelerator and went in pursuit while Remi stood there and wished she had a big rock to hit herself on the head.

What the devil had she just done?

There was no way Alana should have heard any part of that conversation, and it didn't matter that Remi had thought she was either gone or still inside the house with Maybell. The barn wasn't that far from the house. Or from where Alana had parked. So Remi should have guessed that Alana or someone else could have overheard things that shouldn't have been overheard in the first place.

Remi muttered more than a few choice curse words, all aimed at herself, and wished she could time travel and go back a couple of minutes and not start the conversation about Jack. If Egan was hellbent on knowing details of his best friend's affair, Remi should have at least waited until she was certain Egan and she would have some privacy.

A barn didn't qualify as a private venue.

Nope. And there was the added pisser that she shouldn't have even blabbed all of that in the first place. The info should be dead and buried, just as Jack was. Because now that Egan and Alana knew, there'd be no going back and forgetting. It would only add to the grief and regret they were no doubt already feeling.

Remi took out some of her frustrations by kicking every single rock that she encountered on the walk from the barn to the house, and she cursed herself and the situation some more. By the time she made it to the back porch, though, she'd worked herself up to a seriously crap mood and knew she had to do some reining in. Fast. If Maybell, Grammy Effie, Audrey or her dad saw her fuming like this, they'd know something was wrong and would ask her about it. She didn't want to utter one more word about Jack or Alana.

She paced across the porch a couple of times. Did some deep breathing. And ran her fingertips over the badge on her beret. The emblem or flash as it was often called was an angel embracing the globe with the motto "That others may live" emblazoned beneath it. For such a small object, it had always packed an emotional wallop for her.

Apparently, it still did.

As usual, it worked to settle her nerves and get her to focus on the here and now and what had happened five minutes earlier. Remi felt everything inside her level out, and she stepped into the kitchen. No Maybell, but Effie was there. Her grandmother smiled and immediately pulled her into a hug.

The visit wasn't a surprise to Grammy since Remi had texted her earlier to let her know she'd just landed at the military base in San Antonio, and unless something came up in a debriefing she had to attend, she'd be home soon for a short visit. Remi had asked, though, for Effie to keep it a secret just in case there was a hitch in her travel plans.

Effie pulled back from the hug, meeting Remi's gaze. "What's wrong?" Effie asked, causing Remi to silently groan. "And don't say it's about your dad because I saw the commotion going on outside the barn. Want to tell me why Alana hurried off like that and Egan went after her?"

Remi sighed and tried to work out the best possible answer. She finally settled on a headshake. No, she didn't want to explain the *commotion*.

Her grandmother's sigh echoed her own, but thankfully she didn't press Remi further. She might have done that, though, if Audrey hadn't come into the kitchen. *Saved by the general*, Remi thought.

But she thought wrong.

"What happened?" Audrey wanted to know while she, too, gave Remi a welcoming but distracted hug. "Are Egan and Alana all right?"

"They'll be fine." Remi hoped. No thanks to her.

Remi only hoped that Egan caught up with Alana and managed to talk things out with her. Or pulled off a miracle and managed to erase her memory of what she'd overheard.

Audrey studied her eyes a moment, no doubt picking up on Remi's BS answer, but the woman didn't call her on said BS. She smiled, stepped back and gave Remi and her uniform a long look.

"Your dad is going to be so happy to see you," Audrey assured her.

"I'll be happy to see him."

Not a lie. There'd be happiness and maybe, just maybe, it'd tone down some of her worry over him once she saw him for herself. Then again, if he looked like crap, then her worries would be on target to escalate.

Remi turned to her grandmother. "Maybe you and I can do some catching up once I've talked to Dad." Then, she eyed the stash of food that was still on the kitchen island. "And maybe do some eating, too."

Her grandmother smiled and kissed her cheek. "Absolutely. Now, go to your dad. He needs you."

Remi already had plenty of concerns about her

dad, and that added a bit more to the heap. She'd never thought of him needing her, only the other way around. This role reversal sucked.

Audrey put her hand on the small of Remi's back to get her moving toward the stairs. "How is Dad? I mean, how is he really?" Remi asked her once they were out of Effie's earshot.

Remi didn't want any BS about it and thought she'd get the truth from Audrey, but she also didn't want any potential bad news upsetting her grandmother. Remi had already fulfilled her quota on people overhearing stuff that could send them into an emotional spin.

Audrey and she weren't exactly best buds, and Remi never thought of her as a mom. She'd had one of those even if she couldn't remember her. She didn't actually think of Audrey as a stepmother, either, even though she'd been around since Remi had turned six. In the grand scheme of things, Audrey was first and foremost her dad's wife. Then, a high-ranking military officer. And finally, a woman in power who Remi respected. It was because of their relationship that Remi thought she might get the truth.

And she did.

Mercy, she did.

"Your dad's not doing as well as he'll tell you he is," Audrey spelled out as they took a slow walk to the stairs. "That's why Egan had that installed." She pointed to the chair lift that was now on the railing.

"Oh, Dad wouldn't have cared much for that," Remi muttered.

"He didn't object as much as I thought he would," Audrey said. "In fact, he doesn't object much at all."

That didn't sound good. Her dad would have usually fought such things tooth and nail. She recalled when Egan had tried to talk their dad into getting an office assistant to help him with the paperwork and such, and Dad had shut that right down, insisting he could handle anything and everything to do with the ranch.

"Derek's supposed to be taking it slow," Audrey went on, "and the doctor didn't think that should include trips up and down the stairs. Effie said she'd trade rooms with him since her suite is downstairs, but Derek wanted to stay put." Audrey shrugged. "I guess he didn't want her to go to any trouble."

"How long is he supposed to take it easy?" Remi asked.

"We don't know yet," Audrey supplied without hesitation. "I had long talks with both of his doctors before I even got here. Your dad will be able to tackle walking up and down the stairs soon, but he has coronary artery disease. There's no cure for that, but he can minimize the risk of another heart attack and more damage by changing his lifestyle. That includes eating better and not working every waking hour."

That explained why Alana was around with recipe books. It explained, too, why Egan was burning up his leave to be here 24/7. Remi got a punch of guilt over that, but she couldn't take the kind of time off that Egan could. Added to that, she wasn't stationed just an hour away. Still, she hated that the bulk of these lifestyle changes would impact Egan the most.

"I'll be leaving soon," Audrey said, checking the time and continuing the pokey pace for their trek upstairs. "I've stayed as long as I can and have to get back to Germany to put out some fires there."

"I understand," Remi muttered. And she did. Remi was sort of in the same boat since she was within forty-eight hours of her next deployment.

Audrey made a sound that could have meant anything. "I believe you do understand," she said. "But maybe not your brothers."

Probably not. Audrey wasn't talking about her job now but rather her not making more trips to the ranch. After all, general officers accumulated thirty days of leave each year just as other military ranks did, but before this visit, Audrey had spent only two days out of the past three years with her husband.

And that had been Audrey's choice.

The woman hadn't used her superiors as an excuse for the lack of time spent here. Audrey had admitted that her job was her priority and that she intended to give it whatever she felt was needed. Remi and her brothers felt the same way about their jobs, but their dad had a better visible spot on their radars than Audrey had of him on hers.

Audrey came to a full stop at the top of the stairs and looked at Remi. "In hindsight, I could have done a better job of mixing the two worlds, especially earlier on in my career when I didn't have as many responsibilities. It feels right when I'm in uniform.

But this feels right, too, when I'm here with Derek at the ranch." She paused a heartbeat. "I don't think Egan believes it for a second, but I do love your dad."

Remi didn't intend to speculate about Egan's feelings, but she thought Audrey might possibly be right. Not because Egan didn't believe Audrey should have a career but because Audrey herself had hit the nail on the head when she admitted to not doing such a great job of mixing these two worlds.

Of course, at the mention of Egan's name, she thought about what might be going on between Alana and him at this very moment. Remi hoped Egan had managed to catch up to Alana by now and was smoothing things over. Well, as much smoothing that could be done, anyway.

"I've already told your dad goodbye," Audrey went on, getting them moving again until she stopped outside their bedroom door. "So, I won't go back in there. I'm just glad you're here to give him a lift."

Audrey gave Remi's arm a squeeze and headed back to the stairs, moving much faster and with plenty of determination. Remi took a deep breath that she figured she'd need, knocked once on the door and then went in to see her dad.

The rain had already started and was pinging against the large bay window of the suite, but he wasn't at the window, taking in the incredible views he would have had of the ranch. Views that possibly would have allowed him to see Alana speeding away and Egan going after her. Small mercies that he'd avoided that.

Instead, her dad was in a reading chair in the sitting area of the suite, and he was looking at a thick book. No, not a paperback but a photo album, she realized.

For an unguarded split second, she saw the weariness in him that seemed to go all the way to the bone. Of course, he shut that down fast enough and plastered on a smile. Perhaps it was even a genuine one. But genuine or not, it didn't cover up the fact that not only had he been through a scary medical crisis, he was still in the throes of it.

"This is a nice surprise," he said, standing and setting the album aside.

Without trying to make it too obvious, she hurried across the room so that he wouldn't have to go to her. She pulled him into a hug, knowing she was being way gentler than she usually was. Knowing, too, that he would be well aware of that. He did tighten the embrace, but it wasn't as strong as usual, either.

"I didn't see you drive up," he said.

"Because I was being stealthy." She eased him back into the chair and plopped down on the arm so she didn't have to fully end the embrace. "I parked by the gates and made my way through the pasture. Beautiful horses, by the way. Your purchase or Egan's?"

"Jesse's," he supplied, and yeah, he gave her a little look, no doubt to see how she'd react to the man's name.

Remi tried to have no reaction whatsoever, but her dad wasn't an idiot so he'd likely known that Jesse and she had once been *involved*.

"But Egan's been working with the new horses," her dad added. "Working with everything else, too," he said with some frustration in his voice. "He hasn't got time for that."

"Egan is Egan. He'll make time," Remi insisted. It didn't seem fair to put that on him, but even if he hadn't been the oldest, Egan would have taken on the lion's share of responsibility. It was in his nature.

"I'm worried about him," her dad went on. "He's held on to the hurt and anger too long over what Colleen did to him, and the grief about Jack is still eating him alive."

Remi was in complete agreement about the last, but she had hopes about that hurt and anger over Colleen. She had seen the scorching heat in Egan's eyes for Alana. Of course, that might be all shot to hell now that Alana was having to deal with the not so juicy tidbits about her husband's cheating.

"Egan will move on when the time is right," Remi settled for saying. Yeah, it wasn't a clever comeback, but she hoped her dad embraced it. She didn't want him worrying about his kids, not when he had so many health worries of his own.

Her dad nodded, maybe agreeing, maybe just wanting to change the subject. "Did you get a chance to see Audrey before she left?"

"I did for a minute or two." Again, nothing clever came to mind so Remi went with, "She looks good."

This time his nod was definitely of agreement, but his expression had more of that frustration in it. Rather than try to pick apart exactly what was the root of this particular frustration, Remi went with a subject change.

"What's this?" she asked, picking up the album he'd been holding when she had come in.

"Memories," he readily answered. "Of happy times. Of course, most photo albums are happy since people don't tend to hang on to pictures of the miserable times. Effie put this one together. Plenty of others, too, I recently found out. Did you know she'd done albums for each year your mom was here at the ranch? She stopped doing them after your mom passed and then moved on to doing albums for each of you kids."

Remi hadn't known that, but she had seen plenty of family photos over the years. Heck, she'd studied the ones of her mom. Studied hard while trying to recall any sliver of memory that might be buried in the subconscious of her first two years of life. The studying had been a bust, though. There was simply nothing there for Remi to remember.

He took the album from her and turned the pages until he got to one that wasn't under a protective sheet but had rather been tucked inside. Remi knew it, oh, so well. It was her mom when she'd been young, barely eighteen, and a brand new airman fresh out of basic training.

According to the family stories Remi had been told, her mother had joined the military so she could see the world and have an adventure away from Emerald Creek where she'd grown up. Adventures had apparently been had, what with assignments to Turkey and then Alaska. She'd returned home at the end of her four-year commitment, renewed her teenage romance with Derek and the rest was history. Marriage, four kids. Her death.

So many people had asked Remi if it was Audrey or her brothers who'd influenced her to go into the military, but it was neither. It was her mom and understanding the woman's need for an adventure. Remi wanted that rolled up together with the rescues. That didn't dig up any actual memories of her mother, but Remi felt as if she were sort of following in the steps of her mom's own combat boots.

Her dad turned a couple of pages and tapped another photo that Remi had seen many times.

It was of her birth.

Well, slightly after her birth, anyway, with her mother holding a crying gunky-faced newborn while her dad looked on. There was no denying the happiness in their expressions, and Effie had said on more than one occasion that both her parents had been thrilled with their three sons but had also wanted a daughter. They'd gotten one, but her mother only had two years with that daughter. Two years apparently marked with lots of trips to the hospital after her cancer diagnosis.

"I thought I was going to die," her father said, closing the photo album. He continued before Remi could say anything. "While I was on the floor, I thought of you. Of my boys and Audrey. But I thought of your mom, too. I thought of it all."

Again, she didn't get a chance to respond because

her dad turned to her and buried his face against her shoulder. Remi sat there, holding her father while he did something she'd never seen him do before.

He broke down and cried.

CHAPTER ELEVEN

ALANA STOPPED HER car on the narrow gravel road by the creek and barreled out, not caring one bit about the deluge of rain that immediately hit her. The anger and hurt were fueling her now, and she wasn't sure she could feel anything but that.

She wasn't crying and had no plans for it. Though, tears might come. After the hurt and anger had burned their way through her and left her drained and unbearably sad.

Again.

But for now, her eyes were dry—well, except for the rain—and while yanking off her necklace, she marched straight toward the banks of the creek. Even though the creek was about fifteen yards across, the water was fairly shallow in this spot. The creek bed was filled with colorful smooth rocks, and despite the rain, the water was still crystal clear. Not green, though, despite its name of Emerald Creek. Early settlers of the area had called it that because of the thick green foliage that grew on the banks.

She threaded and stomped her way through that foliage, stopping right at the creek's edge, and she opened her hand to hurl the necklace as far as she could.

Alana made the mistake of looking at it first.

A mistake she'd made many, many times in the past when she'd been planning to toss it or hide it away where she'd never have to see it on a daily basis. The chain itself was plain sterling silver, and it had no pendant per se.

Only her wedding band and engagement ring.

Of course, they now managed to sparkle and shine like little beacons, pulling her in and reminding her of Jack. Of when he'd given her the engagement ring with the flashy diamond. Of when he'd put the band on her finger at the wedding.

Alana had kept the rings on her finger for the first year. She'd done that partly because of the guilt she'd felt over his death, but she had also done it for Tilly. Even though the woman hadn't come out and said it, she had needed to see Alana wearing those rings because it allowed her to hang on to some small part of her son. After all, Jack hadn't hurt Tilly, he hadn't done anything to violate his mother's trust in him, and Tilly's grief hadn't been mixed with the other things Alana had felt.

After a year, Alana had moved the rings to the chain, wearing them first in plain sight and then tucking them away beneath her clothes. But those days were over. Hanging on to tiny shreds of her love for Jack was over, too. She was ready to hurl the rings into the water and never lay eyes on them again.

Egan and Remi were almost certainly cursing themselves for what she'd overheard, but Alana knew she should thank them for it. Thank them for putting

it right there in her face so she could once and for all
lay the past to rest. But what she'd overheard had hurt.

Mercy, had it hurt.

Was Jack in love with her, too?

That's what she'd heard Egan ask Remi. Alana
had also heard the part of their conversation before
that about the woman Jack was cheating with.

Alana hadn't waited for Remi's answer because
it hadn't mattered. The woman had loved him, and
that told Alana that the relationship almost certainly
hadn't been just a one-off and that it hadn't been just
about sex. Even if the love had only been one-sided
on his lover's part, it was still there.

That and that alone should be more than enough
for her to toss the blasted rings. But Alana continued to hold them while the rain slid down her face.
While she grieved all over again.

She spotted a lazy daisy, a rain-soaked white pet-
aled wildflower that grew along the banks. A favorite of hers. And the primary decision-making tool
she'd used as a kid. Should she tell her third-grade
crush that she'd love him forever? Well, the lazy
daisy could help with that.

"Do I tell him?" Pluck a petal. "Don't I tell him?"
Pluck a petal. And so on until the last petal revealed
the answer. Usually it wasn't the answer she'd wanted
and that had often caused her to either toss or stomp
on the now bare stem while grumbling about how
stupid flowers were.

That hadn't stopped her, though, from using the
"petal plucking" forecaster again and again.

Alana picked this one. "Should I toss the rings?" she asked.

However, before she had a chance to move on to the second question, she heard the sound of an approaching vehicle. She cursed because she had a good idea who it was, and she got confirmation of it almost right away.

"Alana," Egan called out.

She cursed some more when she heard him coming toward her, understanding that he probably felt as crappy as she did about what she'd overheard. Understanding, too, that she got no satisfaction whatsoever out of a "misery loves company" deal. She'd wanted to do the ring toss for a long time in an effort to finally get over her cheating husband who might or might not have been in love with another woman.

"How did you find me?" she asked when Egan stopped right next to her. Unless the rain had partially blinded him, which was a possibility, he would have seen the necklace and rings she was holding before she squeezed her hand around them.

"I crossed off any places that you might have gone with Jack," he explained. "Jack wasn't a fan of the creek."

True. In fact, Jack hadn't been a fan of water, period, and it was the reason he'd chosen the Air Force over the Navy. He hadn't even learned to swim before he'd gone to Combat Rescue training.

Alana spared him a glance and noted that no, he wasn't partly blind, thanks to his Stetson. The rain was dripping off the brim, creating a little umbrella effect for his face and eyes. His shirt and jeans, though, weren't faring nearly as well since they were just as wet as her dress and hair.

"There was no need for you to come," she insisted. Of course, her insistence wouldn't do any good, but she wanted to spell something out to him. "I'm not here to toss myself in the creek."

He made a sound to indicate that no spelling out had been necessary, and he tipped his head to her hand. "You came here to ask the lazy daisy if you should toss those," he said. Not a question before he did another head tip toward the creek. "The wedding band Colleen gave me is somewhere in there."

Alana frowned. She hadn't known that, and she hadn't guessed it was something he'd tell her now.

"Did tossing it make you feel better?" she wanted to know.

"Not much," he readily admitted. "The moment I hurled it through the air, I thought about the money I could have donated to a charity if I'd sold it. People could have benefited from Colleen's cheating and our marriage ending." He paused. "I suspect there are a lot of diamonds, gold and silver nestled below the creek rocks. Thousands and thousands of dollars' worth."

He had a point since she had, indeed, heard rumors of guys tossing engagement rings after their proposals had been turned down. When she'd been a teenager, Alana recalled Colleen herself chucking in a promise ring given to her by a then boyfriend who'd broken up with her two days before the junior prom.

While Alana contemplated all of that and realigned her thoughts to selling/donating rather than tossing, the silence settled between them. So did some of her anger.

Some.

It was no longer on a full boil but rather the usual perpetual simmer when she thought of what Jack had done.

"You want to talk about what you heard Remi and me saying?" Egan finally asked.

"No," Alana was quick to answer.

It was ironic that if anyone knew what it was like to be cheated on, it was Egan, but there was shame that came with this whole mess. Along with the jabs of inadequacy that she hadn't been enough for her husband.

"If you know," Alana added, "don't tell me if Jack was in love with the other woman."

Or *Miss Things Just Happened* as Remi had called her. Alana smiled a little at that. Apparently, Remi hadn't been a fan of Jack's cheating, either.

"If she was stunningly beautiful, I don't want to know," Alana went on, tossing the unplucked lazy daisy. "Ditto for keeping it to yourself if she was some kind of superhero who saved a bunch of people and brought about world peace."

That came out as the snarky exaggeration she'd meant it to be, but it had an underlying cut to it. Because it might have been this woman's bone-deep heroism and dedication to her country that had drawn Jack to her.

In those minutes she'd listened to Remi and Egan talking in the barn, she had heard Remi say that the woman had been an intel officer. Alana wasn't sure exactly what a job like that entailed, but it was possible she had saved lives with something she'd done.

"I thought about going into the military," Alana went on. "I mean, once Jack had decided that's what he wanted to do, I thought about going in. The Air Force has dietitians so I could have basically been doing the same job I have now. He talked me out of it, though, because he said it would be hard for us to get assignments together."

"It probably would have been," Egan agreed.

Even though it was true, Alana still made a "yeah right" sound, complete with an eye roll. "His argument was I could accompany him as a civilian to the bases where he was stationed and find work there. That's all well and good except he was either deployed or on temporary duty most of the time, and there were assignments where spouses couldn't go. After three years of that, I ended up back home where the plan was for him to visit as often as possible."

And she'd thought Jack had done that. It turned out, though, that some of his "as often as possible" visits hadn't been with her but rather this lover.

"If she was the kind of woman Jack wanted," Alana heard herself confess, "one who was a fellow military officer with hero status, then I couldn't have given him that even if I had been in the Air Force."

Dietitians didn't get many opportunities to save the world and gain hero status.

He made another of those sounds of agreement. "I feel the same way about Colleen's guy. An artist and a poet. The closest I could come to that was making fun of Cal and Blue when we were fighting and I was throwing painted cow shit at them."

Frowning, she looked at him. "You painted cow shit?"

Egan nodded. "Not the super fresh stuff but the partly dried piles. I spray painted them to look like land mines and used sticks to spear chunks that were solid enough for me to hurl." He shrugged when her frown stayed in place. "Brothers don't always have clean fights."

Apparently not. Neither did sisters. "Colleen and I once got in a fight and threw kiddie makeup at each other. I beaned her between the eyes with a Polly Pocket lip gloss."

For one too short moment, that made her smile, and then the other emotions returned with a vengeance. Her eyes burned, not from the rain but from the threat of the damn tears.

"When the grief started, I had no idea it'd go on this long," she admitted. "It didn't start out as me thinking about what it would be like three years from now. It began with me just getting through a second. Then, a minute. I built my way up to hours, then days. Nights. Weeks. But the grief has never gone completely away."

"Yeah." And that was all he said. All he needed to say.

Because Egan was dealing with it, too, only from

a different perspective as the best friend. It wouldn't do her any good to tell him that Jack's death hadn't been his fault. It wouldn't help, either, if he clarified that he hadn't been okay with Jack's cheating. Alana had gotten the gist of his "not being okay" when she'd overheard the bits of his conversation with Remi. She'd seen his face, too, and Egan had not been a happy camper.

"Stating the obvious here, but you're getting wet," he pointed out. "So is your phone."

He aimed a glance at her dress pocket where she had put her phone that was, indeed, getting a soaking. It was hard, though, for her to care about such things when it felt as if she'd stepped into a deep dark hole and couldn't get out. In fact, Alana wasn't sure she could even move at the moment.

The zigzag of lightning changed her mind. It slashed down from the dark clouds, and a rumble of thunder followed.

"Again, stating the obvious, but it's probably not smart to be near water or these trees with the lightning," Egan said.

"No," she agreed, and on a heavy sigh, she turned to head toward her car before Egan stopped her by taking hold of her arm.

"We'd best go in my truck. With this downpour, the road will already be a muddy mess, and you'll get bogged down. I can drop you off at work or home and then have one of the hands come out with the tow chain to get your car to you."

He was right, of course, and Alana had in fact

gotten stuck out here a year ago on another of her grief treks. She didn't want to go through that right now when she was barely holding herself together. It didn't matter so much if Egan saw her fall apart since he'd already witnessed it after she told him all about the final words she'd spoken to Jack.

"I'll need my purse, though," she said, snagging it from her car and putting her phone inside to try to salvage it. She dumped in the necklace and rings, too, and Alana vowed to either find a place to sell them or offer them to Tilly as keepsakes.

She let him lead her to his truck, and he helped her in since it sat so high off the ground. Alana plopped down on the seat and nearly screamed when she glanced down at the front of her dress and saw that the rain had seemingly turned it transparent. Plenty transparent enough to reveal that she'd worn a cobalt blue bra and panties since all her other decent underwear was line-drying in her laundry room.

Good grief.

She might as well have had arrows pointing to the spots that she counted on clothing to hide. Specifically, her breasts and nipples. If Egan had wondered about the size of them, he now had firsthand visual knowledge.

"I didn't look," he assured her a split second before he shut the door. He'd probably noticed her looking down in horror at her body. "Well, I glanced," he added after he was behind the wheel, "but when I realized what was going on, I kept my eyes on your face and feet."

Then he was more of a gentleman than she had been a lady since she'd certainly given his chest a gawking when his shirt had been unbuttoned. Sometime, though, between when she'd run away from the barn and his arrival at the creek, he'd buttoned up.

He started the engine but didn't drive off. "I'm going to say just one thing, and then I'll hush. Jack was an idiot to cheat on you. Most cheaters are. And since we're both the ones who've been cheated on, I believe their affairs didn't have nearly as much to do about us as it did about some weakness in them." He shrugged. "That's how I'm choosing to see it, anyway."

It was a good perspective, one that, surprisingly, took away some of that nagging guilt about not having been good enough and not having saved the world. It didn't eliminate the "really deep pissed off" anger she might always feel for Jack, and herself, but it helped.

"Thanks," she muttered.

"You're welcome." He still didn't make a move to drive away, and after a few moments he turned to her. "Look, about what happened in the barn. Not overhearing the conversation but what happened before that…do we need to talk about it?"

He meant the near kiss and the sweltering heat that had gone along with it. He meant the unwanted attraction. The massive potential problems it could cause if they had gone through with what they'd both been thinking of doing.

"Uh, no, we probably shouldn't talk about it," she

managed to say, knowing full well this was not going to be akin to something out of sight, out of mind. The heat was there and shouldn't be acted on.

That's why Alana stunned herself when she did.

Moving as fast as the next lightning bolt, she leaned across the seat and put her mouth on Egan's. Her heart stumbled over a couple of beats. Butterflies scattered to flight in her stomach.

And the slow trickle of heat started to spread.

Egan seemed to freeze for just a split second, maybe waging a battle against common sense and this clawing need. The need won. Because a deep sound rumbled in his throat before he reached out, his hand sliding around the back of her neck, and he pulled her to him.

Their mouths met for real this time, not just the "testing the waters" peck she had started. This was the "full-on, lip-to-lip, hungry" deal that made her forget all about, well, everything but the kiss.

Egan clearly had some kissing experience, some mouth moves, and he put that expertise to good use by running his tongue along her lips and notching up the already hot and hungry need. He kissed. And took. Alana kissed him back and tried to give as good as she got while the urgency and lust gave her one slam after another.

Thank goodness they had to break to breathe or they might have just started tearing at each other's clothes. Their gazes met and locked during that disconnection where they were both sucking in air. She saw the fire in his eyes. Felt it vibrating. Got another wave of lust.

And just a smidge of common sense.

It wasn't much, but apparently Egan got enough of it, too, that she saw the quick epiphany he was getting. Yes, this was good. Very, very good. And yes, they wanted each other very, very much.

But acting on that want would have consequences. Huge ones. Ones that neither of them might be ready to handle.

Well, crud.

Because his epiphany was spot-on, and it gave Alana just enough time to try to listen to shouts of reason that her brain was trying to send.

Kissing probably wasn't the best way to pull her out of that deep dark hole of grief and misery. But it had worked. For a few precious moments, the only thing she was feeling right now was a hard hungry need. For Egan. For him and more of those scorching kisses.

And she had no idea if that was the best thing that'd happened to her in a long, long time.

Or the worst.

Alana figured one way or another, she'd soon find out.

CHAPTER TWELVE

EGAN HAD NO idea what he was doing, but that didn't stop him from parking his truck and walking up the stone path toward the cemetery.

He had brain fog, as if he hadn't had nearly enough caffeine, but he'd already drank three cups of coffee and was working on his fourth. The odds were the coffee wasn't going to cure the fog that had been there for four days now.

Four days since that rainy kiss with Alana.

Four days since they'd both lost all reason and given into the greedy bastard also known as lust.

Thankfully, the lust had ended with only the kiss and nothing more. Both of them had behaved themselves and sat in utter and seriously uncomfortable silence while he'd driven her home. As she'd gotten out of the truck, they'd both tried their hands at what would have almost certainly been awkward goodbyes. And finally given up when unable to come up with anything that wouldn't spur a conversation about what they'd just done. A conversation that clearly neither of them had wanted to have.

So, for four days they'd had thinking time, and in Egan's case, brain fog, and during that time, he hadn't come up with a single solution that would help. He still wanted Alana. Still grieved for Jack. Still felt guilty as hell. His dad was still struggling with his recovery, along with being even more down now that Audrey and Remi had gone back to their respective bases.

At least Alana and he had managed to avoid seeing each other during those four days. That was in part because he'd stayed holed up in his office or in one of the pastures during her daily visits to the ranch to check on his dad. Not once on those visits had Alana sought him out, and Egan was still trying to decide how he felt about that. She was smart to have stayed away and given him that thinking time, but she obviously had plenty of willpower since he'd been within a breath of breaking down and just calling her.

Sooner or later, he would need to make that call. Or better yet have a face-to-face with Alana. The last thing he wanted to do was add to her guilt because she'd kissed her late husband's best friend, and that meant he owed her an apology. As a minimum. He also owed her an assurance that he would keep his hands off her.

Egan was still working on whether or not he could do that.

Contemplating that, he sipped his coffee and kept on walking. Because he needed to make a quick trip to the base to deal with some paperwork and take a quick meeting, he was wearing his flight suit. To fit that in along with his other duties at the ranch, he'd

gotten an extra early start to the day, and that meant
he'd been able to see the sunrise on his drive to the
cemetery. It also meant it had yet to reach the "hotter
than hell" stage. There was a cool morning breeze,
and the sun was spewing out some beautiful colors
over the tree-dotted landscape.

And the tombstones.

Of course, he knew exactly where Jack was buried since Egan had been at the funeral. He'd had to
do that with a cast on his arm and some bruises,
burns and scrapes. Nothing major. Definitely nothing like the injuries Jack and the others in that vehicle had gotten.

Egan moved off the trail and headed to the tombstone in the far corner. As graves went, he supposed
this was a pretty spot, shaded by two towering oaks
and surrounded by his kin who'd died before him.
His dad who'd died in a car accident when Jack had
been twenty. His paternal grandparents and his infant sister who'd been stillborn.

Someone, Tilly probably, had put fresh flowers on
all three graves, and it reminded Egan that he should
have done that instead of just showing up with his
coffee. Actually, he should have visited before now,
but it was the first time he'd been here in the three
years since the funeral.

Egan stopped in front of Jack's grave and lifted
his coffee mug as he would a toasting drink. Jack
might have gotten a chuckle out of that, but Egan
was in too bad a place right now to think of Jack
chuckling or smiling. And that made Egan realize

why he had made the trek here. The answer finally made its way through the brain fog, and it wasn't an answer he liked much.

He was here to confess to Jack what he'd done to, and with, Alana.

"I kissed your wife," he said aloud.

The words, though, didn't take any of the weight off his shoulders, and the clearing fog led him to other thoughts. How would Jack have felt about Egan doing that? Hard to say since if Jack had survived, Alana and he might not even still be married. They might be bitter exes, the way Egan and Colleen were. Even if that were true, though, Egan still would have had obstacles and guilt over the kiss.

"And Alana kissed me," Egan added.

It still didn't help, but it gave him a reminder of the heat the kissing had generated. Definitely memorable, which meant he wasn't going to forget it or the guilt anytime soon.

"I'm sorry," Egan went on. "Not nearly sorry enough about kissing Alana as I am that I'm here and you're not. I shouldn't have asked you to come. I should have changed seats with you so you would have been the one thrown clear—"

Egan stopped since he was basically launching into another blow-by-blow account of what had happened. He relived that often enough in his nightmares without spelling it out here. Besides, if Jack was truly tuned in from beyond the grave, there was no need for Egan to spell it all out.

He heard the sound of the approaching footsteps

and groaned. Hell. Was this Alana and had she over-heard yet another conversation about Jack? Dreading what he might see, Egan slowly turned around and groaned for a completely different reason. Because it wasn't Alana.

But rather Tilly.

And judging from the way she had her phone lifted, she'd just snapped a photo of him.

"Sorry," she muttered, tapping away at something on her phone screen. "I saw you standing here, and I just couldn't resist. What a picture you made stand-ing there, talking to Jack. I posted it to Facebook so my friends can see it."

Egan wished she hadn't done that, but he knew her reaction could have been a whole lot worse. Es-pecially if Tilly had heard the part about Alana and him kissing. He recalled what Alana had said about Tilly wanting her to stay Jack's wife even after all this time.

"I always want to salute or something when I see people in uniform," the woman went on while she made her way toward him. "So heroic."

There it was, that word that Egan despised, and he had to get his jaw unclenched before he could respond. "Practical," he provided. But he refrained from adding that the flight suit was fire-resistant, comfortable and had plenty of pockets for stashing his wallet and other stuff.

"I have to say," Tilly went on, stopping beside him, "that it made me very happy to see you here. I visit Jack three or four times a week so I can tell him about what's going on, and I bring fresh flowers on Saturdays. I used to run into people all the time. But that's tapered off," she added in a sad mutter.

Three years was a long time. For most people, anyway. Egan was betting it hadn't been nearly long enough for Tilly's grief to lessen over losing both her son and her infant daughter. With her husband having passed as well, it basically left Tilly alone. No wonder she was so determined to be sure Alana remained devoted to Jack.

For just a moment, he wondered how Tilly would react if she learned about Jack's cheating. Not wanting to shatter that "heroic" image of him, she likely wouldn't believe it, and if she did, it would crush her. That was a good reason for her never to learn the truth.

But was it time for Tilly to hear why Jack had died?

Egan ran through what he could say, how he could tell her. Again, she'd be crushed, but she should know the truth. Maybe he could sit her down after the life celebration and spill all. Afterward, she'd hate him, but it had to be done. He didn't want Tilly to keep thinking of him as a blasted hero.

"I can't stay long," Egan explained. "I'm heading to the base for a while." Of course, there was no scheduled appointment for that. His admin officer had said there were training forms that Egan needed to sign and that they would be on his desk.

Tilly nodded and looked up at him. "What's going on with Alana?"

The question threw him, and Egan was thankful

he hadn't sputtered out a cough or some other guilty telltale sign. "What do you mean?" he asked, hoping like the devil that Tilly didn't want to know—

"I mean, there's talk about you and her," Tilly provided.

Clearly, hoping like the devil hadn't worked, but there was no way he was going to spill anything about that kiss. It was possible, of course, that someone had witnessed it if they'd been anywhere in the vicinity of that part of the creek, but Egan hadn't seen anyone. Still, anyone around Alana and him for more than a second or two could probably pick up on the heat between them. He wasn't going to mention that to Tilly, either.

"Alana's been coming to the ranch every day to check on my dad and make sure he's sticking to the diet changes," Egan said. Definitely not a lie.

Tilly didn't respond, and it seemed to Egan that she was waiting for him to add more. She finally muttered, "Of course," but she didn't seem to be feeling much relief that checking on his dad was all there was to the rumors.

"I think the third-year anniversary is weighing on Alana," Tilly went on a moment later. "I suspected it would. Anniversaries tend to do that, they bring it all back to the surface. It was one of the reasons I wanted to go ahead and do a life celebration. I thought the day would be easier, what with so many people around to talk about Jack's finer moments."

He nearly asked if that's why she invited Colleen, but there was no way he could pull off the question and not sound annoyed. Which he was. However, Egan had decided not to dwell on it. Yeah, he'd likely have to face Colleen on the day of the event, but there was no need to give her any mental space before then.

"Take care, Tilly," Egan said, and he started to walk away.

"My friends are all early risers like me," the woman volunteered. "So, I've already got a whole bunch of likes, comments and shares on the photo I posted of you."

Great. Since Tilly's friends were likely the same circle as his dad's, Egan only hoped this blip of attention didn't continue. As far as he was concerned, every day was an anniversary to remember the nightmare of not saving Jack.

He went back to his truck and took the road that would lead him to the interstate and then the base. It also took him straight down Main Street, which thankfully never had much traffic. Including this morning. The only thing to slow a driver down was the posted thirty miles an hour speed limit.

Egan didn't mind the pokey speed, though, because Main Street was lined with interesting, and unusual, mom-and-pop businesses that fed a small town's unique personality. The Sweet Tooth ice-cream and candy shop. Collier's Grocery with its white stucco exterior crammed with vintage and antique signs of foods and drinks. On the other side of it, was the bookstore, One for the Books.

Since this was ranching country, there was a shop where Bobby Medina and his wife, Esther, made custom boots, belts and hats. They hadn't gone with anything catchy back in the '70s when they'd opened their doors. It was just called Boots, Belts and Hats.

Egan stopped at the lone traffic light that was positioned next to Desi's Diner, the town's hot spot for breakfast, and he spotted a familiar vehicle in the parking lot. Grammy Effie's old VW van that she'd refused to part with even though she no longer drove. Egan quickly saw the riddle of how it'd gotten there when he noticed Effie and Maybell at one of the tables that was directly in front of the window.

He might have kept going after the light turned green, but his grandmother waved at him and then motioned for him to come inside. And he got a jolt of worry. Remi had left two days ago to go back to work, and both Maybell and Effie had been at the ranch when he'd left. Since they were here, it meant his dad was maybe in the house alone. Fifteen days ago, before the heart attack, that wouldn't have been any big deal, but it felt like one now.

Egan parked and tried not to do a flat-out run to get inside the diner and find out what was going on. But he didn't manage to get out any questions because the moment he was inside, he saw his dad seated in one of the booths.

With Alana across from him.

"Alana walked up from her office to meet us here," Maybell immediately provided, no doubt because she'd seen the alarm on Egan's face. "She wanted to point out the healthier things on the menu for Derek to order."

Some of that alarm had to still be there in his expression. "Did the doctors give Dad permission to be out and about?"

"They did," his grandmother assured him. "Dr. Abrams gave specific instructions for us to bring him when it wasn't too crowded so Derek wouldn't get overwhelmed with the well-wishers."

Maybell checked the time. "We're also not supposed to stay longer than a half hour, and there's only five minutes left so we'll be heading out soon."

Effie and Maybell clearly hadn't gone with healthier options. They were both eating plate-sized cinnamon rolls that were drowned in icing. His dad, however, was eating what appeared to be a fruit plate with a side of wheat toast. Like him, Alana had coffee, and she met his gaze over the top of her gigantic mug.

Met his gaze and then quickly looked away.

Egan knew why she'd done that. Because they totally sucked at hiding the aftereffects of that kiss, and she hadn't wanted his dad or anyone else to see the heat in her eyes.

Thankfully, though, there weren't many customers to see. Only four others, retired men Egan recognized and knew to be regulars. A waitress was behind the counter, and Egan spotted the cook, Teddy Merkins, behind a cloud of smoke just on the other side of the half wall pass-through to the kitchen. Judging from the smell, he was cooking both sausage and bacon.

The owner, Desi Lovejoy, had obviously embraced

his famous namesake, Desi Arnaz, because there were framed pictures of the actor all over the walls. Even the tops of the tables themselves were covered with Desi photos, coated with a clear protective shield. Egan had always thought it was a little disrespectful to plop down overloaded plates of food and drinks onto Desi's grinning face, but since the particular face took up the entire table, there wasn't much of a choice.

"You on the way to the base?" Maybell asked at the same moment his grandmother said, "That's a good picture of you that Tilly posted." Effie held up her phone as if he might be unaware of it.

He was well past the stage of simply being aware, but it was a shocker to actually see it. The rising sun had caught Jack's granite tombstone just right so that it appeared to be a brilliant white. Like a shining star. With Egan's back to Tilly, he was practically a silhouette.

In a flight suit.

The uniform came through crystal clear, and with Egan's head lowered, it appeared he was paying respect to a fellow fallen officer. Which he hadn't been. Not really. He'd gone there to confess about that blasted kiss.

Maybell stood, putting the rest of Effie's and her pastries in a to-go box that they'd obviously already asked for. "Better get Derek back home."

His dad must have noticed the activity because he got up as well. Obviously compliant of the doctor's orders, but he also looked tired. Too tired. And his color was still off.

It would have been damn hard for Egan to explain why the compliancy was bothering him, though, but it was. His dad hadn't pressed to get back to work. He'd been following the rules, and that likely meant he was scared. Depressed. Or both. Added to that, his dad had had the whammy of both his wife and daughter leaving after what their duty demanded as short visits.

Egan had already asked Alana how his dad was really doing so he wouldn't press her again on it. No, it was best if he had the heart-to-heart talk with his dad instead. A talk that wouldn't make things more worrisome than they already were.

"Son," his dad greeted as he eased himself out and away from the booth. Unlike Maybell and Effie, he didn't box up his leftovers, though it appeared he hadn't eaten much. "Always good to see you in uniform."

The words were right, but Egan thought he heard the worry beneath them. Or rather the reminder that Egan was halfway through his month of leave, and after that, the plan was… Egan decided not to fill in the blanks on that, not with so much still up in the air.

"I won't be long," Egan assured him.

Derek nodded, which had a weariness to it, too, and he moseyed out the door with Maybell and Effie. Not exactly leaving Egan alone with Alana but close.

"Is Dad upset about Remi and Audrey leaving?" Egan came out and asked her.

Alana opened her mouth to answer, and when Egan followed her glance around, he realized they had the attention of the waitress, the four customers and the cook. On a silent mutual agreement, Alana and he went outside.

Not to his truck.

There was a silent, mutual agreement about that, too, since the last time they'd been in a truck, they'd kissed. Instead, they went to the sidewalk, giving a wave to Maybell as she drove away with Effie and Derek.

"Your dad didn't come out and say he was upset," Alana was finally able to answer, "but I think he's feeling a little blue. Remi was worried about that happening, and that's why she stopped by my office on her way out of town."

Egan hadn't known about his sister making that visit to Alana, but it didn't surprise him. Remi had been just as upset as he had over their conversation that Alana had overheard.

"I didn't press Remi for any other details of *Miss Things Just Happened*," Alana added a moment later.

"Neither did I," he volunteered.

Another pause. "Remi guessed that we had kissed," Alana said.

Crap. Of course, she had. Remi wasn't blind. And neither were the town gossips, a reminder that while nothing Alana and he were saying was being overheard, they were being observed. The waitress was now at the window, peering out at them, and the car that drove past crept along well below the speed limit. Added to that, two vehicles had pulled into the parking lot, and while Egan hadn't noticed the drivers, he recognized one of the cars as Tilly's.

"Remi won't say anything to anyone," Alana went on, "but…"

No need for her to confirm that word would, indeed, get around, and that was a good reason for them to say their goodbyes, which they did. Alana headed up the street toward the hospital, and Egan went to his truck. He didn't get far, though, before someone called out to him.

Tilly again.

The woman was out of her car and headed straight toward him. Egan groaned because Tilly was no doubt about to bring up gossip about Alana and him.

Or so he thought.

But the woman was smiling and waving her phone around. "The newspaper's going to put the picture on their website," she gushed out when she was still a good ten yards away.

Egan didn't need any time for that to sink in, and while it wasn't a dreaded chat about Alana and him, it was dreaded. His picture at Jack's grave would be right there for everyone to see. Well, everyone in town who ventured to the website, anyway. Thankfully, it wouldn't be that many people.

Egan soon learned he was wrong about that, too.

"I just talked with Parker," Tilly went on, speaking of Parker Freeman, the editor of the *Emerald Creek Gazette*, "and he thinks the bigger newspapers in San Antonio will post the picture, too, so he's going to write a story to go along with it."

Great. Just great.

"Parker thinks the timing is perfect for a story like that to really take off," Tilly went on, still gushing. "It'll not only be a chance for him to mention Jack's life celebration, but it'll showcase you as our very own local hero."

Something inside Egan snapped. Just snapped. And he heard the words tumble out of his mouth before he could even think about stopping them.

"I'm not a hero," he snarled. "Jack is dead because of me."

Tilly shook her head. "What do you mean? He was on orders in Kandahar."

This was not going to be easy, but that didn't stop him. "Jack was in Kandahar, but he wasn't on a mission at that particular moment. He was in that vehicle because I asked him to come and see me. If I hadn't done that, he wouldn't have been anywhere near that IED, and you wouldn't be having a life celebration for him. You'd have your son."

Tilly stared at him and stared as Egan watched her take in the words, one by one. The words and their god-awful meaning.

"Oh," she muttered. Just *oh*. And she pressed her hand to her trembling mouth.

Tears instantly filled her eyes, and she looked at him, not with hero worship but the truth. The cold, hard, horrible truth that had haunted Egan for three years would now haunt Jack's mother as well.

What the hell had he done?

It was too late to take everything back. Egan knew

he was going to regret this moment for the rest of his life. He could add it to the regret he already felt because of what he'd done to Jack.

Tilly didn't even try to wipe away the tears, but she did back away from him when he reached out in a gesture to steady her. She backed away, and as if looking at the face of a monster, she turned and ran.

Before she even made it to her car, Egan could hear the woman's sobs.

CHAPTER THIRTEEN

ALANA TRIED TO soften her scowl even though it seemed to be her go-to response when a virtual date popped up on her phone screen. That *go-to* should have been her Texas-sized clue to put an end to this particular social activity, but she answered the FaceTime call, anyway, hoping that the next few minutes weren't a complete waste of time and data usage.

"Hi," the man greeted, and while he was smiling, sort of, anyway, there was a definite hesitant edge to it. Maybe he had also been asked about the size of one of his body parts. "I'm Dave," he added, and judging from the way it just rolled off his tongue, that was probably his real name.

"Alana," she said.

Unlike Lucky, Dave's call was right on time, and he didn't look like a teenager. In fact, he looked exactly the age he'd listed, thirty-five, and his profile picture was as close of a likeness as a photo could get.

"So, you're a dietitian," he said. "Do you enjoy your job?"

"Most days." She had to look down at the brief bio beneath his picture to see what his occupation was. A fireman, and judging from what she could see of the background, it appeared he was actually at the fire station. "How about you? Do you enjoy your job?"

"Most days," he echoed, but he flashed a smile to go along with it. "We could probably use the services of a dietitian around here." He leaned in as if telling a secret. "There are three casseroles with the word *surprise* in the fridge right now and at least three kilos of cheap chocolate on the counter."

She smiled, too, but Alana knew hers wasn't anywhere near as bright as his. She continued to glance through his bio and saw no red flags, no weirdo stuff.

And that only deepened her scowl.

She'd thought if she ever had a virtual date with a guy like this, that it would spark her interest in having a relationship. Oh, she had a spark all right, but it wasn't anything Dave the fireman, or any other virtual date could give her.

Crap.

Her spark seemed to be only for Egan, and while she listened to Dave continue to make jokes about fire station food, her mood only got worse.

"Uh, is everything okay?" Dave asked. "I'm babbling too much, I know. Nerves," he added with a chuckle. "I mean, I saw your face on the screen, and I thought, oh, wow, she looks great. Amazing, actually, and I really need to impress her."

"You're impressive," she said, cutting him off. "In fact, on a scale of one to ten for virtual dates, you're a ten."

But he wasn't Egan. She didn't spell that out, but

she wanted to tell him not to waste his time, that this wasn't going anywhere.

At least until she got Egan out of her system.

That kiss had started something she either wanted to finish or fully extinguish, and that wasn't going to happen with her chatting with a hot virtual date.

"Something's come up recently," she tried to explain. "Or rather someone. And I need to work out a few things."

Dave's smile faded, and he gave a resigned nod. "Figures. Like I said, you look amazing so it shouldn't surprise me that someone else is in the picture. I'm disappointed, really disappointed, but I wish you the best, Alana." He paused a moment. "And feel free to call me if this other someone doesn't work out."

This time her smile was more genuine, and she gave a nod. But there'd be no future call. If Egan totally rejected her, then she would go back into sexual hibernation until, well, maybe forever. Or at least until she felt the same things she was starting to feel for Egan. Considering she'd only ever felt those things for Jack, then it could be an extremely long hibernation.

She ended the call and went to her contacts to press Egan's number. Hesitating and worrying, though, she gave herself a moment to settle her nerves and instead checked her messages to see if she'd gotten a response for her "is everything okay" text she'd sent to Tilly earlier. But there was nothing, and that caused Alana to frown.

Something was wrong.

Of course, Alana had already suspected that since throughout the day, three people had mentioned they'd seen Tilly and Egan in the parking lot of the diner. Heck, Alana had seen them, too, but apparently she'd missed the part about Tilly looking upset when she'd left. About Egan looking upset, too.

Alana wondered if something had happened or been said to make Egan change his mind about going to the life celebration. That would have definitely upset both Tilly and him. But it was equally possible this was about the photo that Tilly had taken of Egan at Jack's grave.

Now that the picture was on several newspaper sites, it was getting a lot of buzz, and no way would Egan have wanted that kind of attention. If he'd demanded that Tilly have the photo taken down, then it would have created a sticky, unsettling aftermath.

It'd been the prospect of the "sticky and unsettling" that prompted Alana to send the text to Tilly. She'd expected a quick reply but clearly hadn't gotten one. She made a mental note to drop by Tilly's on her way to work in the morning. For tonight, though, she might be able to get some answers from Egan.

She nearly made the call to him, but then wondered if he was still at the base. He'd been heading there hours ago—twelve to be exact, judging from when she'd seen him at the diner—but maybe he'd gotten caught up in his work. No way did she want to bother him if that were the case, and she didn't want to phone the ranch, either, to see if he was around.

Instead, Alana grabbed her purse and headed out.

She'd drive out to the ranch, and if she saw Egan's truck parked there, then she'd give him a call. Or maybe send him a text. Or maybe she'd just chicken out, she thought with some disgust at all this waffling.

Since her house was on the opposite side of town from the ranch, Alana made the drive out of her neighborhood and onto Main Street. She'd been behind the wheel less than a minute, though, when she did indeed spot Egan's truck. Not at the ranch but at the town's main bar, which was only just around the block from her house.

The Watering Whole, which was a throwback to the Old West saloons, was apparently meant to have been named the more traditional Watering Hole. However, the owner, Freddy Frazier, was a horrible speller, and he'd used the incorrect word when he'd ordered the sign. Not wanting to waste his money, Freddy had installed the sign, and a local institution had been born.

Over the years, some drunks and teens on a dare had climbed up on the steep roof and painted out the extra *W* or *le* in the Whole. Others had tried their talents at graffiti to turn it into Watering Whale, Tatering Hole and other such things, but Freddy had always repainted and kept his misspelling on display for all to see.

Alana pulled into the parking lot and took the empty spot next to Egan's truck. Of course, he wasn't sitting in his vehicle, which meant he was almost certainly inside.

Definitely something that wasn't part of his usual routine.

From what she'd heard over the years, he would sometimes go to the Watering Whole with his dad or his siblings when they were in town. But Alana figured it was a place he'd avoid on his own since he'd have to listen to heaven knew how many people mentioning the hero label that he felt he wasn't worthy of.

She sat there, debating if she should go inside and check on him when the front doors swung open and Egan came out. He was no longer in uniform but instead wearing his work clothes for the ranch. One look at his face, and Alana got more confirmation that something was very wrong.

He stopped when she stepped out of her car. Just stopped. Along with muttering something under his breath that she didn't catch. Alana hoped he wasn't cursing because she was there, but it was possible since they were doing their best to avoid each other.

Well, sort of their best since after all she was here and parked next to his truck.

But she'd temporarily ditched the avoidance because she'd been worried about him and because of the realization she'd gotten with Dave, the fireman. The last wasn't anywhere near a stellar reason, but the first certainly was. Almost certainly, anyway. And even if it weren't, she was here, and she couldn't just leave without saying something.

"I'm not stalking you," she volunteered just as Egan asked, "Are you here for Jesse's birthday party?"

It was possible that both of them looked surprised. She was since she'd had no idea it was Jesse's birthday, and even if she had, she wasn't part of the man's circle of friends and therefore wouldn't have been invited.

"It's Jesse's birthday, and the ranch hands had a get-together for him," Egan explained, and his tone and expression invited her to spill all about her stalking denial.

"I was worried about you," she admitted, "and then I had a problem with my virtual date."

Alana hadn't expected or wanted to tack on that last part, and it put some instant alarm in Egan's eyes. "What kind of problem? Is some guy stalking you?"

"No," she couldn't say fast enough.

No way to explain to him that Dave had been imperfect for her in a perfect sort of way. If she attempted to tell Egan something like that, she'd sound like an idiot. Added to that, she would have to spell out why her mind and body had decided that it wanted Egan and only Egan.

"No stalkings from virtual dates or from anyone else for that matter," she continued. "The date just didn't go as I'd planned so I've decided to put the virtual stuff on hold."

While he swatted a mosquito and its posse, Egan stared at her, maybe trying to suss out what she'd just said. Maybe he thought she'd been trying to tell him that since the virtual wasn't cutting it, she wanted the real deal.

With him.

Attraction could clarify or suggest things like that. It could also suggest really stupid things, like more kissing when this wasn't the time or the place. Or the occasion since she truly had been concerned about Egan.

"I was worried about you," she went on, swatting at the mosquitos, too, that obviously thought they had a fresh buffet to sample. "Worried, because I heard that Tilly and you seemed upset after your conversation at the diner."

Egan blew out a long breath, slapping more mosquitos, and adding some profanity that she heard just fine. Thankfully, not aimed at her but at the bloodsuckers. "We'll need transfusions if we stand out here much longer."

He glanced around as if searching for a solution, and his attention landed on his truck. Since the tight space would make kissing too easy, he seemed to dismiss it right away. Seemed to dismiss her car, too, since it would also be close quarters and therefore a big temptation to giving in to the heat. The car, though, was sort of a vehicular chastity belt since there was no way sex would happen in it unless the participants were contortionists.

"Mind if we walk to your place?" he asked.

The question both threw her and gave her one of those hot tingles of anticipation. She hadn't expected him to want to risk being alone with her. And that told her loads. Egan wouldn't have risked it unless he needed to have a conversation with her where there wasn't a chance of being overheard.

"Yes, let's go to my house," she managed to say after she swallowed hard.

She grabbed her purse from her car and glanced at their vehicles, wondering if someone would question why they were in the parking lot. However, there'd be a lot more questions and gossip if Egan's truck was outside her house for any length of time. Ditto for if she drove him to her place and someone saw them going inside. Of course, walking together would accomplish the same gossip.

"Just a reminder that if we leave together in any way, fashion or form, there'll be talk," she spelled out.

He sighed. "I've decided there'll be gossip if we do anything. Or nothing. So, let's get out of here so I can tell you how I screwed up things with Tilly."

Now it was her turn to sigh. And nod. Alana hoped whatever had happened, that it could be fixed. For Egan's sake since he had that haunted look on his face. For Tilly's sake, too, since she probably wasn't in a good place about whatever had happened, either.

Alana didn't say anything else until they were well away from the Watering Whole. "Is this about the photo Tilly took of you?" Alana whispered just in case there was still someone within earshot.

"No. But I'm not happy about that," he added in a snarl. "I'm pretty sure, though, that Tilly will try to get it taken down."

Oh, no. If this wasn't about the photo but Tilly would likely be doing such measures to remove the photo, then something really bad had happened between Egan and the woman. And it occurred to Alana exactly what that something really bad had to be.

"Crap," she muttered.

"Yeah," and that was all Egan said.

Alana didn't push for any details. She just kept her mouth shut while they walked around the block to her house. The mosquitos tried to follow them, buzzing around their heads and making them pick up the pace so they made the quick trip in record time. Alana unlocked the door with hands she wished were steadier than they were. That applied to the steadiness of the rest of her, too. Egan was likely going to need a strong shoulder to pour out his heart.

And there would be hurt.

It would be amplified because of his own grief and the misery he'd caused Tilly by telling her the truth. Or rather what Egan would have perceived as the truth.

"Should I pour you a stiff drink?" she asked, closing the door behind him. Then, she remembered the only thing alcoholic she had in the house was a fruity wine cooler. Thankfully, Egan declined the offer by waving it off.

He didn't jump into an explanation. He paced across her living room a few times, giving a brief frown to the odd little clay figure on the end table. It was a weird-looking man and had features of both a leprechaun and a Hobbit. She refrained from telling him it was a gift from Loralee. She just waited for Egan.

"Tilly was going on about the *hero* in the photo she took," he finally said. He stopped pacing and met her gaze head-on. "So, I told her what happened, why Jack was where he was when he died."

"You told her that you were responsible," she paraphrased.

"I was," he said, giving her his usual insistence.

Since she seriously doubted it would do any good just to dispute that, again, Alana did some spelling out of her own.

"Fine, we were both responsible," she told him. "You for asking Jack to visit you and me for the argument that would have been a huge distraction that day. In fact, it's possible the main reason Jack agreed to go see you was because he was upset over what I said to him."

She stopped and gave him a moment to let that sink in.

It did some sinking in for her, too. Her argument with Jack may or may not have led to his death, and while that was something that she'd have to deal with for the rest of her life, it did no good to let it consume her.

"We also need to blame the IED," she went on. "And the person or persons who put it there. Heck, the driver of the vehicle could have played a part in what happened, too. Or how about the crews who should have better checked that area to make sure it was safe enough to travel?"

His eye contact morphed into a flat look. "If you're hoping to make me feel better, it's not working."

"I didn't figure it would," she said, her voice suddenly as weary as his. "But maybe that's the point. That nothing we say or do will make us feel better."

"That didn't mean I had to dump that on Tilly," he snarled. "I didn't have to hurt her like that."

"I suspect keeping the truth from her hurt you," she was quick to point out.

But there was no *suspect* to it. Alana knew there'd been hurt not only over what had happened but also because not everyone knew why Jack had been where he'd ended up dying.

As Egan had obviously learned, though, that truth hadn't set him free.

"Have you spoken to Tilly today?" he asked.

Alana shook her head. "I tried to text her earlier, but she didn't respond." And that was her cue to try again.

She took out her phone from her purse and fired off a quick text. Just checking to see if you're all right, she messaged, and then waited for a reply. There wasn't an immediate one, which continued to be odd for the woman since she was usually very prompt at staying in touch.

Even though she wasn't sure she wanted to know the answer, Alana had to ask. "Did you mention Jack's affair? Or that Jack would have been distracted because of the argument I had with him about his sidepiece?"

He both shook his head and muttered a "No."

So, Tilly hadn't gotten a double whammy, which was probably good. "I intend to tell Tilly that Jack and I argued during our last phone call. I want to come clean, too. Or rather partially clean, anyway. There's no reason for her to know Jack cheated. I can just tell her we'd argued and leave it at that."

Egan huffed. "There's no reason for you to say anything at all."

Alana returned the flat stare he'd been giving her while she put her phone back in her purse, which she set on the foyer table. "No reason other than it could give her a better picture of Jack's state of mind when he died."

Egan opened his mouth, no doubt to argue, but he must have realized this whole discussion was a little like a warped spin of the old cliché, what's bad for the goose is bad for the gander. He hadn't wanted Alana to take on even a smidge of guilt or blame. He'd put that all on himself.

She didn't point out that was heroic. Not when he already was fuming and beating himself up. Alana did go to him, though, and despite the risk of it, she pulled him into her arms for what she hoped would be a comforting hug.

It wasn't.

The muscles in his chest and arms turned to iron. He seemed to hold his breath, too. So, clearly not a comfort, but when she started to pull away, Egan put a stop to that. He hooked his tense arms around her and held her in place.

Alana looked up at him, hoping he was about to kiss her, but instead he seemed to be having a fierce battle with his willpower. Unfortunately, the willpower seemed to be winning, too. And just like that day in the truck, she did something about it.

She kissed him.

And there it was. No mere tingle, not this. It was a full-impact kiss that seemed to jump straight from first base to a grand slam. His mouth was just as hard as the rest of him and, oh, so hungry. It seemed as if he was taking out all his frustrations, and pent-up needs, in the kiss.

Within a blink, he deepened the kiss even more, and he tightened his grip as if to make sure she didn't let go. If Alana could have spoken, which she couldn't, she would have told him she had no intention of going away. This, right here in his arms, was exactly where she wanted to be.

Egan, though, clearly had some "going away" intentions. Not away from her but to the back of the door where he anchored her while the kiss raged on. Everything suddenly seemed desperate, urgent and completely vital for survival.

Egan kept taking, kept deepening. Alana also fulfilled a few fantasies by sliding her hands over the tightly corded muscles in his back. Yes, definitely a fantasy fulfilled. The man was built.

She just kept on testing waters by pulling him closer and closer until that incredible chest of his was pressed against her breasts. Her breasts and all the rest of her applauded the contact.

And wanted more.

That was the problem with fueling fantasies and making out with a hot guy. The body wanted to take things up a notch and the stupid parts of her were begging for her to throw caution to the wind and drag Egan to the floor for some down and dirty sex.

Judging from Egan's intensity, he might have been considering the same caution-throwing. He ran his hand between them and touched. Just touched, running his thumb over her nipple and cupping her right breast. He was surprisingly gentle, considering the need was now sky-high and hot as fire.

Alana heard herself moan from the exquisite pleasure of being kissed and touched by a man she'd been lusting after for so long. But she also heard something else. A little dinging sound, and it took several moments for her to realize that it was her phone, alerting her to a text. A text she had no intention of checking.

But apparently Egan had a different notion about that.

He tore his mouth from hers, and with his breath gusting, he looked at her. "It could be Tilly."

Dang it, he was right, and that meant Alana had to press pause on the pleasure so she could check and make sure her former mother-in-law was okay.

Alana reached over and yanked out her phone. It took her a couple of seconds to focus, though, before she could read what was on the screen. Then, she groaned.

Yes, it was from Tilly, and the woman didn't even attempt to reassure Alana that all was well.

Sorry I haven't answered your text before now, but I got some disturbing news today. Please meet me at the city park tomorrow morning at eight because we've got to completely rethink Jack's life celebration. In the meantime, stay far, far away from Egan Donnelly.

CHAPTER FOURTEEN

EGAN DIDN'T EVEN bother to try to caffeinate himself enough to get rid of the headache that was throbbing away at his temples. He just accepted the pain and the fact that this was probably going to be a shitty morning when he finally faced the music.

Or rather when he finally faced Tilly now that she knew the truth.

Of course, Tilly hadn't invited him to this 8:00 a.m. meeting at the park, but Egan had no intention of having Alana meet with the woman alone. Especially since Alana would no doubt just try to excuse away his guilt by bringing up her argument with Jack. Egan was going to try to put a stop to Alana spilling any of that since it would only muddy already muddy waters. That's why he was standing around at the park a good fifteen minutes before Tilly and Alana were supposed to show.

Tilly would be shocked to see him. Probably not Alana, though. The night before, after she had gotten the text that had ended the "scorching kissing" session, Egan had told her that he wanted to be there at the meeting. Alana had insisted that wasn't a good idea, that she could talk to Tilly alone and try to suss out what Tilly was feeling. He'd insisted right back that sooner or later he had to talk to Tilly if only so the woman could shout and scream at him. And he was pretty sure there'd be some kind of emotional reaction on Tilly's part.

Tilly's text to Alana had given him clues as to the possible emotional reactions. She'd said she'd gotten *disturbing news* and *we've got to completely rethink Jack's life celebration*. Definitely not the words of a woman who had glossed over what she'd learned from Egan.

This was all part of the grief process, and while he didn't think for a second that such screaming and shouting would clear the air and heal Tilly, it was better than the pent-up anger eating away at her. Egan knew all too well that wasn't the way to go. Too bad he hadn't found a way to work out that anger at himself.

A little voice in his head disagreed with that.

At first, he blamed that little voice on his headache. But he knew all the kissing and touching he'd done with Alana had given him at least a temporary reprieve. Probably because it was next to impossible to think of anything else while they were going at each other. However, a bit of the buzz he'd gotten from her had carried through the night and here into the morning. It wasn't a cure for all that ailed him, but it didn't make things worse, either.

Well, not on one level.

Of course, down the road, it could lead to disaster, but Egan was toying with the notion that Alana and he could work out some of their feelings and frustrations together. That was the lust's way of thinking, anyway, but since everything else he'd tried had failed, he wasn't ruling out unbridled passion, and really good sex, to put him and Alana on the path to resolving at least some of their misery.

First, though, he had to get past this hurdle with Tilly. Then there was the hurdle with his father. His dad was recovering, sort of, but very soon Egan was going to have to sit down with him and work out, well, everything. It would have been both a blessing and a curse if his dad had been trying to get back to work, to push to have things back the way they were before his heart attack. But he wasn't. It was as if he'd checked out, and while Egan didn't want him going full throttle, he also didn't want his dad to think his life was over.

He felt his body brace at the sound of a vehicle pulling into the parking lot, but the bracing eased some when he saw it wasn't Tilly but rather Alana. She stepped out, not actually huffing, but she looked as if she wanted to. Clearly, though, she'd been expecting him because she got out, carrying a tray with three to-go cups of coffee.

"Tilly's running a little late," she said, walking to him and offering him one of the cups. "Marilu at the diner said you drink your coffee black. Since I knew you wouldn't do the sensible thing and let me handle this meeting, I got you a large."

"Thanks," he said, taking the cup. "You already talked to Tilly this morning?"

She shook her head, had a sip of her own black coffee. "Just a text from her to tell me she had to drop by the hardware store to pick up something before coming here, and it doesn't open until eight."

Which was right about now. The hardware store, though, was just up the street, but that would still give him a few minutes to try to talk Alana out of—

"No," she said, interrupting his thoughts. "I'm telling Tilly about the argument I had with Jack. I'm tired of living with the guilt, too."

There weren't many things Alana could have said to get him to back off, but that was one of them. Egan understood the hungry bites that guilt could take out of you. So could the consequences of the truth. But since it was a "damned if you do, damned if you didn't" situation both ways, the truth just felt like the right thing.

Mostly.

"You're not going to tell Tilly about Jack cheating," he said, not a question.

"No," Alana quickly assured him. "Tilly will get to keep the memory of what she believes was a perfect son. I'll be the bad guy in this. And you," she added with a sigh. "And I suspect after I tell her about the argument, then Tilly will want me to take a back seat at the life celebration."

"I'm sure I'm uninvited," he said, and it surprised him that he felt some pangs of regret about it.

He'd never wanted to attend the celebration, and Tilly had practically twisted his arm to get him to do it. Now that he was off the hook, he could see the big picture he'd been missing because of his own guilt and feelings. He wouldn't be there with the town to celebrate the life of the man who'd been his best friend.

Then again, after what he'd recently learned about Jack, Egan had to admit that best friend had been in name only. He clearly hadn't known Jack as well, or as fondly, as he thought he had. And that lessened another layer of this guilt fest.

Alana.

A month ago, Egan wouldn't have allowed any lustful thoughts about Alana to pop into his head. He damn sure wouldn't have actually kissed her. Obviously, things had changed since he'd kissed her twice and wanted to go for round three. He had to quickly push that urge aside, though, when another vehicle pulled into the parking lot.

This time, it was Tilly, and the woman speared him with narrowed eyes when she spotted him. She got out, hauling a big cardboard box from the back seat. Both Alana and he went to help after Alana set the coffees aside, but Tilly quickly declined.

"I've got it," she insisted and then spared Egan another glance. "I didn't expect you to be here, but maybe this way is for the best." She didn't clarify that, though. Instead, she turned to Alana. "I was hoping you'd help me with the arrangement on the podium for Jack's life celebration."

"Of course," Alana muttered. "But you said you were rethinking that. Are you still going through with it?"

"Absolutely. It'll still go on two weeks from today, just as planned." And her tone indicated that canceling it had never ever been her intention. "But there will be some changes."

She set the box down and pulled out what Egan first thought was a child's paper dolls. But these were blank with the shapes either wearing pants or dresses, and they were attached to foot-long sticks shaped like toothpicks.

"I had Woodrow order these for me," Tilly explained, referring to Woodrow McMillian who ran the hardware store. She used a permanent marker to write her own name and then Alana's on two of the "girl" figures. She wrote Jack's name on one of the boys. "I want to map out the positions, and I thought this would be an easier way to get it right."

Tilly went to the flat grassy area where podium and stages had, indeed, been set up in the past, and she poked Jack's into what would no doubt be the center.

"There'll be a big picture of Jack here," Tilly explained. Then, she staked her paper avatar directly on the right and Alana's on the left. "The mayor will go here," she continued, writing his name on one and staking it next to her. "Then, Reverend Caldwell, who'll do a benediction." He went on the side next to Alana. "Then, Jack's godparents, Nancy and Bill." They went next to the mayor.

Tilly added a couple more, including Jack's favorite high school teacher and his football coach to balance out the side where Alana would be standing, and then she stopped, wrote Egan's name on one of the avatars and looked at him.

"I want to make something clear," Tilly said, her voice as tight as her expression. "I don't want you at my son's life celebration. Not after what you did—"

"Tilly," Alana interrupted. Or rather she tried to do that, but Tilly just rolled right over her.

"I don't want you there," Tilly went on, staring at him. "But I also don't want to have to answer any questions about how or why my son died. I don't want to have to deal with gossip because every morsel dished up will only serve to remind me of his death. I don't want that. I only want to deal with Jack's life. Do I make myself clear?" she tacked on to that.

No, she actually hadn't made it clear, but Egan went with what he thought was a good guess. "You intend for me to be there, but you don't want me to say or do anything that would take away from the celebration."

"Exactly," Tilly snarled, and as if she'd declared war on it, she stabbed his avatar at what would be the very end of the podium.

Tilly hurriedly wrote a name on a girl avatar and jammed it into the ground directly across from his. Not on the podium but what would almost certainly be the crowd watching the event.

Colleen's name.

So, apparently Tilly didn't intend for his ex to stay at the back of the gathering but instead wanted her right in Egan's face. Almost literally. This was punishment, plain and simple, but Egan had no intention of objecting.

Evidently, though, Alana did. "Tilly—" she said, but that was all she managed to get out before Tilly cut her off again.

Tilly marched toward Egan, her glare getting harder and harder with each step. "I won't make this celebration easy for you, Lieutenant Colonel Egan Donnelly." She said his name as if it were poison. "But I will let you stand up on that podium and let everyone believe you're a hero. You're not, and you and I both know that. And when the celebration is over, I never want to see you or hear you speak my son's name again."

The words hit him like heavy artillery, slamming into him and going straight to his heart. She hadn't said anything that he hadn't already said to himself, but now Tilly was hurting. And since she was Jack's mother, he couldn't imagine how deep and hard her pain was. Pain that he had caused, first by getting Jack killed and then not telling her the truth about it.

Obviously finished with him, Tilly turned and stormed away. Not toward her car but back to the box where she grabbed more avatars.

Alana sighed. "I'm so sorry."

But Egan cut her off, too, by shaking his head. "I deserved everything she just said." Everything. "Go to Tilly. See if there's anything you can do to help her. Help," he emphasized. "Don't make things worse by bringing up anything else."

Egan thought that maybe he'd finally convinced

Alana to hold back, and with that mission accomplished, he turned to leave. To get out of Tilly's sight so that Alana stood at least a chance of calming her down. And Alana was clearly trying to do just that. Tilly had allowed Alana to take her by the arm, and Alana was leading them to the shade of a large oak.

Since his lingering would only add to Tilly's misery, he walked toward his truck. He hadn't made it but a couple of steps, though, when yet another car turned into the parking lot, and one look at the driver, and Egan figured he was going to get another round of incoming fire.

Loralee stepped out.

Much as Tilly had done earlier, Alana's aunt scowled at him. That was Loralee's default response, though, when it came to him, so it wasn't unexpected.

"I saw Tilly at the hardware store, and she seemed a little upset," Loralee said as she approached him. "When I spotted all your vehicles parked here, I thought I'd check to see if anything was wrong."

Egan was about to come up with something, anything, that would get Loralee to back off while Alana and Tilly talked, but Loralee's attention shifted to the toothpick avatars.

"Good gravy, no wonder Tilly's upset," Loralee muttered, shaking her head. "This is all bringing back memories of Jack. I was worried this would happen. You can't celebrate a dead person's life without remembering that the life is over."

There wasn't any "pointing the finger" blame at Egan in that remark since Loralee didn't know the truth about that. But some blame quickly sprang to the woman's eyes when she spotted Colleen's avatar.

"Who put that there?" Loralee asked.

"Tilly," Egan provided.

Loralee raised an eyebrow, clearly questioning why the woman had done that, but this time Egan didn't even try to come up with a response.

"Right across from you," Loralee muttered, pointing out the obvious. "I'm not sure who'll be more uncomfortable about that. You or her." She turned to him. "Considering you won't want to spoil the day for Tilly, I expect you'll be on your best behavior. By that, I mean you won't use the occasion to hash out your differences with my niece."

Egan nearly pointed out that the differences had already been hashed out, by Colleen walking out on him, but it would only start an argument with Loralee. Instead, he turned to leave, but Loralee stepped in front of him.

"What's going on between Alana and you?" she whispered in an angry, accusatory tone.

Obviously, this was yet something else that Egan didn't want to discuss, and his silence should have clued Loralee into that.

It didn't.

"I can't stand by and watch you break another of my niece's hearts," Loralee snapped.

This time, Egan ditched the silent approach because it clearly wasn't working. "Excuse me, but I wasn't the heartbreaker for Colleen," he insisted.

"Of course, you were," Loralee insisted. "You

pushed her away from you by bottling everything up and keeping things to yourself."

"Things that were often classified," he inserted. "And I'd say Colleen is the winner of keeping things to herself since I didn't know she was seeing anyone else before she announced she wanted a divorce and left."

Loralee huffed and folded her arms over her chest. "You didn't fight for Colleen," she muttered.

At first, Egan thought he'd misheard her so he mentally replayed it. Nope. He had heard it just fine. "Excuse me?" he challenged. "You told me often that you didn't think I was worshipping your niece enough. And I believe you used that exact word, *worshipping*. You paired it with other words like *the ground she walks on*."

Loralee's mouth tightened. "I said that because I believed it. But I also believed you loved her and had her best interest in mind."

"I did." And he hoped she picked up on the fact that those two things were past tense because he no longer loved Colleen and didn't care about her interests.

"Then, you should have fought harder for her. Instead, you let her walk out with that weirdo."

It was the first time he had heard her say anything negative about Colleen and her man. Then again, it was possible that Loralee didn't make a habit of complimenting anyone involved with her nieces. Egan recalled the woman had often been critical of Jack, too, and she certainly hadn't known the worst about him.

"Anyway," Loralee muttered a moment later. She checked her watch and added under her breath, "I have to go. I have an appointment for a checkup."

But she didn't go. She turned to Egan, staring holes in him. "Don't diddle around with Alana. She puts on a brave face, but she'll fall apart if she's broken again. Don't be the one to break her, Egan. Please. Don't be the one to break her."

Now Loralee did leave, and Egan stood there, wishing she'd delivered that last warning with her usual venom. She hadn't. It had come from the aunt who loved her nieces and wanted the best for them.

Egan was absolutely certain that he didn't qualify as the best for Alana.

With that dismal thought running circles in his head, he watched Loralee drive away, and for a third time, he started for his truck. Just as he heard something that stopped him in his tracks.

A loud gasp.

Egan whirled around, his attention zooming straight to Tilly and Alana who were still beneath the oak. But something had obviously happened. Something bad because the color had drained from Tilly's face, and the woman was staring at Alana as if she were a hired assassin there to finish her off.

Hell.

Alana had told Tilly about the argument. Or worse. And while he was debating if he should try to intercede, Tilly snapped toward him and started his way. Not the slow pace, either. She came at him fast.

"You put Alana up to this," Tilly practically shouted. "I know it was you."

"No," Alana argued. She was right on Tilly's heels, and she tried to take hold of the woman's arm when she caught up with her.

Tilly slung off her grip and kept her attention pinned to Egan. "You told her to say that Jack and she had argued when you know it didn't have anything to do with what happened to him. Happily married couples argue over plenty of little things, period. That wouldn't have been enough to distract Jack."

Egan saw the woman lift her hand and could have stopped it. He didn't. He let the slap come. Tilly's palm struck him hard, but he didn't actually feel it. He couldn't because her pain was ripping him apart inside.

When she went to slap him again, Alana latched onto the woman and spun Tilly around to face her. "My argument with Jack wasn't little," Alana blurted out. "Jack was cheating on me, and I found out. I confronted him during that call, and he didn't deny it. Jack was having an affair," she spelled out.

It seemed as if every muscle in Tilly's body went limp, and she stared at Alana. And stared. Then, she started shaking her head. Little movements at first that quickly picked up speed.

"No," Tilly mouthed, and the response had almost no sound.

In contrast, Alana's voice had plenty of sound. "Yes. I found out when I saw his credit card statements, and he didn't deny it," she repeated, her voice lowering and calming with each new word. "The last thing I said to him was *go straight to hell*. A few hours later, he was dead. If you want to blame someone for that, then put the blame squarely on me."

Tilly shook her head again, and while she was processing the bombshell she'd just heard, Egan tried to figure out a way to fix this. Not a complete fix. That wasn't possible. But he was about to suggest that Alana and Tilly go someplace private so they could talk this out.

"I'm sorry," he said, but that was all he managed to get out before Tilly turned on him again.

"You put her up to this. You made Alana tell this vicious lie so you could save face. Well, it won't work. I know the kind of man my son was, and Egan Donnelly, I see you for exactly what you are."

Tilly slapped him again and stormed away, delivering the rest of what she had to say with her back turned to them. "As far as I'm concerned, you're the one who should be dead, not Jack."

CHAPTER FIFTEEN

FOR A COUPLE of long moments, Alana could only stand there and sigh. Tilly's grief and anger had frozen her in place. Had shaken her to the core. But since Alana knew she was responsible for a lot of that grief and anger, she had to do something.

She started with Egan.

"I'm sorry," Alana told him, and then she went running after Tilly, believing that's exactly what Egan would want her to do.

Later, she could try to make him believe Tilly hadn't meant what she'd said to him, that deep down the woman would soon be sorry for slapping him. But for now, Alana just had to make sure Tilly didn't do something to harm herself. In her state of mind, there was no way she should be behind the wheel of a vehicle.

Thankfully, Alana made it to Tilly's car before the woman could fish out her keys from her purse and drive off. "Please," she told Tilly. "Let's talk, and then if you want, I can drive you home."

Tilly went into the full headshaking mode again, but she also gave up looking for her keys and gripped the steering wheel as if it were capable of grounding her to the earth. The tears came. Of course, they did. Tilly had just gotten a triple whammy. First, hearing Egan's confession. Then, the two-pronged confession that Alana had dumped on her.

Alana had meant to tell Tilly the first revelation about the argument, but the second, the part about Jack's cheating, had just come flying out of her mouth. And while it was the truth, it'd clearly had devastating results. Alana needed to minimize the chance of this turning from devastating to an out-and-out tragedy.

"Tilly, please let's talk," she tried again, and Alana glanced over at Egan as he drove away. He looked as down and out as she did.

The woman didn't let go of the steering wheel, but she didn't issue a flat-out "no, get lost," either. Perhaps because Tilly was trying to hang on to the delusion that her son hadn't cheated and that Egan had put Alana up to saying that. Alana would need to shatter that delusion but not now.

Tilly had a car even smaller than Alana's, and the seats were jammed with other boxes that appeared to be flyers, banners and such for the life celebration. There was no place for Alana to sit without doing a major unloading so she gently took hold of Tilly's arm and eased her out of the car. She was more than a little surprised when Tilly allowed that to happen, and the woman didn't protest when Alana led her back toward the oak tree.

There were no benches or seats nearby so Alana kept hold of Tilly and continued moving until they reached a shaded bench about fifteen feet on the other side of the tree. A quiet spot right in front of a small pond and fountain. The air was filled with the scent of the Grandma's Yellow roses from the bushes that the town council had had planted around the entire perimeter of the water.

On the other occasions when Alana had come here, she'd found it peaceful, but she wasn't counting on water features and the Grandma Yellows to pull off any magic today. Tilly was hurting. And crying now. So Alana just put her arm around her and let Tilly sob.

It surprised Alana that Tilly didn't push her away or yell, scream or slap her. It was possible, though, that the woman had just burned off that initial slam of anger and shock and was moving on to the processing part.

Something that Alana would have to do.

Even though she was trying to comfort Tilly, Alana was still dealing with her own slam of anger over Tilly slapping Egan. Egan hadn't deserved that, but he'd silently taken both blows because he was a decent guy who'd gotten thrust into a nightmarish situation.

One that he clearly hadn't fully processed yet, either.

Alana wanted to spell out to both Tilly and Egan that he hadn't been able to see the future so he hadn't known that Jack would die at that time, that place. Egan had merely wanted to see his best friend, and from there, it'd gone to hell in a handbasket. Ditto for her own argument and last words with Jack. That phone call and argument had been fueled with anger and shock, and there was no way she could have anticipated what would happen next.

When she'd ended that final phone call with Jack, the last thing that'd been on her mind was his death or that her words would be the last thing she'd ever say to him. A divorce, though, had been front and center in her mind, and in her fury, she had already started Google searches for a good divorce attorney. She'd been within minutes of calling one when the notification team had shown up at her house.

So, how much of all of this would Tilly allow her to say? How much did the woman want to hear?

Apparently, not much at all.

As if she'd gained her second wind, Tilly lifted her head from Alana's shoulder, and she dug through the pocket of her dress to come up with a tissue. She started sopping up the tears while she also tried to blink back others.

"I want to erase anything about Jack's last hours from my mind," Tilly spelled out.

"I understand," Alana murmured. And she did. She wanted to erase every word of that argument she'd had with Jack. But that wasn't going to happen.

It wouldn't happen for Tilly, either. The woman was never going to forget Jack's death, or what Alana and Egan had told her. The big picture about Jack had to be a lot easier for a grieving mother if she chose not to deal with those last hours.

"I won't say I'm sorry for slapping Egan," Tilly

went on, and there was a fresh round of fire in her still teary eyes. "Because I'm not sorry. He deserved it and much worse."

Alana sighed. "Egan is eaten up with guilt over what happened."

"He should be," Tilly snarled, moving away from Alana and getting to her feet where she looked Alana straight in the eyes. "And you should be, too, for saying what you did. Jack wasn't cheating on you, and there's nothing you can say or do that'll make me believe it."

There was proof. The credit card statements and Remi's account of seeing Jack with the other woman. But Tilly wouldn't want to see or hear any of that. She was going to try to hang on to the image of her perfect son.

"I think you said those awful things about Jack because you're sleeping with Egan. I'm right, aren't I?" Tilly demanded, but she didn't give Alana a chance to deny it. "You're sleeping with Egan, and the two of you decided the only way to ease your guilt was to smear Jack's good name. Well, I won't have it. Hear me?" Tilly practically shouted. "I won't have it."

With that, Tilly stormed away. Or rather that was clearly the woman's intentions, but she ran right into the dark-haired man who was making his way toward them. Not Egan.

His brother, Lieutenant Colonel Cal Donnelly.

Even if Alana hadn't known who he was, she would have figured it out with just a glance. The Donnelly genes had won out big-time in his DNA, and he was a slightly taller, lankier version of Egan. He wasn't in uniform but rather jeans and a T-shirt that had a picture of a fighter jet on it, but the civilian clothes didn't stop him from looking every bit a military officer.

Alana didn't know who looked more surprised with the encounter. Tilly or Cal. But she thought Cal might win that particular award, and that was possibly because he'd just overheard what Tilly had said.

"Sorry," Cal muttered. "I was driving into town, saw your car and stopped. Is, uh, everything okay?"

Again, Tilly answered before Alana could manage to speak. "Are you here to stick up for your lying coward of a brother?" Tilly demanded from Cal, and everything about the woman radiated the injustice that she obviously thought was going on.

Cal looked at Alana, giving her a long once-over, before his attention eased back to Tilly. "As a general rule, Egan doesn't need anyone to stick up for him. Nor is he a liar or a coward. But I am a little worried about Alana and you. You're looking pale, Miss Tilly, and Alana isn't faring much better."

That only tightened Tilly's face even more, and Alana moved to stop the woman in case she tried to slap Cal. Tilly didn't, though. She snarled out something under her breath and did that storming off she'd attempted seconds earlier.

Cal looked back at Tilly. "Should I go after her?"

Alana thought of those two slaps, of the horrible things Tilly had said to Egan, and she shook her head. If anyone should go after the woman, it should be her, but Alana wasn't in a good place for that, either. This was still the heat of the moment, and with Tilly refusing to hear the truth, it was highly likely that any attempt to help her would only escalate the situation.

"No." Alana sighed. "I think she needs some time to cool off. And if anyone needs to be checked on, it's Egan. I can do that," she said at the same moment Cal said, "I'll take care of that."

Cal probably could. All the Donnelly siblings were close, but Egan was tighter with Cal, probably because they were so close in age.

Alana paused, wondering how much else to say and how much Cal had overheard. Even if he'd heard everything, he probably didn't fully understand what was going on. Heck, she didn't understand, and she knew all the dirty little details.

Cal must have figured out the reason for her hesitation so he helped her out. "From what I gather, Egan and or you told Tilly something she wasn't ready to hear. She's pissed off so she lashed out."

Alana nodded. "That's it in a nutshell."

He nodded as well and glanced around. "I don't know the details of what happened the night Jack died, but I know that Egan blames himself. I figure you're blaming yourself, too. That self-blaming probably extends to anyone and everyone who had a hand in putting those people on that particular transport vehicle in that particular place."

That was probably true, but in Alana's case, spreading the guilt around didn't thin it out. But that still didn't mean Tilly had had the right to say and do those things to Egan. Especially while Tilly was turning a blind eye to Jack's own part in what had happened.

Especially then.

That caused the anger to roll through Alana again, and the anger spurred her mind to replay every ugly word Tilly had said to Egan. Even without the slaps, those words would have been way out of line.

"So, you can tell me to mind my own business," Cal said, getting her attention, "but are you and Egan having sex?"

"No," Alana said, the anger feeding her tone. And apparently everything else. "Not yet. But I intend to remedy that very, very soon."

EGAN HAD THE Andalusian stallion in a full gallop. The hooves chopped into the grass and dirt as he flew across the pasture.

Well, flew for a horse, anyway.

The speed gave him a partial rush, but it wasn't anywhere near what he would have gotten in a fighter jet. Still, it would have to do because there was no way he should be in a cockpit when he was in this state of mind.

A state of mind he'd brought on himself.

Tilly had every right to react the way she had. Toward him, anyway. But it riled Egan to the core that she had turned on Alana that way. Tilly's reaction didn't lessen Egan's blame, but it sure as hell made him a lot less sympathetic to Jack's mom. Yeah, she'd lost a son, but Alana had lost a husband. A cheating one, yes, but Alana had loved Jack, and she had lost him in a horrible way at a horrible time.

The stallion kept up the gallop and seemed to enjoy being out on full throttle, but Egan eased him to a canter when he spotted the rider approaching. At first, he thought it was Jesse or one of the hands since anyone who'd seen him after the park incident would have noticed his rotten mood. But as Egan got closer, he realized it was his brother Cal.

Cal certainly hadn't had time to get home if he'd heard about what had gone on with Tilly so Egan had to wonder what this unscheduled visit was about. Especially since Cal had told him it'd be at least another month before he could get any leave. Egan was about to ask him if he'd been injured or something, but Cal spoke before he got the chance.

"You always were more cowboy than Top Gun," Cal remarked. "That was some good riding."

"Blue's the better rider," Egan pointed out, reining in and studying his brother's face. No injuries, but he knew Cal well enough to see some concern in his eyes. "You were always the better cowboy."

"Remi might have something to say about that," Cal said with a chuckle.

Yeah, she might. "When did you get in?" Egan asked.

"Apparently, about ten minutes after you left the park."

Well, hell. Egan had come out here to get away from all that, and it seemed there wasn't going to be an escape, after all.

"How much did you hear?" Egan pressed.

"Enough. I saw Alana's car, stopped and ended up overhearing some of her conversation with Tilly. Jack's mom clearly wasn't in a good mood. If you want to tell me why that is, I'll listen."

"I don't want to tell you," Egan was quick to answer. Quick to change the subject, too, though he was under no illusions that he'd heard the last of it from Cal. "Have you seen Dad yet?"

Cal nodded, and riding side by side, they started at a walking gait back toward the ranch. "It was a shock. He's always looked so strong. So in charge. He's not in charge now."

"No," Egan agreed in a mutter. "I'm taking care of the office stuff, but my leave is up in two weeks. Decisions will have to be made soon."

Egan was working on that, but first he had to come to terms with it. Once he figured out what he had to do, that is. Then, he'd have to get his dad on board. Since his dad wasn't protesting or objecting too much these days, that probably wouldn't be much of a challenge. The challenge would be to figure out a way to get his dad invested in life and the ranch again.

That might not even be possible.

If so, no matter how much time and effort Egan threw at the ranch, he might not succeed.

"I could get out of the Air Force," Cal suggested.

Egan's huff was so loud that the stallion snorted. "You're a decorated officer. A Top Gun." Egan quickly did the math. "And you've put in nearly thirteen years.

Added to that, you're a Super Troop. Your last promotion was below the zone."

Below the zone, meaning that he'd gotten an early promotion. So, even though Cal had entered the military three years after Egan, Cal was the same rank. Added to that, Cal was on track to make colonel early as well.

Cal shrugged. "I can't put the ranch and Dad solely on your shoulders."

Egan appreciated his brother saying that, but he wouldn't let Cal do any sword falling. "I'll come up with a way to make things work. A way that'll include you staying in uniform. Blue and Remi, too."

Even though they were already riding at a snail's pace, they slowed some more when they went past the limestone and pine cabin just on the other side of the east pasture fence. The backyard was covered with blooming lazy daisies that made him think of Alana and that rainy day at the creek.

"I take it you're not staying there?" Cal asked.

Egan shook his head. "I'm at the main house."

Though the cabin was, indeed, his. His dad had had it built for him shortly after he'd left for college. He'd done the same for all of Egan's siblings, telling them that he wanted them to feel free to keep their old rooms but that they should have their own space, too. Egan supposed his dad had done that so they'd never feel pressured to stay under his roof when they came home.

Egan had stayed at the cabin on occasions when he'd wanted to have friends over. Especially girlfriends. Ironically, not Colleen, though. By the time they'd started dating, she'd had her own place in town. Overnighting there had been more convenient for her. She had sold that place after they'd married, and when they'd made trips to the ranch, they'd just stayed in his bedroom in the main house.

Seeing the cabin now had even more thoughts of Alana flashing in his head. Specifically, the idea of him bringing Alana here. Which would, of course, lead to kissing and sex.

And that meant it was a really bad idea.

"Want to talk about Alana now?" Cal asked, and for a moment, Egan thought he might have unknowingly muttered Alana's name, and that's why Cal was bringing her up. Judging from his brother's expression, though, it was an innocent question.

Well, partially innocent, anyway.

Cal had good instincts and had probably picked up on some kind of vibe Egan was throwing off about Alana.

"No," Egan insisted as they rode in earnest toward the ranch. "I don't want to talk about her." She was already too much on his mind.

"Do you want to talk about Jack's life celebration, what's going on with Tilly or the ranch?" Cal continued.

Again, Egan had to go with "No."

"All right. Then, that leaves Dad, Audrey or the new burger of the week at Desi's Diner. Did you know Desi named it after you?"

"No," Egan muttered again.

"It's called the Lieutenant Colonel Top Dog, Top Gun."

"That's a terrible name for a burger," Egan snarled.

Cal was quick to make a sound of agreement. "A terrible idea for the burger itself, too. A beef patty, topped with hot dog slices, bacon, cheddar and probably a few other things I'm forgetting. I saw it advertised in the window of the diner when I drove through town."

Egan made a mental note to call Desi and tactfully ask him to take it down. No way would Tilly want to see that every time she went by the diner.

Thankfully, Cal didn't ask any other questions, and Egan didn't push him on that stupid notion of him getting out of the Air Force. If the subject came up again, Egan would make sure to shut it down as fast as he could.

When they made it back to the ranch and into the barn, Noah Callaghan was waiting for them. Because Egan had familiarized himself with the new hires, he knew that Noah was the youngest of the ranch hands, barely out of high school, but he'd worked part-time during the past two summers before coming onboard full-time.

"Maybell asked for me to tend to the horses for you," Noah explained.

That shot some alarm through Egan. "Why?"

"I'm to tell you nothing's wrong," Noah quickly added, looking straight at Egan. "Maybell said to make that clear. It's just your dad wants to see you."

Hell. Despite Maybell's insistence, Egan figured

there had to be something wrong. Cal must have thought the same thing because they didn't waste any time handing off the horses to Noah, and they hurried to the house, going in through the kitchen.

Maybell was there, and for the first time in a couple of weeks, she wasn't trying to find a place in the fridge for food that people had brought over. Thankfully, that was tapering off some, but Egan did spot a box from the bakery and a grease-stained white takeout bag from Desi's.

"Your namesake burger," Maybell explained when she noticed it had gotten Egan's attention. "A well-wisher brought it over, but needless to say, your dad won't be eating it."

Judging from the smell, Egan doubted anyone would chow down on it. The burger and the hot dog combo seemed to be at war with each other in the aroma department.

"Did something happen to Dad?" Egan asked her.

Maybell sighed. "I knew you'd be rattled. That's why I told Noah to tell you nothing was wrong. Your dad just wants to talk to you, that's all. No hurry, no fuss."

Yeah, right. If there hadn't been a hurry or fuss, Maybell wouldn't have asked Noah to meet them in the barn.

Maybell took out a can of Cal's favorite soda, Pepsi, from the fridge and handed it to him. "I'm supposed to tactfully find a way to keep you occupied so you won't think there's any trouble brewing," she added to Cal. "Because there isn't," she was quick to assure him. "It's just your dad has some ranching stuff he wants to talk over with Egan."

Cal's gaze met Egan's, silently questioning if he had any idea what this was all about. Egan didn't and shook his head. And then it hit him. If his dad had gotten any whiffs of what was going on with Tilly, he'd want Egan to fill him in on the problem.

"You were always my favorite kid, you know," Maybell remarked to Cal.

Even though there was still worry in his eyes, Cal smiled. "I'll bet you told Remi that."

"I did," Maybell admitted, "but I was fudging the truth there. I swear, you're my favorite."

Maybell continued talking while Egan left Cal and her in the kitchen, and he hurried upstairs. His dad's bedroom door was open, and when he stepped in, Egan spotted him in the reading area. Again, he was looking through old photo albums. Either he'd found more, or he was repeatedly going through the same ones since this was how he was spending his days.

Egan had tried to engage his dad by bringing in copies of prospects for both sales and purchases of some of their livestock, but if his dad had actually read them, he hadn't mentioned it.

"How was your ride?" his dad asked.

Maybe he'd known of the ride because of what had to be Egan's ripe smell or because Maybell had told him. It likely wouldn't have come from his dad personally seeing Egan from the window since he rarely sat there these days.

"It was good," Egan said. Sort of a lie. The ride

itself had been amazing. The thoughts that'd come with it, not so much. "How about you? It was probably good for you to see Cal."

"It was," his dad verified, and there seemed to be a lie somewhere beneath that response. Not because he hadn't wanted Cal there. He would have. But maybe he hadn't especially wanted Cal to see him this way.

"I was thinking about asking Dr. Abrams when he thought it'd be okay for you to go outside and see the new horses," Egan said, testing the waters. "Especially since he allowed you to make the trip to the diner."

His dad nodded, but he didn't show much enthusiasm for the idea. "My ribs are still hurting quite a bit. Even a little cough hurts like the devil. And no, I'm not going to take the pain meds. People get hooked on those."

Egan didn't push on the meds because it was actually good to hear his dad take a stand on something. "I've had a few cracked ribs over the years." Some he'd gotten from being thrown by horses. And others when Jack had been killed. "It takes a while to heal, but you're coming along."

That was perhaps wishful thinking on his part since his dad didn't seem to be improving much.

His dad nodded but then added a weary sigh. "Every time I have a pain, I wonder if it's another heart attack," he muttered.

Well, hell. Of course, he'd think that. This was a form of PTSD, and with those cracked ribs, the pain would happen often, maybe with every single move.

No wonder his dad had mentally corralled himself into his bedroom with the old family pictures.

Egan went closer, taking the seat across from his dad. "I'm listening," he assured him.

His dad looked up, and despite burying the weariness that was also in his eyes, he managed a thin smile. "Yeah. I know." He reached over and patted Egan's knee. "You're a good son."

"You're a good dad," Egan quickly assured him.

His dad didn't outright agree with that, but his smile faded. "You're worried about me."

"I am," Egan admitted and then went with a full disclosure since they seemed to be on the verge of a potential heart-to-heart. "But I have some other things on my mind, too."

"Yeah," his dad repeated. "I got a call from Parker Freeman at the newspaper, and he said Tilly demanded that your photo be taken off the website. I'm guessing that's because Tilly has a beef with you and not because you convinced her to have it taken down."

Even though the timing wasn't great for this, Egan didn't want to risk his dad hearing about it from Tilly. Or from someone else that Tilly might tell.

"I told Tilly that the reason Jack died was because I asked him to meet me," Egan spelled out. "I put Jack in the wrong place at the wrong time."

His dad nodded, but it didn't seem to be in agreement but that he was merely processing it. "Guilt," he muttered. "I know a bit about that. I didn't push your mom to get treatment sooner so her dying is on me."

"No," Egan was quick to argue.

He was about to launch into a spiel about it being the cancer that'd killed her, but he could see the point his dad was making. Still, it wasn't the same. His mom had already had the cancer in her before there'd even been symptoms. Jack had been in solid health when he came to see Egan.

"You wanted to talk to Jack because of Colleen walking out on you?" his dad asked.

"Maybe. In part, anyway. I figured Alana had told him about Colleen, but I'd decided if Jack didn't bring it up, I wasn't going to say anything. I just wanted to see him."

Hindsight, being the greedy bitch that she was, meant that Egan now knew the selfishness of that. Jack was dead because he'd wanted to see him.

"I'm figuring you've told Alana about why Jack was where he was," his dad went on. "Did Colleen know?"

Surprised by the question, Egan shook his head. "Colleen had already left by then."

"Yeah, but I wondered if this had to do with Jack." His dad lifted one of the photo albums, and Egan saw the torn up letter from Colleen beneath it. The one Colleen had given Alana to deliver to him. "Or maybe she's stewing in guilt, too. She could believe her leaving caused you to call Jack and start that whole ball rolling."

"It's possible," Egan admitted in a mutter.

"You want to read the letter to find out?" his dad asked.

Egan didn't even have to think about this. "No."

If Colleen were truly doing any guilt-stewing, then she was on her own. Or she could turn to her significant other. Egan was tapped out in the "healing old wounds" department, and if he'd had any healing attempts to spare, he would have aimed them at Tilly. Or Alana.

At the thought of Alana, Egan's phone dinged with a text, and he saw her name on the screen. He also felt that trickle of heat that should in no way be there, considering their current situation. Since he thought this might be connected to that current situation—Tilly—he immediately read it.

But it wasn't.

Oh, man. It wasn't.

If you've spoken to Cal, then you know what I said to him. I meant it, and it wasn't the anger talking. Well, maybe it was a little anger, but I still meant it. So, are you up for taking a big next step and having a fling with me?

CHAPTER SIXTEEN

ALANA HEARD THE little swoosh to indicate her message had been sent to Egan. And then she panicked. Oh, mercy, she panicked big-time, complete with hyperventilating breath, racing heart and unblinking staring at her phone screen.

What the heck had she just done?

Except the "heck" was replaced by much stronger profanity when that question went flying through her head. She'd typed out that text during the middle of a fresh fuming, and now she was going through the "what the heck?" stage.

Even though it'd been well over five hours since Tilly's outburst and the slappings, Alana's brain seemed to be a hamster wheel where she was reliving it every minute or so. It'd been in one of those reliving moments when she'd composed the text and sent it before common sense returned and she realized what a huge mistake it was.

Well, common sense was back with a vengeance.

At this very second, Egan was perhaps reading the text and going through his own "what the heck?" He'd be shocked. Perhaps would even be doing his own version of panicking.

But she rethought that.

Egan wasn't the panicking type, but he might be wondering if she'd lost her mind. He could possibly be trying to figure out how to respond. She seriously doubted he'd fire back an "I'm onboard for sex" message unless he'd given it some thought. And even then it might not happen if his own common sense held steady.

Egan was attracted to her. Alana had no doubts about that. Ditto for no doubts about her attraction to him. But there was also a big reason why he was holding back, and that reason was Jack. Jack and the fallout gossip that would happen if Jack's best friend ended up hooking up with his widow.

While she tried to calm down her breathing, and the rest of her, she stared at her phone, waiting for a response. And waited. And waited. None came which, of course, could be interpreted as a response on its own. But Egan wouldn't do that, either. He wasn't the kind of man who'd ghost her.

When the seconds dragged into minutes, Alana decided to go with the "out of sight, out of mind" theory. She slid her phone into the pocket of her dress and tried to get back to work on the dietary plan for a new client who wanted to lose fifty pounds before her high school reunion in two months. A reunion where the client would see her old boyfriend and the lying, cheating "tramp" he married after dumping her.

Barring sudden extreme illness, that kind of weight loss was unrealistic, but Alana was mapping out a proposal that would potentially lead to not only dropping fifteen to twenty pounds but also include suggestions for healthier eating in the client's post-reunion world. If followed, the client would perhaps lose those unwanted pounds by the holidays.

Alana made a few notes, checked her phone just in case she'd missed a text reply sound that she wouldn't have possibly missed. Still no reply. So she kept jotting down notes. And kept thinking about Egan and how he might be reacting over what she'd sent him.

So, are you up for taking a big next step and having a fling with me?

There weren't a lot of nonsexual ways to interpret that, and the word *fling* had been around long enough that he'd get the meaning. The word also implied something carefree and casual. A happy launch into something that would…well, possibly screw things up six ways to Sunday.

But Alana wasn't going to look at it that way.

If Egan consented to said fling, she was going to approach it as something she just had to get out of her system. Perhaps after Egan and she sated some of this fire, then they'd realize it was a big mistake and go their separate ways. If that happened, then she'd just have to learn how to deal with it. But she thought even fling failure was better than all this longing and lusting.

Her phone finally made a sound. It wasn't a text, but a call. She dragged in a few quick and hopefully settling breaths before she yanked the phone from her pocket. And cursed.

Because it wasn't Egan. It was Tilly.

Great, just great. Alana couldn't even consider the possibility of letting it go to voice mail since it was possible that Tilly might be calling to apologize. The woman might want to know how she could tell Egan she was sorry. So, with that possibility looming, Alana answered the call.

"Alana," Tilly greeted. There was a cool edge to the woman's voice, but Alana preferred it to the hot knife's edge tone when they'd been in the park.

"Tilly," she greeted back, and Alana left it at that. Best to let Tilly spell out why she'd called since there was a chance that anything Alana might say could be the wrong way to approach this.

"Alana," the woman repeated, and she paused as if waiting for Alana to say the things she'd decided not to say. "I was hoping," Tilly finally continued after several long moments, "that you'd admit you were lying about the things you said about Jack."

Alana sighed. So this was how it was going to be. "I didn't lie. Jack—"

"Don't you dare say it again," Tilly ordered. "I want you to take it back. Take it all back."

Alana wanted to just hang up and hope the woman would soon listen to reason, but maybe that was never going to happen. If so, it was best for Alana to spell out some things.

"I didn't lie," Alana repeated, and she continued before Tilly could get a huff or denial in edgewise.

"I don't want it to be true. In fact, I called him that last time, hoping he could explain everything away. But he didn't deny it, Tilly."

"I think this is the grief talking," Tilly insisted after shaking her head. "I think you're still so distraught and overcome with grief that you don't know what you're really saying."

"I know what I'm saying—" Alana tried to explain.

"You don't," Tilly insisted. "Because every word you're saying is ripping into me. It's tearing me to pieces."

"I'm sorry—"

"If you are really sorry, then don't say it," Tilly demanded. "Honor Jack's name by being the truthful, loving wife that he believed you were."

Talk about a loaded demand. Don't say anything bad even if it's the truth? Honor Jack's name with pretense and lies? And the cherry on top of this particular cake—be a loving wife to a man who'd been dead for three years? A man who hadn't been an especially loving husband since he'd had sex with another woman?

"Tilly," Alana said, trying—really, really trying—to keep her voice calm, "you'll always be Jack's mom. You'll always love him. Part of me will always love him, too, but I'm no longer his wife."

"Well, you should be," Tilly snapped.

Oh, it was hard to hang on to the calm now. "For how long?" Alana asked.

"Forever," the woman insisted. "Because if you

love him, if you're still his wife, then that'll keep a small part of Jack alive."

Only in Tilly's mind would that happen. Alana could have pointed out she on the other hand could continue to honor Jack by moving on. Most people said that, that their late spouse would want them to move on, but Alana believed in Jack's case, it was the truth. In fact, maybe he'd already started to move on himself with the affair.

"I'll be at the life celebration if that's still what you want—"

"It is," Tilly insisted, interrupting Alana. "I want you there as Jack's loving wife."

Alana sighed again. "I'll be at the life celebration," she repeated, "and I won't bring up anything bad about Jack. But you should know that I won't have you dictate my life. And I won't tolerate you lashing out at Egan like that again."

There, she'd said it, but Alana was talking to the air because Tilly had hung up on her.

Obviously, the woman hadn't actually wanted to resolve anything or apologize for her behavior. Part of Alana wanted to forgive the grieving mother, but another part of her was just plain fed up. Fed up enough to text Egan again, not with an explanation of why she'd sent the two other sex-related messages but rather a simple request.

I need to talk to you, she typed out and hit Send.

Alana grabbed her purse and keys so she could go ahead and start the drive to the ranch while she waited for a response. But there wasn't much of a wait at all. She'd barely gotten out the door when Egan replied.

I need to see you, too. Meet me at my cabin on the ranch.

Alana both smiled and frowned within the span of the next five seconds. The cabin was private, a place where their conversation, or anything else, likely wouldn't be overheard.

But this might not be a fling offer at all.

Egan might be seriously down over what'd happened with Tilly. His *I need to see you* might be so she could talk him off a metaphorical ledge. After all, she was the one person on earth who knew exactly what he was going through.

I'm on my way, she texted back, and she hurried to her car to make the drive. A drive that started with a call from Aunt Loralee.

Since her aunt had almost certainly caught wind of Tilly's ire, that was likely why she was calling. Alana let it go to voice mail, but Loralee didn't leave a message. The woman sent a text instead, and Alana had the hands-free read it to her.

Are you okay? Loralee texted.

That definitely wasn't a simple question, and was Loralee asking because she'd seen or heard what had gone on at the park? Alana hadn't spotted her, but it was possible she could have been there. Any response to the text was best reserved for an in-person chat. Still, she didn't want her aunt to worry about her.

I'm okay I'll drop by and see you tonight.

After a couple of seconds, Loralee sent her a thumbs-up emoji, followed by a message of her own.

I'll put off talking to Tilly until you and I have spoken.

Alana replied with her own thumbs-up, and she hoped that by the time Loralee did talk with Tilly that Jack's mom would have calmed the heck down and come to her senses. If not, well, Loralee could handle herself if Tilly flew off the handle again.

When Alana made the turn into the Donnelly ranch, she spotted a few hands in the front pasture. And they obviously spotted her, causing her to sigh. They'd see that she wasn't driving to the main house where everyone and his brother knew she was still doing her daily visits with Derek. The hands would know she was heading to the cabin where they'd probably seen Egan already go. And that meant there'd be gossip.

Correction: there'd be *more* gossip.

Since talk about Egan and her had already been set in motion, Alana decided to go with a "screw it" attitude. That had probably gotten plenty of people into trouble, but she was ready to offer up the same *screw it* to possible outcomes.

She took the narrow road that coiled around the

ranch and soon spotted the cabin. But not Egan's truck. However, there was an impressive looking Andalusian horse chowing down on some grass beneath the shade of an oak just inside the pasture fence. Egan had apparently chosen less visible transportation than she had.

When Alana parked and got out, she heard the music—Guns N' Roses' "Welcome to the Jungle"— and wondered if the tune had just popped up on a shuffled playlist or if Egan was playing it because it matched his mood. If it was the latter, then his mood was pretty much matching hers.

Alana stepped around a patch of lazy daisies and considered picking one to ask if it'd been a mistake for her to come here. But she decided she really didn't want floral advice factoring into this.

She knocked, waited and then knocked again. When he didn't answer, she opened the door and peeked in. No Egan, but from the sound of it, the shower was running. A moment later, the running water stopped, and there was some moving around in what she thought was the bedroom.

"Egan?" she called out to let him know she was inside.

"I'll be right there," he was quick to answer.

While she waited, Alana glanced around. She didn't have to glance much, though, to take in the space since it was fairly small. An open area for the living room, kitchen and a small breakfast-sized nook in front of the bay window that overlooked the pasture.

Like the main house, the cabin had a fireplace, and

there were a few framed photos on the mantel. None of Egan but rather of his dad and siblings. Front and center was an old photo of his mom. Even though the woman had died when Alana had been only four or five, she'd seen other photos of her, ones taken with Jack and Egan, so Alana knew who she was.

"Sorry," Egan said, coming out of the bedroom. He brought the scent of the shower with him. Soap and shampoo.

He also brought a peep show.

He'd put on jeans and a shirt, but the shirt was unbuttoned, and he had missed some spots when he'd dried off. The water had beaded on his chest and was being resupplied by the occasional drops that fell from his hair.

"I was drenched in sweat after I rode out here," he explained, going to the fridge and taking out a Coke. He lifted a second can, offering it to her, but she shook her head. "I figured you wouldn't want to talk with me while I was so ripe."

She hadn't missed the key word in that. *Talk.* So that meant he likely hadn't invited her here to take her up on her fling offer. Bummer. Despite the flurry of sudden nerves she was feeling, her body was still revving for him. And his bare chest was adding fire to the revving.

"Cal's with your dad?" she asked. Small talk while she tried to gauge Egan's mood. Thanks to the small space, she thought mood-gauging might be easy since she had a clear view of his face, but he definitely wasn't showing her much.

Egan nodded, and after he had a long drink of the Coke, he came back into the living area with her. "I decided to come out here to think and to give Dad some time with Cal." He paused and locked his gaze with hers. "I wanted to work out how to answer your text."

"Ah, that," she muttered. "I wondered if you were trying to work out a way to let me down easy."

His mouth tightened just a little, and he set his Coke aside on the coffee table. In the same motion, he hooked his arm around her and pulled her to him. He kissed her before the little squeak of surprise, and relief, could make its way out of her throat.

Yes! Her body shouted that several times, and her mouth would have, too, had she been able to speak. But Alana didn't want to speak. She wanted exactly this. Egan kissing her as if there were no tomorrow. No old baggage, either. Just his mouth on hers while the need and lust coiled and coiled around them.

So, this was his answer to the fling suggestion. Good. It was the only answer she'd wanted, and it spurred Alana to throw herself into the kiss. Not that she wasn't already there, but while Egan was staking a claim to her and firing her up with pleasure, she helped herself to his damp chest by sliding her hands over all those muscles.

Egan made a sound, a sort of growl that she thought was of approval so she kept touching and moved closer and closer to him until they were pressed against each other in some very interesting places.

More heat came. Mercy, did it. A frenzied need that caused her body to start begging for more and to give it to her now. Egan must have picked up on the urgency and unspoken request because he gave her more.

He moved, walking her to the sofa, and he anchored her against the back of it. Good thing, too, because her legs suddenly felt wobbly, thanks in part to the kisses he started on her neck. He did some touching as well. His hands on her breasts, he pushed his leg between hers so that his thigh was right against her center. Delicious pressure that was so intense Alana had to fight to stop the climax from rippling through her.

Needing to gain some control so she could hold off ending this way too soon, she turned the tables on him. Or rather she turned so it was Egan's butt against the back of the sofa. The new position gave her exactly the access she wanted, and Alana ran her tongue over his mouth.

To his neck.

To his chest. Where she lingered a while because, hey, amazing chest.

Then, she went even lower to the equally amazing abs and made some circles with her tongue on his damp skin. She figured she was hitting some of his hot zones when he cursed her.

Alana smiled at the cursing, but Egan, too, went on the offensive by shifting their positions again. He caught onto the bottom of her dress, shoving it up and off. He didn't waste a second going after her bra next, pushing down the cups and doing the tongue-circling number on her nipples that she'd done on his stomach.

Her legs buckled, but Egan was right there with a steadying arm around her waist. The steadying duties didn't stop him, either, from notching up the heat even more. He turned her body into a furnace, one of those super-hot industrial deals, by taking his mouth and hot breath to the front of her panties.

Alana knew the panties were made of a cotton blend, but the fabric seemed to just melt away. And then it actually did. Or rather the underwear just went away when Egan shimmied them off her butt and down her legs.

He kissed her again.

Right there. Right in the center of all that heat and need. Right there where the heat and need just kept rising and rising. Too fast. Too soon.

Somehow, Alana managed to get hold of a handful of his hair. No easy feat, considering he had a fairly short military cut and her fingers weren't exactly steady. Still, she managed it and dragged him back up until they were face-to-face.

"I'm naked," she said. "And you're not."

She did something about that, and once again was supremely thankful for his unbuttoned shirt. Alana shoved it off him and kissed her way back down his stomach while she got to work on his jeans. She made a loud sound of protest when he put his hand over her, to stop her progress.

No way could he say he didn't want this. She could feel him huge and hard behind the zipper of his jeans, but she thought that look in his eyes had "we're stopping" written all over it. Alana hoped a thousand hopes that she was wrong.

"If you get me out of these jeans, we'll have sex. Unprotected sex," he spelled out. "Since I don't have a condom."

Her body was burning for him, and that heat was trying to assure her that it'd be fine, that it was the wrong time of the month. But it might not be. And while she desperately, desperately, desperately wanted to have sex with Egan, an unplanned pregnancy wasn't what either of them needed.

She groaned, then cursed. Then grabbed handfuls of her own hair and pulled hard, hoping the pain would tamp down some of the heat. It didn't.

Egan groaned, too. And cursed. But his had a much quieter edge to it. Almost soothing. Alana was about to tell him that soothing couldn't happen, but he gently took her hand, unthreading it from her hair, and eased her back to him. He gave her another of those "there's no tomorrow" kisses, and for a moment she thought he would toss caution to the wind and go for it.

He went for it.

But not in the way she'd believed he would.

Keeping the kisses ever so gentle, he took his mouth on a slow thorough journey from her mouth down her body. Until his clever mouth landed in just the right spot. In the center of all that heat and need.

Alana had never really been into finishing things this way. She was more of a traditionalist when it came to getting an orgasm. Especially since Egan wouldn't be on the receiving end of this particular "finishing." But any and all protest dissolved when Egan's mouth took the cleverness up a couple of notches. He flicked his tongue, rendering her speechless. Sending her soaring. And leaving her with a single thought.

Exactly what that thought was, Alana couldn't say because all she could feel was wave after wave of pleasure.

CHAPTER SEVENTEEN

EGAN SAT IN the waiting room outside his commander's office and tried to figure out how to answer Cal's question.

"Are you sure you don't want to talk about Alana?" Cal had asked.

The question had come on the tail end of a series of brief discussions that had started when Egan and Cal left the ranch an hour earlier and continued on the drive to the base. Some of the chat had been Cal informing Egan of his travel plans. Plans that included Egan dropping him off at the San Antonio airport as soon as Egan was done meeting with his commander, Colonel Phil Joyner. Once Cal was back at his own base in Virginia, he'd try to arrange another short leave so he could return to the ranch in about six weeks.

There'd been more discussion about Egan keeping Cal posted on any medical updates for their dad. From there, there'd been talk about Blue's possible visit and with Egan reiterating that he didn't want Cal to consider getting out of the Air Force. Period. Egan hoped he'd made it clear that it'd be unacceptable and unnecessary. He wasn't sure how he was going to make things work at the ranch and with his dad, but he sure as hell didn't want Cal throwing himself on the sword.

Thankfully, Cal had steered clear of any mention of Tilly and what had gone on in the park four days earlier, and the steering clear had lulled Egan into believing that Cal wasn't going to bring any of it up. But the question Cal had just thrown at him proved otherwise.

"Yes, I'm sure I don't want to talk about Alana," Egan insisted.

Even though they were alone in the waiting area, Egan still kept his voice at a whisper. The commander's executive assistant was in the office with him, but Egan hadn't wanted to risk yet another conversation, or in this case, denial, being overheard, especially since it was a highly personal subject.

It was true. Egan didn't want to talk about Alana to Cal or anyone else for that matter. That didn't mean, though, that Egan hadn't thought about her plenty. And was still thinking about her even though he hadn't seen her in the four days since she'd come to the cabin.

Or rather she had come *at* the cabin, his dirty mind interjected.

Since the cabin, they'd texted and called, but Alana had stayed away, telling Egan that she wanted to give him time to spend with his brother. She'd even shifted her appointments with his dad so they were virtual instead of in person. Maybe she had done that to give herself some time and space, too.

And that gave Egan a far more unsettled feeling than he wanted.

"I just figured you'd want to talk about Alana," Cal went on, "because you muttered her name a couple of times on the drive here."

Egan turned toward Cal so fast that his neck popped. He scowled when he saw Cal's grin to let him know it was a joke. A lousy one. And Cal's grin faded plenty quick enough.

"Stating the obvious," Cal went on, "but I hate for either you or Alana to get burned. You two have already had enough burns for a lifetime or two."

There was no disputing that, and Egan had been thinking the same thing about not wanting Alana to be hurt by this fling. That's why Egan had stopped her from yanking down his jeans in the cabin, though that was clearly what she'd had in mind. Seconds after she'd come back to earth from her climax, she'd wanted to go after him the way he'd gone after her. He'd stopped it, though, not because he hadn't wanted that. Damn right, he'd wanted it. But thankfully he'd had a few functional brain cells left, and he'd known this was going to have an effect on Alana.

Perhaps a good effect in the short term.

But the long-term stuff could be a bitch.

As things stood between them now, if Alana got hit with the motherload of guilt and grief, then she would maybe reason that things hadn't gone so far between them. She could rationalize it all away as a lapse that couldn't be repeated if she wanted to be able to live with herself.

Egan still wasn't sure how he was going to reason and rationalize things. Wasn't sure how he could press pause on the heat, and other feelings, he had for her. Hell, he wasn't even sure he wanted to pause at all. Sometimes, like now for instance, he wanted her more than his next breath.

If that weren't a big-assed red flag warning, then he didn't know what was.

"Dad talked about Alana," Cal went on. "He's heard talk about you two, and he thought it was time for you to settle up any unfinished business."

Egan was sure he looked puzzled because he was. "What unfinished business?" he demanded.

Cal promptly pulled something from one of the many pockets of his flight suit, and the sight of it caused Egan to groan. It was Colleen's letter again. The damn thing was like a bad penny. Two of them since it was still in halves.

"Dad thought it would be a good idea for you to go ahead and read it," Cal spelled out.

Egan scowled. "I don't have any unfinished business with Colleen so there's no need to read it."

However, Egan did end up shoving it in the pocket of his own flight suit when the commander's executive assistant came out of the office. "Colonel Joyner can see you now," the exec relayed, stepping aside so Egan could enter.

Egan automatically went to put his phone away as well, and he realized he wasn't holding it. He glanced back and saw it was on the chair next to where he'd been sitting, but since Cal would be there to keep an eye on it, Egan went ahead into the commander's office.

Even though the colonel wouldn't have expected it, Egan reported in, anyway, by saluting his superior officer, but his salute wobbled a bit when he saw the woman on the sofa of the seating area.

Audrey.

She was sipping what appeared to be a cup of tea, and while Joyner was standing, he immediately sat down in the chair across from Audrey.

"Phil and I were just catching up," Audrey said. "We've known each other for years. But don't worry. I won't be horning in on your meeting." She set her cup aside on the table. "I was about to leave."

Egan recalled Joyner mentioning that "knowing each other for years" at some time or another, but he sure as heck hadn't known Audrey would be here. "Are you going to the ranch?" Egan asked.

She shook her head, checked her watch. "I don't have time. I flew in for a meeting that ended early so I came to see Phil. I'm flying back out in about fifteen minutes, but I'll call your dad on my flight to the Pentagon." She took a step and then stopped. "You'll probably hear talk that I'm up for the deputy commander position at Third Air Force."

"Third Air Force," Egan repeated. "At Ramstein, Germany."

She nodded, though it wasn't necessary for her to confirm it. "My mentors and advisors believe it's a good way for me to earn a second star."

It probably was, and that's why Egan made a sound

of agreement. It was a high-visibility position with a lot of responsibility. It would also mean Audrey would be thousands of miles away from Texas and her husband. Ironic, since Egan had adjusted his career so he could be closer while Audrey was considering an assignment that would take her as far away as possible.

"I'll talk to Derek about it," she added. "In fact, once he's up to it, I'll see if he wants to make a trip to Germany to see the base."

Egan held back on saying "good luck with that" since he probably wouldn't have been able to keep the sarcasm out of it. His dad didn't make trips, period, and if he hadn't gone to Audrey before now, Egan doubted he would start with a place as far away as Germany. Especially considering how down he'd been since the heart attack.

"Well," Audrey muttered when Egan didn't say anything. "I'll keep you posted about the assignment." And with that, she walked out.

Egan considered giving her a heads-up that Cal was in the waiting room, but he decided he'd let her figure that out for herself. Besides, any encounter with Cal would be a short one. Cal had a knack for getting along with everyone.

"Take a seat," Joyner insisted, motioning toward the sofa that Audrey had just vacated. "That's possible good news about Audrey," he said and slid right on to a new topic. "How's your dad?"

Egan had known the question would come. Had known, too, that he was going to have to tell the truth, which meant spilling all about things that his dad probably wouldn't want anyone outside the family to know. Still, Joyner had to have at least the big picture to understand why Egan was here.

Well, understand why he might be here.

Egan wasn't sure exactly what he was going to ask, but something big had to be done. Then, once it was all settled, then he could fill his siblings in—and yes, Audrey—on what had all been decided.

"My dad's not doing as well as his doctors expected," Egan started. "He's still in a lot of pain and has limited mobility and hasn't been able to step into his usual duties at the family ranch."

Of course, some of those limitations were due to the pain and the lack of medication that make it at least tolerable. Egan was worried about his dad's physical problems, but he was just as concerned about his dad's emotional ones.

"I know my leave runs out in eleven days," Egan went on. "But I want to see if I can extend it for another two weeks. If that's not possible—"

"It's possible," Joyner interrupted. "You've got it. Just submit the paperwork, and I'll approve it." But then he paused. "Any thoughts, though, as to what you'll do if your father is unable to go back to work full-time?"

Oh, yeah. Plenty of thoughts, none of them ideal, especially since his dad had repeatedly nixed the idea of having an office manager. "I could continue to stay at the ranch and make the one-hour commute here to the base. Again, if you'll grant permission."

Squadron commanders were expected to live on base where they'd be easily accessible, but waivers could be given.

"Done, I'll approve the waiver," the colonel was quick to assure him. "As far as I'm concerned, you can continue the commute for the entire duration of your assignment."

That would buy Egan almost two years. Plenty of time. But even that might not be enough. There'd been a lot of damage to his father's heart. Maybe so much that he'd have to avoid even minimal stress for, well, the rest of his life. That was almost certainly one of the reasons, that and the depression, his dad had yet to jump back into his duties.

"I can use the next two years to see how things go at the ranch," Egan went on. And he dreaded down to the marrow what he needed to say next. "If things stay as is, though, in four years, I'll have my twenty in."

Egan saw the shock on the colonel's face. Not because the man hadn't known how much time Egan had in uniform but because Joyner wouldn't have been expecting him to bring up the R-word.

Retirement.

Egan could, indeed, retire after twenty years on active duty, but before his dad's heart attack, he hadn't considered the possibility of retirement for at least another decade. With his track record, he was on pace to make full colonel. Maybe even general. No way would that happen if there were any signs that he was cutting his career short.

This was the definition of a rock and hard place.

If he followed his career plan, it would put the responsibilities of the ranch on his dad's shoulders. Maybe he'd be able to handle it, but at the moment, that was a very big maybe.

"Well," Joyner said, obviously processing that. "I'm guessing none of your siblings could step up?"

They could. But Egan wouldn't ask any of them to do that. They were all on the fast track, all decorated officers with stellar career potential ahead of them. Egan was the oldest, and whether it was fair or not, he believed the responsibility of the family ranch was his.

Egan shook his head. "None of my siblings is as close to twenty years as I am," he settled for saying.

"Any other relatives who could take over?" Joyner pressed.

Again, Egan shook his head. His dad had some nephews, but they weren't close. In fact, they hadn't visited the ranch since they were kids.

Joyner nodded and then stayed quiet a few more moments. "All right, then let's hope your dad makes a full recovery. It sounds as if that'd be the best-case scenario for everyone involved. Just in case that doesn't happen though, let's brainstorm some possibilities."

Egan had already done the brainstorming and mulled over the possibilities. None of which were ideal.

"You'll be the squadron commander here for another two years," Joyner spelled out, "and you can apply for a one-year extension, which I believe you'd get. That'd close the gap for retirement. Then, you could finish out your career at headquarters here on the base."

That would keep Egan both in uniform and on the ranch. Mainly on the ranch, though, since he'd be living there. Part of him wanted to mentally groan at being in the fishbowl of Emerald Creek, but he also didn't want to go the high and dry route by leaving his dad.

Or Alana.

That brought on some more mental groaning and cursing. A fling, that was all she wanted from him. But if he was worried about leaving her, then Egan had to accept that this particular fling clearly had some feelings attached to it. And that was probably the last thing Alana wanted. He could take out the *probably* when he applied that to himself. No way did he want to fall for Alana when part of him would likely always consider her to be Jack's.

"A final option," Joyner threw out there, "you could always try to finish up your time in the reserves."

Egan was sure his mouth tightened. His gut, too. It was a good choice for plenty of military members, but the notion of being on duty only one weekend a month and two weeks in the summer had never appealed to him. Mainly because he'd always thought of himself as a full-time career officer.

But he was a son, too.

"Lots to consider," Joyner added. "But for now, let's see if the leave alone is enough time for you to get some things resolved." He leaned back in his chair and studied Egan's expression. "Audrey mentioned something about a memorial for your CRO friend who was killed a few years back. How's that going?"

Once again, Egan went with the mental groaning and cursing. He'd already dumped enough of his personal life on the colonel, and he had no intention of adding more.

"It's going fine," Egan lied.

Joyner stared at him as if waiting for more, but when Egan didn't offer up any details, he stood. "Good. Go ahead and do the request for additional leave so I can get that approved. And tell your dad that I wish him a speedy recovery."

"I will," Egan assured him, standing as well. He ended the meeting with a salute and walked out of the office.

Egan was grateful that Audrey wasn't there since he definitely didn't want any more questions about why he'd asked for this meeting with Joyner. He didn't want questions about Jack's life celebration, either. Or Alana. The bottom line was he was just glad that he didn't have to sort through any more details about the civilian, private part of his life.

"I'm ready to go," Egan immediately told his brother and didn't even bring up the subject of how Cal's meeting had gone with Audrey.

Cal smiled, and for a moment Egan thought the particular facial expression was connected to their stepmother.

It wasn't.

Cal lifted his phone and held it face out for Egan to see. That's when Egan realized it wasn't Cal's phone. But his. That's when he also realized what Cal had wanted him to see.

The photo that had been texted.

"Sorry," Cal muttered. "But I automatically looked when your phone dinged and I saw it."

The text was from Alana, though there was no written message, only the picture. Of a pack of condoms.

"Anything you want to tell me?" Cal asked.

Egan snatched his phone and shoved it into his pocket. "No," Egan couldn't say fast enough. "There's absolutely nothing I want to tell you."

CHAPTER EIGHTEEN

ALANA KNEW SHE was being watched. Not in a "creepy stalker" kind of way. Well, not totally. But the other shoppers in the town's Fresh Pickin's grocery store always "observed" whatever she put in her cart.

Normally, those observers were enough to prompt her to at least try to buy the stuff that was good for her, but she was feeling a little mutinous and added a bag of sour gummy bears to her healthy stash. An addition that caused Marilu Dennison to audibly gasp. Since Marilu was one of the town's biggest gossips, word of the indulgence would soon get around and might diffuse the other talk.

Especially diffuse the buzz about Egan and her.

Yep, there was buzz all right, and Alana had even heard that many believed Tilly had had Egan's picture taken off the newspaper web page because she was irate over Alana and him hooking up. Tilly was certainly irate, and it was possible some of it was because of the hooking up, but Alana knew the bulk of it was because Tilly had had her illusions about Jack shattered.

Welcome to the club.

Alana had had her illusions about him shattered,

too, when he'd confessed to the affair. She was try-ing not to dwell on that, though. Trying not to dwell on Jack, either, and that's where the hooking up with Egan was helping.

Or rather the partial hooking.

Technically, they hadn't actually had sex, not the full-blown variety, anyway, and Alana figured that was intentional on Egan's part in case she was hav-ing to deal with any guilt since they had hooked up. She wasn't. Well, not much, anyway. But she was dealing with a whole lot of confusion.

The day before, she'd sent Egan the photo of the condoms she'd bought. Not a purchase she'd made in town but rather at the mini mart out by the interstate. Egan had responded with a thumbs-up and then had added that he was on his way to drop off Cal at the airport. About an hour later, he'd followed up with a further explanation about being tied up at the base for a while and that he would call her later.

He'd tried that call, but she'd had to cut it short since she'd been with his dad for their daily appoint-ment. It hadn't felt right to make sex plans with Egan with Derek right there in the room. So Alana had asked Egan if they could "talk" later that night. That had earned her another thumbs-up, but when night had come around, Egan had had to cancel because of an injured horse.

Egan hadn't committed to another time for them to get together, and Alana had decided not to push. He was obviously going through a lot right now. He didn't need anyone or anything else pressuring him. Especially her since it was possible he was going through his own battle with guilt and the past.

Unfortunately, this fling limbo was making Alana want him even more. And, apparently, it was making her antsy and rebellious, too, because she added some cake mix to the cart. She reasoned that she'd probably never get around to actually making the cake before it expired, but the box would be in her pantry if she got the overwhelming urge to indulge in something other than Egan.

Alana heard the sound of rapidly approaching squeaky wheels of a grocery cart, and she glanced back, expecting to see someone trying to get a better look at her rebellious items, but the person right on her heels was Aunt Loralee, who fell in step right alongside Alana.

"I think you caused Marilu to faint in aisle three," her aunt muttered, glancing into Alana's shopping cart. "Eating your sorrows?"

"Indulging myself," Alana amended and purposely added the nearest bag of chips to her stash. It was sour cream and onion, a flavor combo she detested, so the bag would likely meet a slow death on the shelf with the cake mix.

"Indulging because of Egan or Tilly?" Loralee pressed.

It was a loaded question, especially since Alana hadn't spilled anything to her aunt about her park encounter with Tilly. And Alana especially hadn't spilled anything about Egan giving her an orgasm.

That just wasn't something you could work into a conversation with a mother figure.

"It feels empowering to buy these things," Alana said, dodging the subject of both Tilly and Egan. "It's my version of an adrenaline rush. Sort of like a mini toned-down experience that Egan gets when he flies fighter jets. Sort of," she tacked on to that in a mutter.

Loralee made a sound that was barely audible but still managed to sound like a full-volume disapproval. "I just got off the phone with Tilly," her aunt said, still keeping her voice low. "She's very upset because the artist she'd commissioned to do Jack's memorial broke both his arms in a car accident. He can't finish the painting."

Alana went through a quick-fire round of emotions. She felt sorry for the artist, but maybe this meant—

"Tilly's not canceling the life celebration," Loralee said, dashing Alana's hopes that the event might be called off. "In fact, this is a case akin to jumping out of the frying pan and into the fire."

Alana had to shake her head. "What does that mean?"

"It means that Tilly contacted the only other artist she knew. Or rather an artist I knew."

And it hit Alana then. Frying pan, fire. Yep. "Colleen's lover, Anton Ewing, is finishing the painting."

"Bingo. It's really a huge favor since he'll have to work lots of hours to finish it up. Then, of course, Tilly will want him at the unveiling so she can publicly thank him for filling in."

"Of course," Alana repeated like profanity.

Now Egan would not only have to face the ex who'd walked out on him, but he'd also have to see the man she'd walked out with. Alana had no idea just how much that would bother Egan. She suspected, though, the answer to that was "a lot."

"I don't think Egan knows about the artist substitute," Loralee went on. "I can call him if you like so he doesn't have to hear it through gossip."

"No," Alana couldn't say fast enough. Best not to encourage interaction between Egan and her aunt. "I'll tell him."

Of course, Loralee frowned at that, probably because she suspected there might be more than just mere conversation going on between Egan and her niece.

Loralee kept up the frown and the whispered voice when she continued. "Well, you might not be able to tell Egan in person once his leave runs out," she went on. "I heard from Maybell that Egan will be commuting from the base to the ranch. It means he'll be on the road back and forth a lot."

This was the first Alana was hearing about a commute, and it made her wonder why she hadn't heard it from Egan. That only added to her antsy uncertainty, causing her to toss in a can of bean dip and another of queso. Clearly, she was going to have to figure out a less caloric way of handling this relationship stuff.

Heck, what she had with Egan might not even qualify as a relationship.

Considering what had gone on, and not gone on,

between them, their status had more of a "loosey-goosey limbo" feel to it.

Then, her phone buzzed.

And everything changed.

Alana's heart tapped out a little dance and her stomach fluttered when she saw Egan's name on the screen. Loralee must have seen it, too, because she huffed loud and long enough to extinguish a whole bunch of birthday candles. Alana turned the phone so her aunt wouldn't be able to see the message and the photo Egan had sent.

Good thing, too, because this was as private as private got.

I've been trying to convince myself that I should spare you the gossip and leave you the hell alone. I'm failing big-time. If you're not busy, I can come by your place later.

Beneath those joyful, mood-lifting words was a picture that spelled out the rest of his sentiment.

A photo of a jumbo box of condoms.

EGAN HURRIED INTO his bathroom at the ranch to take the fastest shower in history, just enough to wash away the stench of the horses and the barn. Then, while he dressed, he tried to tamp down all the things that were making him feel like a randy teenager.

The heat and need for Alana were there. Man, were they. But even though he wasn't going to try to talk himself out of seeing her, he wanted his brain to fully understand that this could be a mistake. So far, he was failing at that, and it was the reason he'd ended up sending Alana that photo of the condoms.

Exactly as a randy teenager would do.

Still, he had to smile at her response—three rows of thumbs-up—at his suggestion of coming to her place. Yeah, it would spin even more gossip, but Egan was almost past the point of caring. Almost. He thought maybe a night with Alana might even rid him of the *almost*.

Grabbing his phone, he hurried out of his bedroom but then slowed when he saw the door of his dad's room open. Egan came to a full stop after seeing his dad not in his usual sitting area but rather standing at the window.

Egan cleared his throat, making his presence known, and his dad glanced at him from over his shoulder before motioning for Egan to join him. Egan did, and he soon saw what had gotten his father's attention. One of the trainers was working with an Andalusian mare in the front pasture.

"Remi used to name all the horses, remember?" his dad asked. "I miss her doing that."

Egan smiled because he'd missed his dad talking about anything ranch-related. "The hands give some of them names. But yeah, Remi's were better."

His sister had usually gone with characters in her favorite books, and she did have a knack for matching the name with personalities of the horses. That's how they'd ended up with a Hermione, Bella, Voldemort and Primrose.

Even though Egan had been in a hurry to get to Alana's, he mentally slowed himself down. "Would you like me to have the hands bring more horses into the front pasture so you can watch them? Or I can walk with you outside so you can better see them."

"No," his dad said, but he didn't jump straight into that denial. It seemed to Egan that he gave it a little thought. "Maybell mentioned that you got your leave extended." He glanced at Egan, their eyes meeting for only a second before he returned his attention to the window.

"I did, and once my leave is up, I'll commute for a while."

His dad nodded. "And I understand you saw Audrey."

With everything else going on, Egan hadn't given that chance meeting much thought, but he should have. Audrey's plans impacted his dad, which meant in turn they had an impact on him, too.

"Yes, I saw her at the base," Egan said, and he waited to see how his dad would respond to that. He didn't want to spill about Audrey's possible assignment if she hadn't gotten around to telling him.

"I know about the job she's up for in Germany," his dad volunteered. While he didn't voice any disappointment or disapproval about that, Egan thought he heard some in the weary breath his dad dragged in. "I also know what's going on with Tilly and Alana."

Egan frowned, again debating how much to say. He went with a noncommittal "Oh?"

His dad did more than glance this time. He gave

Egan a full look, studying his eyes. "Tilly did an interview with Parker at the newspaper, and the big papers in San Antonio and even a couple in Austin have picked up the story. Reporters are going out to Tilly's to do a more thorough interview."

Egan's frown deepened, and the worry came. "Did Tilly bad-mouth Alana in the interview?"

"No," his dad said. "She didn't bad-mouth you, either. According to Maybell and Effie, Tilly took a different approach and told the interviewer that the life celebration was going to be *mighty* hard for her and Jack's still-grieving widow, that Alana and she would almost certainly shed some tears over their heart-crushing loss."

"Good grief," Egan muttered.

His dad made a sound of agreement. "But Tilly added that she believes the event will celebrate Jack and remind Alana just how much she loves and misses her soulmate."

Egan groaned, and he could almost hear Tilly repeating some of that in the speech she'd no doubt give at the life celebration. The woman was trying to shame Alana into ditching any plans to put aside her widowhood status and move on with her life. Tilly might be trying to repair her own illusions about her son, too, so Egan figured both Alana and he were going to have to steel themselves up for whatever Tilly threw at them. Not just at the life celebration but afterward, too.

Tilly might believe the interview would cause Alana and him to rethink this fling they'd started.

But it only made Egan more resolved to go through with it.

Even if it turned out to be a mistake.

"Let me know if you want to go outside and have a better look at the horses," Egan said, giving his dad's arm a gentle squeeze.

"I will." But his tone didn't show much interest in him doing that. "You're heading to see Alana?" he asked.

That hadn't taken any ESP on his dad's part. If Maybell and Effie had filled him in about Tilly and the interview, then one of them would have also mentioned the gossip about Alana and him.

"I am," Egan verified.

"Good," his dad said, surprising him. "Any fool can see how she feels about you. I figure that's why Tilly's giving her so much backlash, because she can see that Alana's falling in love with you."

That stopped Egan in his tracks, and he shook his head. He nearly blurted out that if people were seeing anything in Alana, it wasn't love for him. It was the blazing attraction.

Wasn't it?

Yeah, it had to be. Egan had just gotten used to the notion of a fling, and he didn't have the emotional bandwidth to go beyond that.

Egan's pace wasn't quite so hurried as he said goodbye to his dad and went down the stairs and out the door so he could head to his truck. He didn't make it there, though, before the silver Mercedes turned into the driveway. Egan didn't recognize the vehicle nor the blond-haired driver behind the wheel, and he wondered if this was someone here about a meeting Egan had forgotten or hadn't known about.

A man wearing khakis and a white shirt stepped out, and judging from the way his attention zoomed in on Egan, he knew who Egan was. He came closer, extending his hand for Egan to shake.

"Egan," the man said. "We meet at last. I'm Anton Ewing."

Egan had already moved to shake his hand, but he stopped. And cursed. Not silently, either. Because he knew who this was.

Colleen's lover.

Even though this was the man Colleen had left him for, over the years Egan had purposely avoided photos or any gossip that might come up about Anton. He'd done that because he hadn't wanted one tidbit of info about him in his head. Now, here he was, right in front of him where he was impossible to avoid. But not for long.

"I'm on my way out," Egan said and started toward his truck again.

"I thought we should meet, and that way if we had any differences to settle, we could do that before Jack's life celebration," Anton called out to him.

Egan stopped again, turned and faced him. A lot of questions fired through Egan's head, but the only one he managed to voice was, "What?"

Anton sighed, not in a "smug asshole" kind of way, either. "I guess neither Tilly nor Loralee told you," he muttered.

Egan didn't like that particular pairing. Tilly, the woman who wished he'd died instead of her son, and Loralee, the woman who wished him, well, probably all sorts of bad things.

"How bad is this?" Egan came out and asked.

Anton sighed again. "Bad."

And his ex-wife's lover filled him in.

CHAPTER NINETEEN

EGAN WENT UP the steps to Alana's house, ready to knock, ready to tell her everything he'd just learned from his dad and Anton. But before he even made it to her porch, the front door opened.

She looked amazing, of course. That was the default for her. Her hair was down, spilling onto the shoulders of the pale green dress she was wearing. Even though he'd come with a starter of bad news, he couldn't help but feel the punch of lust he got at just seeing her.

"You've heard," she said almost right away.

So she already knew what he needed to tell her. Maybe. "You know about the interview Tilly did and Anton doing the painting?" he countered.

She nodded, sighed, took hold of his arm and tugged him inside. "I also know that Tilly is having Colleen and Anton do the unveiling while she, you and I are supposed to watch with teary-eyed anticipation. We're to follow that up with more tears to show everyone how much we love Jack."

That had been Anton's version of the plan, too, and even though Tilly probably hadn't told Anton about the details of Jack's death, the man had clearly picked up on a bad vibe from Tilly.

"How'd you find out?" Alana asked.

"From Anton himself. He paid me a visit at the ranch just as I was leaving to come here."

Her eyes widened, and her gaze combed over his face as if searching for any injuries. "I don't see any bruises or open gashes."

Egan managed a smile. "Nope. No bloodshed. Anton just wanted to explain that Tilly's plans weren't his idea and that he'd actually tried to talk her out of it. He says if she sticks to her guns, that he'll feign some kind of stomach flu and skip the ceremony so she won't be able to rub him in my face."

Alana smiled, too. "Well, good for Anton." She shut the door once they were both inside. "So, your meeting with him was civil?"

"Civil enough," he clarified. "I doubt we'll ever be best buds, but I didn't want to break any bones when we shook hands."

"Baby steps," she muttered.

Alana leaned in and brushed her mouth over his. That stirred some fresh heat, but Egan put that heat on pause while he studied her eyes. Then, he studied the kitchen counter that was loaded with all sorts of junk food.

"Are you upset about Tilly's interview?" he came out and asked.

"No," she was quick to assure him. "Baby steps that it didn't upset me. But there could be more to come. More that could require much bigger steps."

On a sigh, she motioned for him to follow her into the kitchen where she got herself a Coke and offered him a beer, which he accepted. He didn't question her about the junk food stash, or the bad news that had prompted her to buy it. Egan just sipped his beer and waited her out.

"I ran into Aunt Loralee at the grocery store," Alana eventually continued, "and she seems to think with all these petty things Tilly has been doing, that she might have a big finale planned for the life celebration."

Hell. He didn't like the sound of that. "Is Tilly going to publicly out you for seeing me?"

Alana shook her head. "Loralee doesn't know the specifics of Jack's death but thinks that Tilly is planning something big. I figure Tilly will publicly try to out *you* for what she'll say is you betraying your best friend by leading him to his death and then moving in on his wife."

Egan mentally repeated his *hell* and added a few more curse words. It took him plenty of long moments to rein in his anger. More moments to try to figure out a way to counteract Tilly's bombshell so that he could keep Alana out of it.

"Maybe I should make my own statement about being the reason Jack ended up where he was," Egan threw out there.

This time, she didn't hesitate. "If you do that, I'll counter it with a statement about the 'hell on wheels' argument I had with him. And where would that get us, huh? It would get us talking publicly about things that are private and painful for us."

Yeah, it would do that.

"It would punish us," Alana went on, "and whether or not Tilly realizes it, it would punish her, too. Because people won't be wearing their 'see no wrong in Jack' glasses and they will believe wholeheartedly that he cheated. That, in turn, will bring down Tilly's illusions like a house of cards."

Egan didn't spell out that he'd always believe he should be punished since Alana no doubt felt the same way. Besides, just because they would always feel the guilt, it didn't mean Tilly had a right to use it as a weapon. He almost wished for that "house of cards" effect, but he was afraid a truth like that wouldn't end with Tilly slapping him again. It could end Tilly, period. It could take away the woman's reasons for living, and Egan thought he owed it to Jack to make sure that didn't happen.

"We could both come down with Anton's stomach flu," Alana suggested, forcing a smile.

Egan would go for it if he thought it would silence Tilly. But if the woman was truly hell-bent on doing a tell-all with her particular slant on things, then their absence wouldn't stop her. The best Alana and he could do was try to weather the storm and make sure they all—including Tilly—got out of it alive.

Setting her Coke aside, she went to him and forced a smile. She fanned her hand over the bags of junk food. "I can offer you high caloric, zero nutritional options for working out your frustrations."

"I see that," he said, setting his own beer aside so he could take hold of her waist and ease her closer. Because he thought they could both use it, he kissed her. Nothing scalding, but there was heat, of course. Heat was inevitable when it came to Alana and him.

"I also know a noncaloric way of working out our frustrations," she muttered.

This time, her smile wasn't forced. But it was short-lived because Egan put his mouth on hers and kissed that smile. She made a sound of pleasure, a purr that came from deep within her throat, and she melted against him.

Egan was glad about the melting because it put them body to body, and he felt his pulse rev up into the stratosphere. He'd braced himself for the kick of adrenaline and fire. Not enough, though.

Not nearly enough.

He couldn't manage to rein in any part of him so this could be the start of some really good foreplay. The hungry kiss catapulted them from the start to near the very end where his brain and body were already looking for a place to take Alana now, now, now.

Alana was clearly in the same mode, too, and it occurred to him that this was what happened when sex and fierce attraction kept getting put on hold. Eventually, the dam would break and land them right in bed. Or on the floor since it was closer.

Just as he'd done during their other make-out session, Egan reached for the bottom of her dress, but she stopped him, causing him to curse. Not her but himself. Had he misread the signals? He was battling with the answer to that when she kissed him.

No misread signals.

"Turnabout is fair play," she said, going after his shirt. "You stripped me last time, and now I get to do the same to you."

He wasn't wearing a button-up shirt today, but Alana quickly took hold of his T-shirt and shoved it up, up, up until she had it over his head and off. Then, she sent it flying. She put her hands on him, touching and sliding her palms over his chest. Flaming the fire that was already too hot to contain.

Her breath was coming out in quick rough gusts now, and that intensified the kiss that she dropped on his chest. Everything intensified even more when the kiss turned French, and she slid her tongue from his chest to his stomach.

Alana was either trying to replicate what he had done to her the other time they'd been together at his cabin. Or else she was trying to drive him mad. She was doing a very good job at both. Alana kissed, making full use of her mouth and tongue and even her teeth while she continued that tortuous trail down his stomach.

Onto the front of his jeans.

Oh, yeah, she was definitely trying to drive him over the edge and along with her mouth, tongue and even teeth, she was putting that hot fast breath of hers to good use.

Her hands got in on the act, too, as she reached for his belt buckle. That slowed her down a little but not much. She got the belt undone, got him unbuttoned, lowered his zipper and used the same mouth, tongue, teeth and breath trick against the front of his boxers.

That did it.

Egan could take no more. Rather than pull her up to him, he dropped to his knees, taking her with him and adjusting their position so they were face-to-face again. So he could take her mouth with a hot hungry need that she had ignited inside him.

"Condom," she rasped. "They're in the bedroom."

"I have one closer," Egan assured her, extracting the foil packet from the pocket of his jeans. "First, though, you're getting naked."

"*We're* getting naked," Alana amended. "We're doing this together this time."

"No arguments from me," Egan muttered.

And there wouldn't be. There was no argument he could give himself to rethink what they were about to do even if rethinking would be smart.

He went after her dress again, and this time she didn't stop him. Alana let him slip it off over her head, and Egan tossed it onto the floor, somewhere. He went after her bra next, and once he unhooked it and removed it, he did some kissing of his own. On her breasts, taking one of her nipples into his mouth.

Oh, mercy. This was good. Beyond good. He enjoyed the hitch in her voice and took pleasure in the sound that she made. He enjoyed the way she latched onto him and demanded, "More."

He very much intended to give both of them *more*.

He got rid of her panties next, but he ran into a little interference when she also tried to rid him of his jeans. There was some awkward fumbling around, but they finally worked it all out. And after he moved the panties down her legs, he had exactly what he wanted.

A naked Alana right in front of him.

Apparently, Alana wanted the same for him because with more maneuvering, she pulled off his boots and jeans. He had to land on his back for that to happen, and she took full advantage of that. She pulled down his boxers and gave him a kiss that he was reasonably sure he wouldn't forget even if he had full-blown amnesia.

Since more of those kind of kisses would put a quick end to this and wouldn't in any way complete that "together" promise, Egan had to reluctantly put a halt to it. Instead, he did another maneuver, rolling on top of her.

He kissed her long, hard and deep, all while he did more fumbling around, this time to get the condom open and on. Alana tried to help with that as well, and they nearly ended up having unprotected sex, after all.

After steeling himself up, Egan finally managed to get his hands working again so he could get the condom on. But he didn't just push into her as his body was begging him to do. No, he took a moment to savor the moment. This moment with Alana where they would become lovers.

That gave him a heavy emotional punch that he hadn't been expecting. It seemed to give Alana one as well because her gaze connected with him, and she held the stare for several moments. Moments filled with the need for each other even more out of control than their breathing.

Oh, man. One way or another, they were going to pay for this. He hoped the payment would be good, that there would be no regrets. But they would pay.

That thought/worry quickly faded, though, when Alana's mouth came back to his for a kiss that jump-started their big finale. Egan did push inside now, but he kept his gaze on her. Watched her take him in. Watched what the pleasure and need did to her face. She was stunning, and no, he didn't think that was just because they were having sex.

Because the need for her became overwhelming, Egan started to move. Slow gentle strokes. Strokes that one by one skyrocketed in the heat. Escalating it with each move. With each breath. With each whispered sound of pleasure. And there were plenty of whispered sounds of pleasure coming from both of them.

Egan tried to catalog each of those sounds she was making, wanting to hang on to each one. Wanting to hang on to this moment. But that was the problem with really good sex. It couldn't last forever. The thrusts inside her became harder, faster. More frantic with both of them dictating the need and the pace. And it was that need and pace that sent Alana straight up to that climactic edge.

Egan felt the orgasm ripple through her. Felt it squeeze around him, urging him and carrying him to the only place he could go. And he went over that edge right along with her.

The wave of intense almost overwhelming pleasure came, crashing and consuming, both sating and
exhausting his body. But not exhausting the need for
her. Nope, that was still there. He cataloged that as
well, and as soon as he was able to catch his breath,
he shifted just a little so that he wouldn't be dead-
weight on her.

Alana rolled with him, moving until they were
side by side, face-to-face and breath to breath. Egan's
gaze was pretty blurry right now, but he could still
see the curve of a smile on her mouth. A smile that
showed she was very pleased with the outcome. If
the guilt was going to come, it wasn't going to come
right now.

He held her there, the floor feeling harder and
harder with each passing second, and when he felt his
butt cheek falling asleep, he finally let go so he could
get up and make a quick pit stop in the bathroom.

When he came back out, he found Alana still
naked on the floor, but she was no longer lying there.
She was sitting up and had clutched the front of her
dress to her bare breasts. The smile was gone, and
she was looking a little alarmed.

"I think someone's on the porch," she whispered.

Egan was sure that put some alarm on his own
face. Even if everyone in town suspected there was
something going on between Alana and him, he
didn't want that verified by someone peering in the
window and seeing them naked.

He glanced around for his boxers, but when he
didn't see them, he gave up on that search and grabbed

his jeans instead. He yanked them on, zipped up and then located his shirt.

Alana was putting on her clothes, too, but he couldn't help but notice that she hadn't located her panties, either, and the back of her dress was lifted up over her butt. Even though Egan rather enjoyed that particular view, he pulled it down for her and opened the window to peek out. And he nearly got the hell scared out of him.

When someone peered back at him.

Egan garbled out a slew of profanity, and then he cursed even more once he recognized the face looking back at him. Not a nosy neighbor, but his youngest brother.

Blue grinned in that cocky way that only he and some Greek gods could have managed to pull off.

"I wanted to make an entrance like Remi said she did, but I couldn't find any rope or a nearby hayloft," Blue said, his tone as cocky as the rest of him.

Still cursing, still scowling, Egan checked to make sure Alana was fully dressed. She was.

"Should I go find some rope and come back while you finish up whatever you're doing in there?" Blue asked while still grinning.

A grin that caused Egan to scowl, but then he remembered that technically Blue hadn't interrupted anything. Well, nothing other than what would have no doubt been an amazing aftermath to the amazing sex. Egan also remembered that he actually wanted Blue here in Emerald Creek. He just hadn't wanted him right here at this exact moment.

"Brothers," Egan grumbled.

Knowing full well that Blue would know exactly what had just gone on between Alana and him, Egan opened the door and let the ribbing begin.

CHAPTER TWENTY

ALANA FELT A little cowardly as she checked the window for anyone who might be out there when she went to her car.

Not Blue.

She definitely wasn't expecting him and hadn't seen him since he'd shown up two days earlier and given Egan some playful ribbing about seeing her. However, others had dropped by in the past forty-eight hours. Neighbors, casual acquaintances and such who all had one thing in common. Or rather two things.

They were nosy and Tilly's friends.

Most had been pleasant enough, saying they were just checking to see how she was or to tell her how excited they were about the upcoming life celebration for Jack. Others mentioned they'd seen Egan at her place and in a roundabout way had wondered how he and his dad were doing. None had come out and asked if Egan and she were seeing each other, but Alana had no doubt that's why they had come by.

The nosiness, gossip, nor Tilly had caused Alana to put a halt to seeing Egan. Duty, though, had done a darn fine job of keeping them apart so they hadn't been able to have a repeat of that stellar sex on the floor.

For the past two days, her schedule had been slammed with working up nutrition plans for five new clients. Egan had been in the same equally slammed boat since he'd made some trips to the base to meet with a group of newly assigned pilots to his squadron. Yes, he was on leave, but Egan had explained that he was still the commander, and he hadn't wanted to delegate that initial meet and greet to someone else.

The back and forth had given Alana a glimpse of what life might be like in two and a half weeks when he would be making the commute daily and then coming home to take care of ranch business.

There wouldn't be a lot of free time for a fling, but she was hoping the busyness wouldn't put an end to things between them. In fact, Alana couldn't bear the thought of it. And that was an "in her face" reminder that she'd done something she knew she shouldn't have done.

She'd fallen hard for Egan.

Sex had broken down some of her resolve, but it was more than that. The sex had fueled both the attraction and her feelings for him, and since she didn't like to lie to herself, Alana didn't think these feelings were just going to vanish because there weren't enough hours in the day.

But gossip and ill feelings toward them weren't going to vanish, either.

Tilly, and others, weren't simply going to forget

that she was Jack's widow. Nor would they forget that Egan had been married to her sister. That meant there would always be talk. Always be those who felt Egan and she shouldn't be together no matter how strong their feelings were for each other.

Sighing over that, she peeked out the window again, and when she didn't spot anyone lying in wait for her, she grabbed her purse and went outside. The papers fluttered from the now open door, and Alana sighed again when she saw what they were.

A new revised flyer for Jack's life celebration.

Not just one copy but at least a dozen. They landed like a unit of paratroopers at her feet.

She glanced around, wondering if Tilly herself had tucked them there, but she doubted it. Tilly had been avoiding her, communicating only through group texts and emails that included Anton, Colleen, Loralee and the minister. It was more likely that Tilly's circle of friends was distributing these flyers all over town, and that circle wanted to make certain she didn't miss out.

Alana picked one of them up and saw the revised announcement that included the time, date and place. What Tilly had taken out were any words that had to do with death.

Memorial. Remembrance. Memories. Widow.

Alana's name was on the flyer, but she was now listed as Jack's loving wife, and she would apparently be giving a brief speech to *mark the occasion*. There was no mention of Egan, but there was this new addition. *Everyone attending will be treated to the life celebration unveiling by special guest Anton Ewing.*

She seriously doubted Egan would be bothered by being removed from the festivities. Just the opposite. It'd be a relief. It'd be a relief to Alana, too, when it was finally over.

Unlike the versions of the previous flyers, this one didn't have a blank backside, and when Alana turned it over, she saw the eight-by-ten image of her own smiling face. Front and center with a smiling Jack, Tilly and Colleen.

The photo had been taken on their wedding day, a candid shot that had originally included Egan at Jack's side, but Tilly had obviously cropped that out. Alana was surprised that Tilly hadn't tried to do the same to her, but that would have no doubt caused questions that Tilly wouldn't have wanted to address.

She left all the flyers on the porch, hoping the wind would scatter them to parts unknown, and Alana hurried to her car. She made it in just the nick of time since her "across the street" neighbor, Doris McGill, was heading her way. Alana smiled, waved and called out that she had to get to an appointment. It was the truth, too. She was headed to the ranch to see Derek.

And maybe Egan.

She'd dreamed about him all night, and she'd woken up aroused and with high hopes that their schedules might finally mesh so they could get together again. If the meshing didn't happen, though,

Alana just wanted to see him even if it turned out to be only for a minute or two.

As usual, there was very little traffic on the road so it didn't take her long to reach the ranch, and despite it only being eight thirty in the morning, the place was already busy. She spotted Jesse in the corral with one of the trainers, and Blue was in the pasture on the west side of the house. He was riding a chestnut horse and in the process of herding some Angus away from the fence.

Despite the picture-postcard setting in front of her, Alana's mood dipped a little when she didn't see Egan or his truck. Blue waved at her and grinned as she made her way from her car to the house.

Following her usual routine, Alana went to the back and knocked on the kitchen door. Maybell followed her usual routine, too, and let her in. The woman greeted her with a quick hug.

"Food drops-offs have picked up again," Maybell grumbled. "It's because of Blue. He attracts cooking women like flies."

"Anything good?" Alana asked. "The food, I mean. Not the flies or cooking women."

"Stuff with words like *sin* and *sex* in them." Maybell rolled her eyes.

"It's Blue's pretty face," Alana said. "Women just can't help themselves."

She'd said that lightheartedly, but there was a lot of truth to it. Blue was just plain likeable with the infectious grin and face that had gotten a very generous DNA combo. A combo that apparently prompted some women to bake their hearts out.

"Egan's at the base," Maybell said when Alana glanced around.

"I figured as much, but I was looking for Derek." Normally, he took their appointments in the breakfast nook in the kitchen.

"He should be down soon," Maybell said, checking the time. "But I'll text him to let him know you're here."

"Derek's on his way down," Effie said, coming into the kitchen. She gave Alana a quick hug. "His mood's a little better now that Blue is here," she added in a whisper.

Good. Because Derek's mood definitely needed some lifting. "How long will Blue be home?" Alana asked.

"Three days. He'll miss the life celebration." Effie paused. "Egan's still going."

Even though it wasn't a question, she answered it as one. "As far as I know, he plans to be there."

Effie's gaze stayed locked with hers, and Alana heard the woman's unspoken concern loud and clear. She wasn't sure how much Effie knew about Jack's death, but it was obvious she knew enough to worry about her eldest grandson.

There was a shuffling sound, and a few moments later, Derek came in. Alana certainly didn't see an improved mood so she took something from her purse that she thought might give him at least a temporary high.

"Dr. Abrams said your latest cholesterol results were improving. Your low iron levels, too. So, I thought you'd like to add a few treats to your diet."

She handed him the printout that included some recipes for marginally indulgent cookies and suggestions for items he could have from the menus at the diner and the Sweet Tooth. Alana gave copies to Effie and Maybell since they'd likely be the ones to actually make the cookies or take Derek to the ice-cream shop.

Derek sat at the table and glanced over the sheet. Emphasis on glance. Apparently, he wasn't eager for any new treats.

"I'm worried about Egan," Derek came out and said, and since he was looking directly at Alana, the comment was meant for her. "I was hoping you'd tell me what's going on with him. And what's going on between you and him."

"Uh, Effie and I need to take some of this baked stuff out to the hands," Maybell suddenly remarked.

Effie quickly agreed, and they were clearly heading out so that Derek and she could have this chat in private. Alana waited until the women had gathered up some of the plastic containers and left before she said anything to Derek.

"Have you talked to Egan about what's going on with him?" Alana asked.

Derek nodded. "He sugarcoats everything because he doesn't want me to worry, but the sugarcoating makes me worry even more."

"Fair enough," she muttered. "But I wouldn't feel right spilling—"

"Is he burning bridges with his career so he can be here at the ranch?" Derek interrupted.

Alana chose her words carefully. "I think he's finding the right balance."

Derek stared at her as if trying to decide if more sugarcoating was coming from her. But then he nodded. "I just don't want to hold him back. But I need him," he added in a mutter.

"And he needs you and this ranch," she assured him. But what she wouldn't spell out was that Egan needed his job as well.

"Egan's burning the candle at both ends," Derek said under his breath.

Again, Alana had a debate with how much to say. Or not say. "But that's temporary, right? I mean, down the road you'll be able to do some of the things you used to do."

"Down the road," he repeated without a whole lot of conviction.

She heard the doubt in his voice that even if he did return to duty in some way, it wouldn't be the same. Of course, it wouldn't be. His heart had been damaged, and Dr. Abrams had made it clear that Derek wouldn't be able to do 100 percent again.

"Egan's worked up this schedule," Derek went on. "A calendar of when his brothers and sister will be here. I think he did that to take some of the guilt off me. More sugarcoating," he concluded.

Alana thought it was more than that. Egan was trying to find that elusive balance. And there was something that might help with that.

"Have you thought of hiring an office manager?" she asked.

Since Derek showed absolutely no surprise over that question, she had to believe he had considered it. And dismissed it. Maybe because he'd been hoping for a miracle recovery.

"Oh, well," she quickly added, "maybe that's something Egan, Jesse and you can discuss."

"Maybe," Derek muttered in that same lack of conviction. He lifted the paper she'd given him. "Thanks for this," he said, getting up. "I think I'm going to head back upstairs for a quick rest."

She debated offering to help him to his room, but he made a waving gesture with his hand that seemed to dismiss any such offer. On a sigh, Alana went out the back door, intending to find Maybell and Effie and let them know about that *quick rest*. However, she didn't see them but rather Egan. He was already out of his truck and making his way to the house.

The smile he gave her warmed her all the way to her toes.

Alana smiled back, wishing she could go to him and give him a scalding kiss. Not a good idea, though, considering that at least half a dozen people would witness it. No need to give anyone visuals to go along with the gossip.

"I didn't think you'd be back from the base this soon," she said.

"I just had to do some paperwork." He kept his gaze on her, making her think that he was having the same "scalding kiss" thoughts.

They stood there until Alana snapped herself out of the fantasy she was having about him, and she remembered his dad. "I just finished up with your dad, and he said he was going back upstairs to rest."

That clearly snapped Egan out of fantasyland, too. "Is he okay?"

Not wanting to go the sugarcoat route, Alana shrugged. "Maybell said he was happy that Blue is here, but he's clearly worried about you. Maybe worried about us, too," she tacked on to that.

Yes, there was an *us*. And yes, that would give Derek some concern since he'd know that would take jabs at their old painful wounds along with having to deal with the pesky gossip.

"I'll check on him," Egan said, giving her hand a quick squeeze. "And if you're not busy, maybe I can come to your place later?"

She nodded, smiled. Fantasized. "I'm free the rest of the morning," she said. That was sort of true. She didn't have any appointments until the afternoon and had planned on devoting the next few hours to paperwork and scheduling, but she could play hooky with Egan.

"See you in about an hour, then," he said. Another hand squeeze. Another smile. Then, he seemed to say to heck with it, and he brushed a quick kiss on her mouth before he muttered a goodbye.

Alana thought maybe she floated to her car. It'd been so long since she'd had feelings like this, and it was exciting and magical. Scary, too, but she wasn't going to focus on that. She was going to take this "us" status one day at a time and see where Egan and she ended up. If they ended up apart… She stopped stomping on the magic and excitement and repeated that "one day" vow.

She was still floating and buzzing on the drive home, and thankfully there was no one outside her house to tamp down her giddiness. Alana practically danced her way inside and saw something that had her smile widening.

Egan's boxers.

They were peeking out from the edge of the sofa where they'd apparently landed during their frantic undressing. She picked them up just as her phone rang. And her giddiness and joy went south when she saw Tilly's name on the screen.

Crud.

She considered not answering it, but if Tilly truly wanted to speak to her, she only lived two blocks away and would probably just come over. Alana decided a phone call was better than a face-to-face.

"Tilly," Alana said, trying to keep her voice as neutral as possible and hoping that Tilly would do the same.

"Alana," Tilly greeted right back, and while it

wasn't a totally neutral tone, it wasn't exactly hostile, either. Not yet, anyway. "I was wondering if you had time for me to come over so we can chat."

Alana thought of Egan. He had said he would be over in about an hour, and while that was still forty or so minutes away, Alana definitely didn't want Tilly there when he arrived.

"I'm sorry but I can't," Alana told her. "I have some free time this afternoon after four o'clock."

"I can't make that," Tilly insisted. "I still have a lot of details to finalize for the life celebration." The woman paused. "Actually, you're one of those details."

Of course, she was, and that caused Alana to sigh. "What exactly do you want?" Alana came out and asked.

Tilly didn't hesitate to come out and answer that, either. "I want you to stop seeing Egan. I want everyone's focus on Jack, not on Egan and you. And the best way to shift that focus is for you to stop seeing him."

Alana muttered another mental but equally derogatory, *Of course*. Why else would Tilly have been calling?

"No," Alana said, and she purposely didn't add any other words to that because she didn't want Tilly to get confused over her answer.

The sound Tilly made was plenty derogatory, too. "If you won't do this for me, then do it for Jack."

Alana nearly blurted out "Jack's dead," but there was no reason to hit the woman over the head with that particular sledgehammer.

"All right," Tilly went on, her tone turning to a full-blown snarl. "Then, just stop seeing Egan until after the celebration. That's only five days. Surely, you can do the right thing for that short period of time."

Oh, that did not sit well with Alana, and she had to bite her tongue again to stop herself from bringing up that Jack sure as hell hadn't done the right thing when he'd screwed around with another woman while he'd been married. Instead, Alana took her riled response in another direction.

"I'll abstain if you'll apologize to Egan for slapping him," Alana threw out there.

Tilly made a gasping sound as if Alana had just suggested she jump off a cliff. "I have no reason to apologize, and I won't. Egan deserved those slaps and a whole lot more. More that I wish I could give him."

Alana didn't have the same gasping reaction, but it sure sounded to her as if Tilly had just implied she wanted Egan to be permanently out of the picture.

There was a knock at her door, and Alana let go of some of her ire when the relief washed over her. She'd tell Egan about this conversation—after they'd done some kissing and maybe some other stuff. Alana didn't want to keep it from him in case Tilly had truly gone off the deep end.

"Tilly, I have to go," Alana said.

But Tilly clearly wasn't ready for this conversation to be over. "I really want you to consider not seeing Egan. Five days, that's all I'm asking."

No, it wasn't. Alana had no doubt that Tilly would try to advocate for an extension. Perhaps a permanent one.

"Tilly, I'm sorry," Alana said, throwing open the door, "but I'm not going to stop seeing Egan."

Alana got a déjà vu moment that was no doubt similar to the one Egan had gotten two days ago when Blue had shown up. Because it wasn't Egan at the door. Nor was it Blue.

It was her sister, Colleen.

Alana replayed the bit of the conversation that Colleen had almost certainly overheard, and then she glanced down at what she was still holding. Egan's boxers. While there was no way Colleen could know for certain that the boxers belonged to her ex-husband, apparently the underwear paired with the conversation had clued her in.

"Good for you," Colleen remarked just as Alana punched the End Call on her phone.

"Excuse me?" Alana asked, stepping aside as Colleen came in.

Colleen motioned toward the phone. "Good for you."

"Uh, you might not say that if you knew what Tilly was talking about."

"I know what she was talking about. She wants you to stop seeing Egan. It's the reason she asked me to come here and have a heart-to-heart chat with you."

Alana didn't know whether to be pissed or not, but she was experiencing some confusion. "You came here to tell me not to see Egan?"

"No, that's what Tilly wanted me to say." Colleen shrugged. "But I'd rather give you my own opinion of just what I think."

CHAPTER TWENTY-ONE

EGAN WAS WELL aware that this visit to Alana would fuel the gossips. Gossips who'd see his truck in front of her house and figure out the reason he was there.

He didn't care, though.

Not that he wanted to invite any more gossip for Alana, but he couldn't see a way around it. The best he could hope for now was that people would soon tire of the talk and move on to something else. With Blue in town, that something else might be chatter about him. Blue tended to stir things up whenever he was around.

Egan hadn't bothered to change out of his flight suit. After he'd seen his dad and had one of their usual talks where actual talk was in short supply, Egan had told Effie and Maybell that he was heading out for a while. Considering that Maybell had asked him to bring some "hotter than sex" cookies to Alana, the woman knew exactly where he was going.

He knocked on Alana's door and caught the sound of voices. Two women's voices, causing him to mutter a *hell* or two. Tilly might be in there, and if she was, then she was almost certainly giving Alana some grief. No way did Egan want that to continue so he knocked again. This time, there was the sound of running footsteps, and a moment later Alana opened the door.

She had a wild sort of look in her eyes, and if he hadn't heard that other voice, Egan might have thought the wildness was because of the anticipation of sex.

"Colleen's here," she blurted out.

Egan had already stepped forward to go in, but that caused him to pause. He looked over Alana's shoulder and saw his ex on one of the living room chairs. Colleen gave him a perky little wave. Egan didn't return the greeting. He decided to reserve judgment, and wrath, until he could figure out if Colleen was here to verbally bash or browbeat her sister.

If any of that—the bashing or the browbeating— was going on, Alana wasn't showing it. There were Cokes and snacks on the coffee table, and Alana had kicked off her shoes. He paused again, though, when he spotted his boxers on the end table next to Colleen.

Colleen followed his gaze and seemed to guess that he'd been the topic of the sisterly conversation, but his ex just smiled and shook her head. "We weren't talking about that," Colleen assured him. "Well, not much, anyway."

Egan had to admit, he was very confused. Colleen and he hadn't had a civil word between them since she'd left. Actually, they hadn't had many words at all, and the few that had been spoken had been strained and drenched with all the feelings and emotions that went with a divorce. But right here, right now, Colleen seemed, well, happy.

"Uh, I didn't know you were here," Egan said, stating the obvious.

"I was at the diner and left my car there and walked over. Got here just in time, too, because Tilly was talking to Alana on the phone, and was trying to convince her to do something stupid."

That got his attention, and Egan studied Alana's face to see if there were any clues as to what this was all about. "What happened?" he asked as Alana took him by the hand and led him to the sofa.

Alana didn't dismiss it, but she also didn't launch into an explanation until she'd handed him a can of Coke. "Tilly wanted me to quit seeing you until after the life celebration."

As demands went, that was pretty tame coming from Tilly, and soon, very soon, he'd want to know just how hard Tilly had tried to push Alana.

And how Alana had responded.

For now, though, he needed to wrap his head around the fact that Colleen apparently knew that Alana and he were seeing each other and that she wasn't pitching a fit about it. That required some rethinking because Egan had been certain that Colleen wouldn't want his hands on her kid sister.

"I'm not going to bite you," Colleen assured him. "And I'm sure as hell not going to slap you the way Tilly did. I didn't know about that, by the way, until

Alana just told me. If I'd known, I wouldn't have agreed to even attend the life celebration."

That made Egan wonder how much more Colleen knew, but he didn't have to wonder long.

"Alana told me about Jack's cheating," Colleen spelled out. Anger flared through her eyes. "FYI, I didn't cheat on you. Yes, that's a technicality since I fell in love with another man, but I didn't have sex with that man until I'd left you."

Egan wanted to roll his eyes. Or at least he thought that was what he wanted to do for a couple of seconds. Ditto for doling out a reminder that cheating of the heart was worse than cheating with other parts of the body. But then he realized that Colleen was a lot like the gossip.

And that he just didn't care.

Not about why she'd left. Not about what she'd done after the leaving. He had his life, and she wasn't part of it. Well, only a small part since she was Alana's sister. But the anger he'd once felt for her was long gone.

It was about time.

And if this mess weren't going on with Tilly, Egan was sure he would have felt a smidge of something he hadn't felt in years.

Peace.

He got another smidge of the feeling when he turned to Alana, but the worry soon set in. "How hard did Tilly push when she asked you to stop seeing me?"

"Hard." Alana brushed a quick kiss on his mouth.

"I pushed right back. I didn't come out and say go to hell, but I said enough that she might decide she doesn't want me at the life celebration, after all."

If that happened, Egan figured it would be a mixed bag of emotions for Alana. She'd want to be there, maybe, to see Jack being honored. But she might not want to be there so she could miss any of Tilly's drama and misinterpretation of her son's life.

"Alana told Tilly no," Colleen verified. She lifted her hand as if on the witness stand and about to take an oath. "I heard it with my own ears. Now, maybe Tilly will hear it with hers, too, because I personally think it's high time that Alana moved on with her life. You, too," she added to Egan.

Who the heck was this woman? That was the snarky question that popped into his head. But when the snark flitted away, he nodded in thanks.

Colleen nodded back. "While I'm going on and on about what I'm thinking, Tilly should apologize to you for those slaps."

Egan shrugged, shook his head and might have said something if Colleen hadn't continued.

"Don't you dare say you deserved it," Colleen insisted, and then she paused. "Tilly filled me in about you asking Jack to come to see you. Well, I suspect you wanted to see him because I'd left you, and you wanted to pour out your heart to your best friend."

Egan couldn't deny that because it was true.

"So, if we use your logic or Alana's, then I'm just as much to blame as the two of you are," Colleen went on. "But you know what? I'm not going to take any of that blame, and you shouldn't, either. Jack was there because he chose to be, and he was killed by someone who probably didn't even have him as a specific target since it was a combat zone."

That seemed to take some of the wind out of her, and she settled back into the chair.

"Every time you deployed or got in the cockpit, I was terrified," Colleen admitted. "Alana felt the same way about Jack. Tilly, too. But we all knew what could happen. We would all pray that it wouldn't. And that's okay. Praying and being scared is okay. It's not okay, though, to lay the blame on someone who loved Jack as much as you did."

Colleen had tears in her eyes when she glanced first at Egan and then at Alana.

"Sorry," Colleen muttered. "I might have overused the word *okay* there."

The apology wasn't flippant. Nope. Egan knew those tears were the real deal and that all of this had been gnawing away at Colleen, too. Apparently, guilt was claiming multiple targets.

"Sierra Hotel, are we there yet?" Egan muttered. Of course, that caused some confusion with both Alana and Colleen. "That was the last thing Jack said."

Alana's eyes widened, and she pinned her gaze to his. "Sierra Hotel?" she questioned.

Egan nodded. "Slang for Shit Hot. I'd told Jack that one of the other pilots had flown in some steaks with all the trimmings. I also told him that Remi had sent me a long video of all of us together. She'd taken it at Christmas, but she'd forgotten to message me a copy. It was a video of Cal, Blue, Colleen, Remi, Jack, you and me playing a very sloppy military version of beer pong."

Alana nodded, and he knew she was tapping into those memories. A rare ice storm that had kept them housebound for what was supposed to have been a short get-together to celebrate the holidays. Lots and lots of food and beer, of course. Lots of fun and laughter, too. The game had evolved into simulated aircraft carrier landings with each of them taking turns gliding across the wet pong table while "trusting" others to catch them.

"When I told Jack about the steaks and the video," Egan went on, "he said *Sierra Hotel, are we there yet?*"

Egan wasn't sure why he'd never told Alana that. And then he remembered why. If he'd told her, it would have meant talking about Jack. Specifically, talking about those last minutes. Egan hadn't been able to do that because of what had followed those minutes.

And keeping quiet about that was a mistake.

The kind of mistake Tilly was making by not wanting to believe anything but the good about her son. The big picture could often give you a hard kick in the gut. But it could also give you priceless memories. Egan wouldn't ever forget the explosion, but now he had the image of a grinning Jack in his head to go along with it.

"Well," Colleen muttered, getting to her feet. "I should be going."

She leaned in and kissed Alana on the cheek. She turned as if she might do the same to Egan but settled for patting him on the arm instead.

"Oh, did you ever read the letter I sent you?" Colleen asked him as she started for the door and then stopped to look at him.

Egan shook his head. He hadn't. But ironically he had it with him. He'd discovered that when he'd been at the base and rifled through his pockets to locate a pen and found the letter instead. He could *thank* Reba, the housekeeper, for that. The woman had insisted on doing his laundry, and when she found it, she must have put it back once the suit was clean and dry.

"Ah," Colleen muttered, as if disappointed but not especially surprised that he hadn't read it. "I figured you'd just tear it up and toss it."

"I tried that, but it didn't work," he muttered.

She didn't ask for details. Colleen gave her sister another hug and left, closing the door behind her.

Alana looked at him. He looked at her. And Egan tried to steel himself up in case Alana had any questions about Jack's last moments, but she was smiling a little when she moved to sit on the sofa next to him.

"I think we just waded our way through a lot of boggy ground," she said.

"Yeah," he agreed. "Are you okay?" He pushed her hair away from the side of her face and kissed her cheek. Not one of those heat spiking foreplay kisses but one that he hoped would soothe.

She nodded and kissed his cheek, too. Except hers did feel like foreplay because, well, because she was Alana. "My advice?" she asked. "Either read the letter or burn it to ash so you put it to rest once and for all."

Alana had a point. As long as the letter existed or was unread, then it was basically unfinished business. And it no longer felt as if he had any of that with Colleen.

Egan took out the letter, and when Alana started to move away, probably to give him some privacy that he didn't want or need, he took hold of her hand and pulled her back to him.

"You're sure?" she asked.

He nodded. Kissed her. And intended to kiss her a whole lot more once he got the letter out of the way. It felt a little like the reading of a will.

Egan opened the taped up envelope and saw that the letter itself hadn't been repaired. He held the two sides together and saw the handwriting. Not much of it, though. It certainly wasn't a long pouring out of Colleen's heart. Nor was it a rant and rave about their failed marriage.

Egan, this is me trying to make amends for things that probably can't be amended, but here goes, Colleen had written. *I'm sorry, and I wish you the best.* He smiled at the last line. *Damn the torpedoes. Full speed ahead.*

Well, hell. He hadn't expected to feel as if a weight

had been lifted from his shoulders, but he did. Apparently, sometimes old baggage did get unpacked and put away. Now that it had been, he moved on to better, more pleasurable things.

Egan pulled Alana onto his lap and kissed her hard, long and deep.

ALANA MUTTERED A bad word when her phone dinged with a text. She muttered another bad word when she saw the time. It was one o'clock, which meant it was only an hour until her client came in for an appointment.

Normally, cursing wouldn't have been her go-to response for work, but in this case, work would mean leaving a naked Egan. After he'd read the letter, they'd made it to the bed for their latest round of sex. Incredible sex that had obviously worn them both out since they had fallen asleep. It was wonderful to wake up to the sight of Egan's superior butt while he was sprawled out on his stomach on her bed. Alana was certain if he rolled over, there'd be an equally arousing view for her. A view she could savor—and perhaps toy with—for a quickie, anyway.

She moved away from him to check the text and was instantly sorry she had. Because it was from Tilly.

"What does Tilly want?" Egan asked, lifting one eyelid and looking at her.

"How'd you know it was her?" Alana said.

"The tone of your groan."

Well, she had been groaning a lot about Tilly lately

so the response probably was immediately recognizable.

Alana didn't bother with the repeated response when she glanced through the rather lengthy message. "She's reminding me of the agenda and specific times for the life celebration. She's also reminding me that she expects you to be there but not cause any waves."

He didn't groan, either, but rather gave a flash of a dry smile. A smile that vanished when he focused on her face.

"Don't let her upset you," he insisted.

"I try not to, but I don't like the way she's treating you. In fact, I've considered boycotting the celebration to let her know I don't approve of pretty much anything she's done in the past couple of weeks."

He sighed, nodded. "I've considered not going, too. But if I stayed back, it would be to punish Tilly, and I'm holding on to the notion that the day isn't about her. It's not about us. It's about Jack."

There it was. All spelled out and in a nice little nutshell. Jack wasn't Tilly, and he wouldn't have approved of what she was doing. Still, Jack would have probably appreciated the town celebrating his life.

And that's what Alana would do, too.

She moved back closer to Egan and ran her hand over his fine right butt cheek. Then, she ran her hand over the equally fine left one. He responded by rolling onto his back and giving her that front side view she'd been fantasizing about.

"How long before you have to leave for work?" he asked.

Alana checked the time again. "A half hour."

Egan didn't waste a second of those thirty minutes. He pulled her down to him for one of those kisses that made her wish there were more time but thankful that it'd be enough for a quickie.

Alana returned the kiss, adding some little nips on his mouth while her hand went exploring. She climbed on top of him so she could slide her palm over all those muscles and found him hard and ready. She smiled and took his mouth again while she multitasked by fumbling around in the nightstand drawer for one of the condoms she'd put there.

"We could play carrier landings," she murmured, sliding the condom on him. Apparently, she tortured him more than a bit while doing that because he grimaced, groaned and begged for mercy.

"I'm guessing you're the deck of the carrier," he gutted out.

"Oh, yeah. And you're the fighter jet, which by the way has a phallic shape. So, let's see if you can land it just right."

He did.

Without any trouble whatsoever.

He piloted right into her and sent her body into a reverse tailspin. Her breath vanished. Her heart went haywire. But the rest of her was already climbing high with the slam of pleasure.

It took some doing to get her body to move and not just hover over him and absorb that pleasure. She wanted Egan in on this, too. And he cooperated, all right. When she started the thrusts that slid him in and out of her, he caught onto her hips and helped.

They found the rhythm. The right rhythm that meant he was landing in just the right spot for that pleasure to consume every part of her. When she couldn't fight the climax any longer, she moved in and captured his mouth with hers. That was the only afterburner needed to finish her.

Moments later, she finished Egan, too.

Alana accomplished her "landing" when her now sated, limp body dropped onto his. Until they were chest to breast and still mouth-to-mouth. Pre-sex kisses were amazing with Egan, but the post ones were equally stellar.

She wasn't sure how many of those minutes had passed, but Alana decided to refuel by staying in place and getting some post-sex jollies by feeling his body against hers. While her breathing and heart rate leveled, she tried to count off the minutes until she had to get up.

There was still a minute or two on her mental clock when there was another sound, not a text this time but a call. Alana automatically cursed, but then she realized it wasn't her phone but rather Egan's.

He maneuvered himself to the side of the bed, dug through his flight suit on the floor and came up with his phone. "Blue," he grumbled. He jabbed the Accept as if ready to blast his brother for the interruption.

But he didn't.

Alana didn't hear what Blue said, but whatever it

was, it caused Egan to scramble off the bed and start dressing. "I'm on my way," he rattled off to Blue.

Egan ended the call, pulled on his flight suit and met her gaze. "It's Dad. He's been taken to the hospital."

CHAPTER TWENTY-TWO

EGAN HAD ALREADY known that some conversations just stayed with you. Like the last one he'd had with Jack, for instance. But Egan was certain he wouldn't be forgetting what he'd just heard Dr. Abrams say.

"Derek went into cardiac arrest," Abrams explained. "And we nearly lost him."

That *nearly* didn't help tamp down the slam of worry and fear. The words that rang through loud and clear were *lost him*.

His dad had come close to dying, again.

"What is cardiac arrest?" Blue asked, thankfully voicing the question that was on Egan's mind. Probably on Alana's, Maybell's and Effie's, too, since they were all huddled in the doctor's office, waiting to hear the medical verdict.

"It's an abrupt loss of heart function, breathing and, in your dad's case, consciousness," Abrams said. "The good news is it happened during a routine appointment here at the hospital so he was able to get immediate treatment. He's stable."

"You said that after his heart attack," Egan pointed out, trying not to sound bitter. Because he wasn't.

He wasn't blaming the doctor for any of this. He just wanted to know how long *stable* would last.

Abrams nodded. "He was, but cardiac arrest can happen before or after a heart attack."

"What caused it?" Effie wanted to know.

"Derek will need more tests, but at this point, we believe he has arrhythmia. An irregular heartbeat," the doctor clarified. "If it's just that, he'll need to go on some medication."

Some of the tightness eased in Egan's chest. Medication and not more surgery. Though, if surgery had been the fix, Egan figured his dad would have accepted that since it was far better than the alternative of having another incident like this.

"I talked with the heart specialist who's on his way, and he suggested something called an implantable cardioverter-defibrillator, an ICD." Dr. Abrams pointed to the area around his collarbone. "It's a battery powered implant that monitors the heart rhythm and can make adjustments if the heart rate spikes too high or goes too low."

The tightness in his chest returned, and Egan groaned and scrubbed his hand over his face. It helped when he felt Alana give his arm a gentle squeeze.

"Does Dad know all of this?" Egan asked Abrams. Because if so, he hadn't said anything about it in the couple of seconds that Egan had been allowed to see him in the ICU.

The doctor nodded. "I told him right before I came here to talk to you." He paused. "Of course, Derek will need some time to process this. All of you will. But he seemed…resigned."

"Yeah," Egan said just as Effie, Blue and Maybell voiced their own agreements. And maybe his dad felt that way because he'd sensed that the massive heart attack wouldn't be the last of it.

"Can he make a full recovery?" Blue asked.

Abrams dragged in a long breath. "Yes, but I need to put an asterisk on that," he was quick to add. "He can recover with proper treatment, medication and diet. It's imperative that he work on his health, but if he does, he could be an even better version of his old self in just a matter of months."

All right. That was something, at least. It meant Egan could stick to the plan of commuting. His dad would get any and all medical treatment he needed, and then slowly, over that *matter of months*, Derek could return to managing the ranch that he loved. A win-win for everyone.

"When can we see him?" Blue wanted to know.

"You can have a short visit with him now," the doctor said. "Short, as in a minute or two at most," he emphasized, and then he shifted his attention to Egan. "Since he asked specifically for you, why don't you go in first?"

Egan immediately got to his feet and tried to give the others a reassuring glance. Especially Effie. Like the rest of them, she'd already been through so much with Derek, and this had to be wearing her down.

"I won't be long," Egan told them.

Blue nodded and took out his phone. "I'll call Cal and Remi to let them know."

"And I'll call Audrey," Maybell volunteered.

Egan certainly hadn't forgotten about any of them, but he'd wanted to wait to contact them until they'd gotten word on his dad's condition. At least now it wouldn't be all gloom and doom when they were notified.

Egan gave Alana one last glance and followed Dr. Abrams out of the office and down the hall to the ICU. It'd been less than a month since his dad's initial stay here, and it seemed as if the same nurses were on duty as had been then. He stepped inside the ICU, expecting to find his father asleep or heavily medicated. But he wasn't. His dad's eyes were wide open, and he saw another of the nurses by his bedside.

"He asked me to call his wife," the nurse, Cora Kolstad, explained. "She didn't answer, but I left a message for her. I'm sure she'll call as soon as she hears the voice mail."

Since Egan only had a couple of minutes, he didn't waste that on speculation as to what Audrey might or might not do. He went to his dad and took hold of his hand.

"How are you?" Egan asked.

His dad wasn't quick to answer. "Been better," he finally said. He didn't add anything else until Cora had walked away. "I had a gut feeling that something like this would happen."

He wasn't surprised his dad felt that way, and it was probably one of the reasons he'd been so down.

"Dr. Abrams says you'll get better," Egan spelled out for him. "In the meantime, what can I do?"

Egan expected a pat answer like you're already doing it, or maybe a request for him to contact his siblings or stepmother. But his dad shook his head and locked gazes with him.

"I know what I'm asking is huge," his dad muttered. "But I can't see another way around it."

"Another way around what?" Egan questioned.

"I don't think I have much time left," he said, and he lifted his hand to silence Egan when he started to dispute that. "As soon as I'm able, I plan to join Audrey at wherever she happens to be stationed."

Egan stared at him. And stared. He also had to do a couple of mental double takes to try to figure out if his dad had just said that.

"You want to be with Audrey?" Egan spelled out.

"I do." His dad groaned softly but didn't break eye contact. "It hurts to be at the ranch, to see, hear and be around all the things I can't do."

Egan wished he didn't know how his dad felt. But he did. Because this was one of his own battles. Fighter pilots didn't have lifelong careers. Sure, they could remain in the military for thirty years or more, but flying wouldn't be their primary or even their secondary jobs. Far from it. Egan was damn close to that point now.

"I understand," Egan muttered.

"Good." His dad closed his eyes and gave a weary sigh. "I hate to do this, Egan, I just can't do this anymore. The ranch is yours now."

EGAN TRIED TO stay on autopilot while he sorted through the upcoming weekly tasks for the ranch. Something he'd already done for the things he had on his schedule for his job at the base.

Over the past five days since his father's announcement that the ranch was his now, Egan had tried to adapt that autopilot mode as much as possible. Later, he'd have to process the emotion and the reality of it, but for now, he just kept moving.

He glanced over a proposal that Jesse had worked up for the purchase of some horses that would add some prime breed stock to the ranch. Unlike the invoices and such, this wasn't mundane work. This was the heart of the ranch, and it could affect the profits and the ranch's reputation for years to come. If he approved this new direction Jesse was suggesting, then...

Egan stopped short of mentally spelling out the impact, but he couldn't deny the kick of adrenaline it gave him. Not exactly like being in the cockpit, but he could understand why this had been enough to keep his dad going.

Of course, that was no longer true for his dad, and before Egan could throttle back into autopilot, he went back through the other things that would be happening today. His dad would be released from the hospital this morning and then later in the day, there was Jack's life celebration.

The hospital release was great news because it meant his dad was recovering on his new meds and monitor. The second event, however, could end up being a hornet's nest. Egan was just hoping that Alana came through it unscathed.

He missed her. Bad. Not just the sex, either. He missed being with her. They'd managed a few short visits over the past five days, but their work schedules and Egan's trips back and forth to the hospital had all but eliminated any free time. He hoped that changed after today.

Then again, a lot of things were going to change.

The latest email from Audrey reminded him of that, and he glanced through it to see if there was anything new. There was no firm date for his dad to join Audrey at her current assignment at the Pentagon, but his stepmom was onboard with her husband being with her. So onboard that she'd insisted she could arrange medical transport for him and could set him up with a new doctor at the top-notch medical center in nearby Maryland.

Egan responded to Audrey's email with a thanks for keeping me updated, and he checked the time. It'd be at least an hour before his dad was released, but he wanted to get there ahead of time since it would also be his chance to say goodbye to Blue. His brother had extended his leave an extra day but had to fly back to his base at noon.

He hurried downstairs and found Effie and Maybell, not having their usual morning coffee but rather sorting through the latest round of food that people had brought over. Both women immediately stopped and gave him long once-overs. Something they'd been doing since his dad's announcement.

I just can't do this anymore. The ranch is yours now.

Alana and Blue had done it as well, no doubt looking for signs that Egan was about to crack. There might be cracks, but he had no intention of even trying to deal with his own feelings until his dad's release and the life celebration were behind him.

"Reba picked up your dress blues uniform from the cleaners," Maybell let him know. "I figured you'd be wearing that to the festivities."

Egan hadn't considered what he'd wear. Too bad cloaking devices for clothes wasn't a real thing since he intended to attend but didn't want to stand out. Something that Tilly would want as well.

"Tell Reba thanks," he said, "but I'll probably just wear what I have on." Which was jeans, a blue button-up shirt and his cowboy boots. That meant he'd look like at least half the other attendees.

Maybell made a "suit yourself" shrug that she'd probably meant to look casual, but she was still examining him to make sure he was okay. Ditto for Effie, so he tried to diffuse their concerns by kissing them both on the cheek and grabbing a huge chocolate chip cookie from the "get well soon" stash. He was hoping it'd be hard to worry over someone who could chow down on what appeared to be a kilo of chocolate for breakfast.

"You want to take a cookie out to the woman waiting in the car?" Effie asked him, stopping Egan in his tracks.

"What woman?" he wanted to know.

"Don't know," Maybell piped in. "She was parked

out there when I came in for work about an hour ago. A pretty brunette. I figure she's one of Blue's conquests. And yes, I know what your brother gets up to," she added. "But I've never seen her before."

Egan frowned. "Did you talk to her and ask her what she wanted?"

"I said hello and asked if I could help her, and she said she was here to see you. It could still be about Blue," Maybell tacked on to that.

Yeah, it could be, but if so, it'd likely be bad news. Like maybe she was pregnant or something. Still, if that were the case, then Egan couldn't figure out why she'd wanted to see him instead of Blue.

He didn't grab the second cookie that Effie was offering but instead made his way out of the kitchen and around to the front of the house where he saw the vintage cherry red Mustang parked in the circular drive. He also saw the attractive brunette who stepped from it.

One look at the woman and Egan understood Maybell's initial impressions. She was exactly Blue's type. Long hair tumbling over her shoulders, snug jeans and an equally snug top. Before he'd joined the military, Blue had had some success in the rodeo as a bronc rider and had had his share of what some referred to with the unflattering term *buckle bunnies*. Egan thought this might be one of them.

"Lieutenant Colonel Donnelly," she greeted, causing him to rethink that unflattering label. The rank had just rolled off her tongue as if she were accustomed to saying it. And Blue was a major, not a lieutenant colonel.

He nodded and went closer, trying to pick through her features to see if there was anything he recognized about her. He didn't. "I'm sorry, but do I know you?" he came out and asked.

She hesitated. "I thought you might."

Egan sighed. Blue didn't make a habit of spilling any details about the women in his life, but perhaps this visitor believed he had. "Look, if this is about my brother Blue, he's at the hospital with our dad."

"It's not about your brother," she insisted and then paused again. "I'm Melinda Gorman."

As Effie and Maybell had just done, this woman studied him, and he was pretty sure she was looking for some reaction. And Egan had one, all right. But probably not the reaction of recognition that she wanted.

He shook his head.

"Major Melinda Gorman," she supplied.

Still nothing. Well, nothing other than it told him she was military, army, Marines or Air Force since major wasn't a Navy rank.

He suddenly got a bad thought. "Are you here about one of the pilots in the squadron I command?" he asked.

"No. I'm here about Jack," she muttered, her voice barely a whisper.

Of all the things Egan had thought she might say, that wasn't one of them. Nor was it something he

wanted to hear because his mind had no trouble filling in the blanks.

"Jack," he repeated.

She nodded. "I was the woman he was, uh, seeing."

Yeah, Egan had already gone there, and he automatically took a step back. It'd been a little less than
a month since he'd learned that his best friend had
been cheating.

Cheating on Alana.

During that month, he'd built up a lot of resentment
for this other woman. He'd built up some resentment
for Jack, too, and he was certain that was coming
through loud and clear because Melinda moved back
as well.

"I'm sorry," she said. "But would it be possible
for us to talk?"

He didn't want to talk to her. He didn't want to see
her because it made Jack's affair even more real. It
brought the past back, and it slammed the hell right
into him. Again.

"My dad's being released from the hospital today,"
he managed to say. "I was on my way there now."

She nodded, glanced around, and that's when he
saw that she was blinking back tears. "Maybe I could
ride with you and we could talk along the way? It's
important," she added when he'd been about to shake
his head. "There are some things I need to tell you
about Jack."

Until she'd added that last part, Egan had been prepared to go through with the headshake and a refusal.
He wasn't sure he could handle this, especially not

today, but he also couldn't just go back in time and prevent this woman from showing up out of the blue.

"All right," he finally said. "But it's a short drive."

"That's okay. If it's all right, can I leave my car here? Then, I can Uber back to get it."

Egan didn't point out that Uber services were in short supply in Emerald Creek, but there was a taxi. Sort of. Henriette Miller, who was pushing seventy, had bought a used taxicab and provided that service when the mood suited her. Still, he wasn't going to worry about how Melinda got back to the ranch. That was her problem.

"Look," he said as they walked to his truck, "if you're thinking about going to Jack's life celebration this afternoon, that's not a good idea."

He didn't get into the details about what it would do to Alana or Tilly to have the other woman show up. It'd be a hard blow for both of them. Well, for Alana, anyway. Tilly would likely just keep on believing that Jack hadn't had an affair and cause Tilly to believe Melinda was lying.

"I hadn't planned on going to that," Melinda said. "But I have been keeping up with the details about it on social media." She didn't add anything else until they were in his truck. "Uh, does Jack's wife know about me?"

Egan took a moment to decide what or what not to say. "She knows he had an affair." He set the cookie on the dash, started the engine and glanced at her as he drove away. "Why did you come to see me?"

She took a deep breath. She also took her time

answering and must have decided the scenery was a good way to avoid eye contact with him because she pinned her gaze to the window.

"You were his best friend," she finally said. "Jack worshipped you. Loved you. I just figured if anyone knew about me, it'd be you."

Egan cursed, and he didn't bother to keep it mild or under his breath. "Well, he didn't tell me so that blows your theory about him worshipping me."

"It doesn't," she assured him. "If he didn't tell you, it was probably because he wouldn't have wanted you to think the worst about him."

"I sure as heck would have done that since he was cheating on his wife," Egan snarled, but he immediately had to amend that. "No, I wouldn't have thought the worst about him, but I would have given him hell for what he was doing."

Melinda smiled, but he didn't think there was any humor in it. "Yes, he said you would. Jack also said he was going to tell you."

"Well, he didn't." Egan's voice was still a snarl, but some of the fury was gone. Some. Not enough, though, for him to ease the white-knuckle grip he had on the steering wheel.

"I guess he didn't get the chance."

"Yeah, there was a lot of that going around." Alana hadn't gotten the chance to try to resolve things with her husband. Egan hadn't been able to talk to his best friend about Colleen walking out on him. And Jack hadn't had time to spill about his dicking around with this woman.

Egan reined in and cursed himself. All right, maybe he would have thought the worst about Jack, but his reaction was being filtered through the feelings that Egan had developed for Alana.

Deep feelings.

That made him hurt as much as she had over Jack's affair. Back then, though, three years ago, Egan figured he would have had an entirely different mindset.

"I drove Jack to RAF Mildenhall where he was flying out to go see you," Melinda continued after several moments. "He told me that his wife had found some charges on his credit card and that she'd confronted him." She swallowed hard. No smile now. "Jack broke things off with me. He said he loved his wife and that he wanted to make things work with her."

Oh, that brought back some of the fury. "If he loved her, then why did he start seeing you in the first place?"

"It's complicated," she insisted.

"Don't you dare say it just happened," he snapped when he remembered what Remi had told him.

"Okay. Then, I'll say it shouldn't have happened, but it did."

"Maybe you can justify that if it'd only been once, but it wasn't. You had an affair with a married man." Once again, he reined in. "And a married man had an affair with you."

"Jack and I were together for three days. So, I guess that's technically an affair, but for part of that, we were together for a memorial service."

Egan frowned and pulled into the lot of the hospital. He parked and turned to her, waiting for an explanation. Before she could say anything, though, he caught the movement from the corner of his eye and turned to see Alana making her way toward him.

Shit.

Talk about the worst timing. He didn't want her to see Melinda, but here Alana was, already tapping on his truck window. She was smiling, but that evaporated in a hurry when she saw the woman in the passenger seat.

Egan had no idea what he was going to say to Alana, but he lowered the window, hoping that he would come up with something that would spare her an emotional bashing.

He didn't.

Her gaze fixed on Melinda. "Oh," Alana said.

Just that. That one little word that was proof that the emotional bashing had happened, anyway.

Alana repeated her "Oh," but this time it seemed to have a bunch of denials and a string of no's attached to it. She did a fast about-face and hurried away.

CHAPTER TWENTY-THREE

ALANA WISHED SHE could sprout wings and fly at the speed of a fighter jet. That would get her away from Egan and the woman in his truck. That would get her to a hiding place where she could try to wrap her mind around what she'd just seen.

The shock gave her enough adrenaline to help with her speedy exit out of the parking lot, but she didn't get far before she heard the running footsteps behind her. Without looking back, she knew it was Egan. He'd come to apologize, explain, maybe even grovel.

None of which she especially wanted to hear.

Egan made it inside the hospital only seconds after she did, and he jogged until he was right by her side. There were people milling around so she thought that might earn her a few seconds where she didn't have to respond to anything he might say. But she was wrong.

"She's not an old girlfriend or anything like that," Egan whispered, taking hold of her arm.

"No," she whispered back. "She was Jack's girlfriend."

His grip tightened on her arm a bit, and he looked at her. What he thankfully didn't do was try to slow her down. Probably because he understood this was not a discussion best had in a public place. He held off saying anything else until they were in her office.

"How did you know?" he asked the moment the door was shut.

Alana felt the weariness and a whole bunch of other feelings seep all the way to the bone. "The look she gave me. It wasn't an 'oops, I just got caught in the truck with your lover' expression. It was a much deeper guilt. I've seen it plenty of times when I look in the mirror," she added in a mutter.

He cursed, put his hands on his hips and stared at her as if he might dole out a lecture about guilt. But then he backed off and groaned.

"What does she want?" Alana came out and asked.

Egan shook his head and looked as weary as she suddenly felt. "I'm not sure. Forgiveness, maybe."

Of course. What else? Guilty consciences spurred all sorts of reaction. "Well, I hope she doesn't try to get that from Tilly. Or me." Then, something occurred to her. "Or you. Why did she go to you?"

"She seemed to think I knew about the affair. And I believe she wanted me to know that Jack had broken things off right before he got on the aircraft to come and see me."

"So, she blames herself for his death," Alana grumbled, and she would have laughed had it not made her want to cry.

"Maybe," he admitted. "This could be sort of like that letter Colleen wrote me. She could want to make amends, and she might have started with me to test the waters before coming to you. She won't be coming to you," Egan insisted.

It sounded very much like a military order. And part of Alana appreciated it. He was trying to protect her. But that wouldn't work. Jack's lover was here in Emerald Creek, and even if Alana never set eyes on her again, she would always have the image of her.

"She's beautiful," Alana admitted. "Then again, why cheat with someone ugly, huh?"

On a sigh, Egan went to her and pulled her into his arms. "You're prettier than she is."

That made her smile. For a split second, anyway. "I want to talk to her."

Egan was already shaking his head before he even eased back to face her. "You don't have to do that."

Again, he was the hero to the rescue, trying to protect her. "I know. But this seems to be a good day for opening up old wounds. Maybe clearing out the gunk. And re-healing."

He kept shaking his head. "I don't think you'll get all of that from her."

"Probably not," Alana agreed. "But I'd still like to talk to her. Can you get her in here so that can happen?"

Oh, the debate came, and she could see every bit of the battle playing out in his eyes. She must have had enough resolve, though, in her own eyes to make him finally nod. After he cursed some more, that is.

"I'll go get her," he griped, and he turned and started for the door.

"By the way, what's her name? I'd rather use her name than call her skanky husband screwer."

Egan's breath came out like a sigh. "It's Melinda Gorman. Major Melinda Gorman," he clarified. "But if you go with skanky husband screwer, I'll back you up."

She nodded, and they shared a brief dry smile before he left to go fetch the woman who had given Alana plenty of sleepless nights, elevated blood pressure and mega jolts of anger over the past three years.

Alana cursed herself when she took out the cosmetics bag from her desk and touched up her makeup. This wasn't a "who's prettier" competition. But in a way, it felt like one. After all, her husband had been attracted enough to this woman to ditch his vows and land in bed with her.

It only took a couple of minutes before there was a single knock at her door, and after she managed a "Come in," Egan did just that. His expression seemed to ask if she still wanted to go through with this so Alana nodded. That caused Egan to step out of the doorway so that Melinda could enter.

Even though Alana had gotten a good look at the woman when she'd been in Egan's truck, she took an even more thorough one now. Definitely beautiful, but it was more than that. Alana suspected that when Melinda wasn't in the groveling mode, which she clearly was at the moment, she exuded a boatload of confidence and charisma.

"I want to stay," Egan immediately said.

Alana wasn't surprised. However, she wished she'd

better thought this through. She was all for hearing the truth, but what would hurt her could also hurt Egan. If things turned in that direction, Alana would put an end to this visit. Or maybe she could do that even sooner.

"You're here to take your dad home," Alana reminded him.

He checked the time. "I have about a half hour, and Blue is with him."

Apparently, that was Melinda's cue to start talking. "If you want to hear any apologies from me, then I'm sorry," she said, looking straight at Alana. "I'm so sorry that you were hurt. Sorry that Jack got hurt as well."

"There weren't many winners in this," Alana conceded, still studying Melinda and hating that it felt as if she were sizing up the competition. "So, other than an apology, what do you want to tell me?"

Melinda lifted her shoulder. "I'll tell you anything you want to hear. Anything. Damn the torpedoes," Melinda muttered. "Full speed ahead."

All righty, then. If the woman was going to offer up one of Jack's favorite sayings, then Alana would take her up on it.

"Did Jack come onto you or did you come onto him?" Alana asked.

"I came onto him," Melinda insisted without even a moment of hesitation and while looking straight at Alana.

Alana studied the woman's eyes, which she supposed some would call sparkling blue. "Liar," Alana concluded.

Some of that sparkle vanished. "All right. It was mutual, I guess. Jack and I were in ROTC together so we were old friends. Also, Taylor had just been killed, and Jack and I were dealing with that. We ended up together at the memorial service. And then afterward, too."

"Taylor?" Alana repeated, and she thumbed back through her memory. "A CRO buddy of Jack's who died during a rescue?" She recalled Jack mentioning him in their next to last phone call.

Melinda nodded. "Taylor was also my kid brother. Jack was his supervisor and insisted on going with the notification team to tell me. I was stationed at a base in England then, and Taylor's girlfriend was from London. She's the one who arranged a memorial service that Jack and I both attended. We were sort of grieving together…and I'm sure you don't want to hear this."

"You're right," Alana verified. "I don't want to hear it, but I also don't want to spend another minute trying to figure out why I wasn't enough for my husband." Egan groaned and would have no doubt gone to her for his special brand of Top Gun TLC, but Alana waved him off. "I just want to know what was going on in Jack's head. I want to know why."

She could tell Egan still didn't care much for this line of questioning, but he nodded, letting her know that he understood. Of course, he did. It hadn't taken this meeting with the other woman for Alana to know that Egan understood so very much of her life. And so very much about her.

"I could say the affair wasn't about you," Melinda answered, "but that sounds insulting. It's the truth, but it's still insulting."

"Then, what was it about?" Alana demanded, already guessing where Melinda would go with this. Guessing, too, that it would be the truth.

"The affair was about the grief," she said. "We were just trying to get through a really bad time."

"Then, Jack should have come home to me to help him get through that *really bad time*."

Alana's voice broke on that last word, and she cursed the response. Cursed, too, that she had to fight back tears since it was that first sign of tears that had Egan going to her side and pulling her to him.

She welcomed the comfort but, oh, there was an irony here. She was cursing tears for Jack seeking comfort with another woman while she was seeking comfort with his best friend. Of course, the difference was—and it was a massive one—had either Egan or she been married, then the comforting wouldn't have led to sex. No way.

And that was a line that Jack had crossed.

"Yes, Jack should have gone to you," Melinda admitted, "and I should have acted out on my grief elsewhere."

There it was. The admission that Alana had wanted to hear. An admission didn't fix squat. At the end of the day, why did the reason even matter?

It didn't.

And that was quite a nice revelation to feel. It didn't matter because that part of her life was over. Jack was dead and buried, and while a part of her would always love him, and never actually forgive him, he was her past. So was this woman standing in front of her.

"You should know that I didn't come here today to see you," Melinda went on. "I came to talk to Egan to help me make up my mind about what I should do. Whether or not I should talk to you or Jack's mother."

Alana stumbled over her first attempt to answer. "It would be a lousy idea to tell Tilly that you cheated with her son. I've already tried, and she doesn't believe it."

Melinda's eyes widened. "You told her that Jack had an affair with me?"

"Well, I didn't say specifically with you because I didn't know your name, but yes, I gave her the broad strokes. I regret that, by the way. I was angry when I said it and I should have kept it to myself." Alana paused to do more studying of the woman's expression. "Why would you want her to know, anyway?"

The color drained from Melinda's beautiful face, and Alana saw the hesitation. And more. Unfortunately, Alana didn't have time to steel herself up for what Melinda was about to say.

"Because the affair isn't just about me," Melinda said. "It's about Easton. Jack's son."

EGAN WASN'T SURE who was more stunned by what Melinda had just said, but he thought it was a tie between Alana and him. This was the absolute first time Egan had heard even a whiff of Jack having a son.

"Uh, you got pregnant?" Alana asked, her voice

wobbly. Since she seemed wobbly, too, he slid his arm around her waist.

"I did," Melinda admitted in a whisper. "Jack didn't know. I didn't find out until weeks after he died."

"And you decided not to tell anyone?" Egan asked at the same moment Alana said, "Where is he? Where's Jack's son?"

Apparently, Melinda decided to go with Alana's questions first because she turned toward her. "He's with my mom in Austin. He's two now. Would you like to see a picture?" she asked, taking her phone from her pocket.

"No," Alana said, and she repeated it in a hoarse whisper.

Hell, this was going to cause Alana to spiral straight back to that pit of grief. Or maybe worse. Because the affair wasn't just an affair that she could possibly dismiss. There was a child involved. Jack's child.

Melinda looked at Egan. "And, no, I didn't tell anyone except my mom who Easton's father was. At first, I was just so bogged down with the pain of losing Jack that I didn't think to tell anyone else. I especially didn't want you to know because it would have hurt you."

Yes, and it was hurting her now. Egan wanted to get Alana the hell out of there, but leaving wasn't going to fix this. This wasn't something Alana would just be able to forget.

"Then, I saw the social media posts about the

life celebration," Melinda went on. "I could tell that Jack's mother was desperately missing him, and I started to think that I had no right to keep Easton from her. After all, she is his grandmother."

True, but for Tilly to accept that, she'd have to first accept that Jack had, indeed, had an affair, and he wasn't sure the woman would ever be ready for that. Then again, the little boy would be proof that maybe even Tilly couldn't deny.

"So, do you think I should tell Tilly about Easton?" Melinda asked.

Egan didn't have a clue, and he didn't want to waste any mental energy trying to figure it out. Right now, his mental energy belonged to Alana.

"I don't know," Egan muttered.

Melinda nodded as if that was exactly what she'd expected him to say. "I booked a room at the inn here in town," she said. "I'll take the day to think about it." She turned to Alana, then. "You should know that Jack loved you very much."

Alana shook her head, turned away. "He obviously didn't love me enough."

Melinda opened her mouth, no doubt to try to convince Alana otherwise, but Egan hurled a few eye daggers at the woman to get her to back off. There was nothing Melinda could say now to make this better. Nothing she could do, either.

In fact, this whole shitstorm could end up getting a whole lot worse if word got out that Jack had had an affair and fathered a child. That would throw Alana right into the mix of the gossip and the fresh grief.

"I need to check on my dad," Egan muttered to Alana. "Any chance you'd go with me for that?"

Of course, she shook her head again. "I think I just need a minute or two to myself."

That came as no surprise, but he didn't like the idea of leaving her. Especially not leaving her alone with Melinda. The woman didn't seem to have malicious intentions, but she could still carve out more pieces of Alana if she went on and on about how much Jack had loved his wife.

Egan stared at Melinda until she came to the right conclusion. "I'll just be going," she said. She opened her mouth as if about to add more, but Egan's stare must have changed her mind about that, too, because she muttered, "Again, I'm sorry," before she left the office, shutting the door behind her.

Egan pulled Alana even closer to him, trying to give her whatever he could to help ease the pain she had to be feeling. He expected her to break down and cry. Or curse and yell.

But that didn't happen.

She stayed in his arms for a couple of minutes, and then she eased back to meet his gaze. There were no tears in her eyes now. Just a whole lot of sadness that cut him to the bone.

"You should go see your father," she insisted. "I'll be okay."

That last part had to be a lie. Well, a lie at the moment, anyway. Alana had already been through hell and back, and while this would no doubt be a serious setback, she would weather it.

Just not today.

"Go see your father," Alana repeated. "We can talk after you've got him back home." She checked the time and did do some cursing. "Or maybe after the life celebration."

Of course, she'd still insist on going to that. He would, too, but Egan hoped it would be short appearances for both of them.

He wasn't going to think about how the next couple of days would play out if Melinda did tell Tilly about her having Jack's son. For now, he was just going to get through the morning and life celebration, and then he could try to help Alana deal with all of this.

"I'll be right back," he assured her. Though, he wasn't sure how he was going to manage that, but he'd work out something with Blue and his dad.

Egan looked down at her, giving her one last check to see if those tears had started. They hadn't. So he dropped a kiss on her mouth and hurried out, hoping to quickly resolve things with his dad so he could get back to her.

He hurried away from her office and around the hall to his dad's room, and he spotted Blue on the phone outside the door. Blue spotted him, too, and finished up the call right away.

"Dad's on the phone with Audrey," Blue explained. "I thought I'd give them a minute or two." He stopped and looked at Egan. "Is everything all right?"

Obviously, Alana wasn't the only one who looked

shell-shocked from Melinda's confession. "Tough day," Egan settled for saying.

"Does it have anything to do with the woman who showed up at the ranch this morning?" Blue asked, and then he added. "That was Granny Effie on the phone. She saw you drive away with her, and she was worried about you. She wondered if the woman had anything to do with Tilly's visit to the sheriff's office."

Egan shook his head. "What visit to the sheriff's office?"

Blue huffed and clearly wasn't happy about being the messenger for this. "Tilly wanted to get the sheriff to file charges against you for endangering Jack's life. She's apparently already written a letter to your commander, asking for the same thing. She wants you charged and court-martialed."

"Oh, for Pete's sake," Egan grumbled.

A couple of weeks ago, Egan would have believed wholeheartedly that he deserved those charges. That was despite his being cleared of any wrongdoing during the official military investigation of Jack's death. He'd never felt as if he deserved total absolution, but he was getting damn tired of Tilly coming at him like this. Didn't the woman know that nothing she did was going to bring back her son? And that all these angry maneuvers would only end up hurting Alana by constantly bringing up the past?

"No, the visitor doesn't have anything to do with that," Egan said, and he decided to go with the condensed version. "That was the woman Jack had an affair with."

"Oh," was all Blue said for several moments while he clearly tried to process that. "And this woman…" He waved that off. "How's Alana?"

"It's been a tough day," Egan repeated. "In fact, I need to ask you a favor. Will you still be able to make your flight if you take Dad home? If not, I'll see if Jesse can do it."

"I can take him," Blue insisted, "and if I miss my flight, I'll just get another one." He paused. "Exactly how tough is it for Alana?"

Egan had a quick debate and went with the truth. "This woman who showed up says she's the mother of Jack's son."

"Holy shit," Blue said. "You believe her?"

"Yeah, I do." In this day and age, it would be too easy to prove paternity, and besides, he couldn't see a reason for Melinda to lie. "She's in town, trying to decide if she wants to tell Tilly that she has a grandchild."

"Holy shit," Blue repeated, but this time his tone wasn't solely one of surprise. There was some dread mixed with it.

Egan went with a repeat response as well and muttered a "Yeah."

Alana was already reeling from the news, but the reeling was only going to escalate. Especially if Tilly found out. And as much as Egan hated to admit it, Tilly did deserve to know. Heck, Jack's son should know as well so he could have the chance to be around his grandmother.

"Where's Alana now?" Blue asked. "She's not with this other woman, is she?"

Egan shook his head. "She's in her office. The woman, Melinda Gorman, should be on her way to the inn."

And that would cause some gossip, too, with folks wondering who Melinda was and why she was in town. Then again, the life celebration might be the perfect cover for her arrival if people believed she'd come for that.

"Go to Alana," Blue insisted.

Egan considered just doing a quick check on his dad first, but one look at his face and his dad would know something was wrong. Once his dad was back home and he'd made sure that Alana was as all right as she could be, then Egan would explain everything to him.

"Thanks," Egan told Blue.

He hurried back down the hall to Alana's office and knocked once before he opened the door. And saw that Alana wasn't there. Egan didn't curse. Not yet, anyway. Instead, he checked the vending area.

No sign of her.

He then knocked on the door of the women's restroom, and when there was no response, he opened the door a fraction. "Alana?" he softly called out.

"I saw her leave a couple of minutes ago," someone said from behind him. It was a nurse, Nellie Parsons, and she smiled as if happy to provide that info.

But Egan sure as hell wasn't happy. "Any idea where she went?" he asked, trying not to sound so worried that it would alarm Nellie.

It was already too late for that, though. Nellie was clearly alarmed. "I'm not sure. Uh, is she upset because the life celebration is dredging up so many bad memories for her?"

Egan made a sound that could have meant anything, and he headed back to Alana's office to see if she'd left her purse, and therefore her keys and phone, behind. She hadn't. However, there was a note on the center of her desk.

Now he cursed and wanted to throttle himself for not staying with her. He should have called Blue to let him know there was a problem and not have left her side.

Hell. He had to find Alana now.

CHAPTER TWENTY-FOUR

AFTER SHE ENDED her call, Alana sat in Egan's cabin and stared out the window. Waiting for Egan, knowing he'd come because he would be worried sick about her.

Even though she'd left him a note on her desk, one where she'd insisted she was *all right and just needed some time to think*, there was no chance that Egan would just accept that "all right" status and not check on her himself.

Since there wasn't any place in Emerald Creek she could go where Egan wouldn't have found her, she'd opted to come here. A sort of hiding in plain sight along with killing two birds with one stone. It would put Egan on the ranch where his father was. And it would give them some privacy while Egan tried to do the only thing he could possibly do.

Be her hero.

She wasn't sure if that particular trait was because of his DNA or if it'd been drilled into him during his military training. Maybe a combination of both. Either way, he would try his damndest to make things better for her, to soothe her old wounds. The new ones, too, that Melinda's confession had given her. Egan would try to kiss it all away.

Alana just might let him try, too.

But he'd fail.

Because this was too big of a fix even for Egan.

For now, though, she pushed aside the inevitable doom and gloom and welcomed the quiet moments where she could sit at his breakfast table. Moments where she could try to clear her mind enough so she could start sorting through the stew of feelings that were boiling and bubbling inside her.

Thankfully, the cabin hadn't been locked, and the view outside Egan's kitchen window was ideal for peaceful thoughts, serenity and yes, even a little mind clearing. The picture-perfect acres of pastures and the horses that looked regal and expensive. A rider was on what she thought was one of the ranch's cutting horses and was herding up some of the Andalusians, maybe to move them elsewhere.

The rider made the turns and maneuvers look effortless, and she was pretty sure there was some kind of life lesson in that. But Alana couldn't figure out what.

Beside her on the table was a pile of flower remains. Petals, stems and leaves from the handful of lazy daisies she'd picked and brought into the cabin with her. According to flowers number two, five and six, she shouldn't be here. According to numbers one, three and four, she should be.

Since it was a tie, Alana had decided the tiebreaker was the ladybug she'd accidentally brought in with her flower stash. Before Alana had put the bug back outside, it had crawled over what she was certain was a petal from the number three daisy, and that had been enough to get her to stay.

She heard the sound of the approaching vehicle. Egan, no doubt. She checked the time and saw that it'd been less than a half hour since she'd arrived so that meant one of the hands, Maybell or Effie had seen her car heading toward the cabin and told him. Of course, she'd known that would happen and secretly counted on it.

Sighing, she got up from the table and flicked away the photo that she had pulled up on her phone. That was another element of the emotional stew that she'd save for another time.

She walked toward the door, stopped, and then decided to do something that just might convince Egan that she wasn't about to lose her mind. Then again, he might think this was proof of such mind loss. But for a minute or two, it would distract him, and therefore, it would distract her.

Alana yanked off her dress to the sound of the vehicle door shutting and then got into a battle with her bra. The hook jammed or something so she twisted it around. Not the best idea she'd ever had because the right cup was still clinging to her right breast while the other one was jammed in such a way to make it look as if she were wearing some kind of extreme push-up device meant to show off her cleavage.

Alana stopped the battle when she heard the footsteps and got a horrible thought. What if this wasn't Egan? What if it was Blue, Jesse or one of the other hands? That sent her scrambling for her dress.

Just as the front door opened.

It was Egan, and the sound of relief she made was loud and contained a lot of breath gushing. That could have been the reason he froze because he wouldn't have been expecting her to be relieved about much of anything. But Alana figured the near nudity was playing into his reaction as well.

"Are, uh, you okay?" Egan asked, stepping inside and shutting the door behind him.

Alana couldn't help herself. She laughed because clearly she was far from okay. The laughter jangled with nerves. And yes, some fear. Fear that her life would always be that jangle she was feeling now.

She went with another impulse. "For now, please don't be the good guy you are," she said.

His forehead was already bunched up, but that created even more bunching. Obviously, she needed to explain that. Which, of course, wouldn't be easy, but she gave it a try.

"I don't want you to keep your hands off me because you think I'm not capable of making a wise decision." All right, not her best attempt so she tried again. "You wouldn't kiss a drunk woman, but I don't want you to think of me as drunk. Or drunk-ish." She fanned her hand over her body. "I know this will lead to sex, and it's what I want."

She glanced down at herself and laughed again. With her bra still at odds with her and her dress wadded up in front of her stomach, she wasn't exactly a vision of a sex goddess.

Egan pulled in a long breath as if he was certain

he was going to need it and others. He went to her, slipped his hand around the back of her neck and brushed a too-tame kiss on her lips. When he sniffed her breath, she realized he was, indeed, checking to see if she was drunk.

"You wouldn't be taking advantage of me," she insisted.

"I'm not so sure about that," he muttered. He grimaced and groaned after she bumped her body against his. "I don't want to do anything you'd regret."

"See?" Alana said, as if that proved her point. "That's why I told you to not be the good guy. I want someone a little lecherous. I want lusty and randy." She drew a blank on any other synonyms. "I want… you," she clarified.

"Why?" he countered. "I mean, why do you want me now?"

She hated the logic. Hated that he was right to question her. She just wanted to forget, and that meant she was using him. Or rather *trying* to use him.

When she blew out a string of sighs, he scooped her up and carried her to the sofa. "You should be with your dad," she muttered.

"My dad's fine. He's at home being pampered by Maybell and Effie." He sat down with her on his lap. "I think at the moment you need me more than he does."

She did. Mercy, did she. She hadn't had cardiac arrest, but the crushing pain in her chest was almost physical.

Using just the tip of his finger, he gently moved a

strand of hair off her cheek. "Do you want to talk or would you rather I get that bra untangled from your nipple?" he asked. "It's sort of poking out there between the jammed up and twisted strap."

She glanced down to confirm that was true, and with more groaning, she buried her face against his shoulder. "Please tell me that you were at least a little tempted to jump me where I stood and that you weren't just feeling pity for me."

"Oh, I definitely had thoughts of jumping you. Still do," he whispered, giving her earlobe a nip. "But I guess I just can't ditch that good streak."

Truer words had never been spoken, and that only added to her misery. Because Egan would always think of her as Jack's widow. Correction, as Jack's wronged widow. Egan would never be free to love her.

That left sex.

If that was all they could have, then so be it. It would have to be enough.

"Just sex," she heard herself say. Just a mind-blowing distraction that she desperately needed.

Figuring she was risking rejection, Alana kissed him. She felt the resistance, all right. His muscles went hard. The tension came off him in waves. But the instant erection was a good sign.

"I'm sure," she said, murmuring it against his mouth and taking the kiss to the next level. "I'm really, really sure."

She would have added a thousand reallys if necessary, but those two seemed to do the job. That and she ran her hand between them and pressed her palm to his erection.

Egan cursed, maybe aiming it at her, maybe at himself, but he lost the choke hold he had on all that goodness. He returned the kiss, and the hot and hungry urgency came through loud and clear.

His mouth went to her breasts, kissing whatever parts were not covered by the bra. He was moving fast, maybe so it wouldn't give him a chance to change his mind. Alana went with that and upped the speed, too, figuring this was going to be a desperate kind of quickie.

She didn't bother with his shirt but instead went after his belt. Thankfully, it cooperated and gave her speedy access to his zipper. Alana shoved it down, immediately sliding her hand into his boxers.

He did more cursing and yanked off her panties. Not down her legs, either. The thin fabric ripped, and he tossed them aside. Egan reached in his pocket, pulled out a condom and had it on in record time. He took hold of her hips and thrust inside her.

Yes, this was where battle and speed mattered. Apparently, so did extreme, intense pleasure. Because that's exactly what he gave her. He moved inside her. Harder, deeper, faster. Until Alana lost her breath and didn't care if she ever found it again. She just held on and let Egan give her exactly what she'd asked for.

Sex, with him.

Yes, it was enough. Not just for their future but for the climax he gave her that had her skyrocketing to that amazing place of pure pleasure and mindlessness. She felt him go down that same slippery slope as he came.

Alana didn't move. Couldn't. Her muscles had disappeared. But that was okay, too, because it meant she could just stay put with her head on his shoulder. Body to body. His breath mingling with hers while he was still inside her. She wanted to just stay like this for hours. Maybe even longer.

But she couldn't.

She also couldn't avoid eye contact, either. He wouldn't see the guilt that he no doubt expected to see there, but Alana suspected he'd be able to see something deeper. That tangled mix of still-healing wounds and fear.

"I'm still planning on going to the life celebration," she said. Talk about an inappropriate post-sex subject. "But my suggestion is that you stay away."

His eyebrow rose. "Why?"

"It's not that I don't want you there," she quickly qualified. "But there's going to be trouble. Right before you got here, I called the inn and spoke to Melinda."

His eyebrow lifted even higher, and he adjusted his posture, sitting up straighter. "Why?"

"I invited her to the life celebration," Alana admitted. "I figure it's time for a good air-clearing."

"AIR-CLEARING, MY ASS," Egan muttered as he stepped from his truck at the town's park. He had another word for what he was sure was about to happen.

Shitstorm.

It definitely wouldn't be the life celebration that Tilly had meticulously planned. Then again, what Tilly had planned was a tribute to the perfect son who never existed. Tilly wanted a whitewashed version of Jack to be hailed and praised. Which wouldn't have been so bad if the woman hadn't created that whitewash by trying to stomp down the truth. In doing so, Tilly had stomped down Alana, too.

Egan figured Alana had reached a breaking point. Not a snap but more so fed up with the lies. He couldn't blame her for that, but he still thought she was going to regret inviting Jack's lover to this event. That's why he'd tried and tried to talk her out of it. But those attempts had failed.

Of course, it was possible that Melinda simply wouldn't show. She might not even accept Alana's invitation, and Egan held on to that hope as he made his way from the truck and toward the already-gathered crowd.

Alana hadn't driven with him. After their quick round of sex, she'd headed home to shower and change, and Egan had gone to the ranch house to check on his dad. That hadn't been an especially long visit since he'd been on the phone with Audrey again, but Effie, who was skipping the celebration because of the heat, had said she'd keep an eye on him.

Even though the wind had kicked up from a storm front that was moving in, the heat was still a factor. It was the same for the dress blues uniform that Egan had decided to wear for the occasion. Even though the shit show component of this event might indeed materialize, he wanted to pay his respects to Jack. Well, partially pay respects, anyway. It occurred to him that if Jack were alive, Egan would want to punch him in the face for the mess he'd created.

With that unsettling reminder coursing through him, Egan made it to the edge of the crowd and stopped, peering over the sea of cowboy hats and even some umbrellas to try to spot Alana. He saw her on the makeshift covered podium positioned to the side of the draped easel that he assumed was holding the painting.

Tilly was there, too, dressed in mourning black, complete with a gauzy thin black scarf that looked more like a veil that'd just slipped off her head. In contrast, Alana was wearing a yellow skirt and top.

She looked pissed off.

And amazing.

Then again, Alana always looked amazing, but the riled expression might surprise some. If Tilly had noticed it, she wasn't reacting. She was waving and responding to the well-wishers who were calling out to her.

Colleen and her significant other, Anton, were there as well on the other side of Tilly. So, Anton had apparently decided not to stay home "sick" after all and Egan didn't think he was projecting when he thought both Anton and Colleen seemed to be wishing they were anywhere but there. If Alana had filled them in on what had happened, they were perhaps bracing for that shit show, too.

As the flyers had promised, there was food. An

entire school cafeteria–length table set up under another awning. The table was loaded with all sorts of dishes. Ditto for the second table behind it that had an assortment of drinks.

There was no sign of Melinda, and Egan was going to take that as a blessing. That didn't mean, however, that Alana wouldn't go through with the air-clearing. If so, and if there was the fallout that Egan was anticipating, then both Alana and Tilly were going to be hurting, bad, before this was over.

"Egan," he heard someone say, and he turned to find Jesse making his way toward him. When Jesse reached him, he glanced around the crowd just as Egan had done and then leaned in and whispered, "I'm guessing you've heard that Tilly's trying to have charges filed against you."

Egan wanted to groan. Or curse. He didn't do either. The sound he made was more of a sigh of resignation. He'd apparently made an enemy for life with Tilly.

"I've heard," Egan assured him.

"Lissa overheard the conversation Tilly had with the sheriff," Jesse went on, he said referring to Deputy Lissa Whitlock, his sister, "and Tilly also wanted to know if she could press charges against Alana."

Egan turned so fast to look at Jesse that his neck popped. "What the hell for?"

"Slander," Jesse supplied. "Or rather possible slander if Alana voices any lies about Jack."

Well, crap. The old guilt reared its ugly head to remind Egan that the woman's venom was justified.

But it wasn't. Not when the venom was aimed at Alana.

Suddenly, Egan wasn't so worried about any waves or trouble that Alana might cause at this gathering. Just the opposite. He might want to stir up some trouble of his own.

"I thought you should know," Jesse added. He tipped his head to Tilly. "She could be planning some kind of ambush to publicly smear Alana and you."

As if on cue, Tilly went to the microphone, tapped it and did the testing-testing thing that people always seemed to do. Egan's eyes automatically narrowed, and he began to thread his way through the crowd just in case he did have to come to Alana's defense.

"Hello, everyone," Tilly greeted. The wind chose that moment to flutter her veil/scarf. Flutter the drape around the painting, too. There was also a distant rumble of thunder that had the guests casting baleful glances at the sky. "Thank you all for coming to this celebration of life for United States Air Force Major Jack Davidson. As you all know, Jack isn't just my son, he's the town's true hero."

That was no doubt a dig at Egan, but he didn't object. Not to the title, anyway. But rather to the woman's use of present tense. On the surface, it didn't seem like that big of a deal, but Tilly's refusal to even acknowledge Jack's death and shortcomings was spilling over on to Alana.

Tilly looked down at a paper she was holding. "I talked to Jack's friends, teachers and fellow officers to ask them their favorite stories about him. I want to share some of those with you…"

There was another gust of wind that whipped up the scarf and blew it around Tilly's face like a muzzle. The gust also rattled the easel enough to get Tilly, Colleen and Anton scrambling to make sure it didn't tip over. The three ended up ramming into each other, which in turn caused them to ram into the easel.

Gasps and other sounds of concern rippled through the crowd, but Anton managed to get hold of the easel to steady it. Apparently, though, the wind wasn't finished because another gust lifted the fabric covering the painting. Anton moved again to stop it, but the wind won this battle. The fabric flew right up, revealing the painting.

Or rather paintings.

One was positioned on top of the other.

More sounds rippled through the crowd but none were as loud or shocked as Tilly's own reaction. Her mouth fell open, and her eyes seemingly doubled in size. She started shaking her head while she turned those widened eyes on Anton.

"It was only supposed to be this one," Tilly insisted, flinging her finger at the painting on the bottom. It was of Jack in his CRO uniform.

To Egan, it almost looked like an official portrait, void of any of Jack's personality. It seemed more suited for a promotion folder or a press release.

The painting on top wasn't like that.

And it was very familiar to Egan since it was essentially a painted reproduction of the photo of Jack and him that Alana kept in her office. The brothers-in-arms shot taken when Egan had just won Top Gun. Anton had nailed the moment. The happiness. Yeah, even the brotherhood of it. It was like being slammed with two competing oceans of grief and joy at once.

Egan's muttered profanity was drowned out by Tilly, who had apparently forgotten she was still holding the microphone.

"I didn't pay you to do that." She did more finger flinging at the top painting while her angered gaze locked on Anton. "And I don't want it here. Or anywhere else," she spat out. "I want it burned to ash. Do you hear me? I want it—"

The microphone screeched out a sound that had people covering their ears. It also stopped Tilly, and she looked around as if just recalling that she had an audience for her tirade. She swallowed hard and made a visible effort to regain her composure. However, she applied no such energies to regaining her calm.

"I didn't hire the artist to paint that," she said, speaking to the crowd now as she pointed to the top painting. "I don't want it to exist because the painting is a lie. Everything you know about that man is a lie."

Tilly wasn't pointing at the image of Jack but rather Egan, and that got people turning to him.

"Egan Donnelly lured my son into a vehicle where he was killed," Tilly went on. She wasn't crying, and Egan figured that was possibly because the muscles in her face were too tight to let any tears come through. "My son wouldn't have been anywhere near that—"

"That's not true," Alana called out, her voice somehow managing to be louder than Tilly's despite her not having a microphone.

"Hell," Egan grumbled, and he started weaving his way through the crowd again to get to Alana.

But Alana just kept on talking. "Jack and I had an argument, a really bad argument," she emphasized, "and he wanted to talk to Egan. FYI, Egan was on that transport vehicle and could have been killed, too. And he was on that vehicle so he could see Jack."

Tilly looked ready to implode. "Egan is responsible." And the woman's gaze seemed to dare Alana to disagree.

Alana dared. "No, the IED is responsible, and since this has turned into a tell-all, let me do some telling."

Tilly actually darted toward Alana, but Anton hooked his arm around the woman's waist and held her back. Even if Tilly had managed to tackle Alana, Egan wasn't sure that would have stopped her. Alana certainly didn't stop when he made it to the podium to try to talk her out of this. Instead, Alana grabbed Tilly's microphone and got to spilling.

"Jack and I had argued because he'd been having an affair," Alana announced. "With her."

Alana's pointing finger had everyone, including Egan, turning to see Melinda at the back of the crowd. Melinda looked as if she wished a big hole would swallow her up. However, it was Tilly's reaction that was the stunner. Because there was no "stunned" to it. Tilly didn't look at Melinda as the stranger who'd bedded Jack. No.

Tilly recognized her.

WTF? Had Jack told his mother about his lover? That didn't make sense, but Egan was suddenly very certain that Tilly had not only been aware of the affair but had also known the identity of Jack's lover.

"Don't do this," Tilly warned Alana. No shout this time. Just angry whispered daggers. "Don't put something out there that you can't take back."

"How did you know about Melinda?" Alana asked, clearly picking up on Tilly's reaction, too.

"She's Jack's friend," Tilly insisted. "His *friend*," she emphasized. "And Jack turned to her during his time of overwhelming grief. That's all it was. Grief. It's exactly what's happening between Egan and you, and it'll be over like that." She snapped her fingers. "And then you'll have to live with the regret of what you both have done."

Egan figured Tilly had managed to land the intended blows with those words. Words that he wished he could sure as hell deny, but there was the possibility that regret would rear its ugly head in the future.

The mutterings of the crowd grew louder, and that's when Egan realized people were moving closer. Now that the microphone wasn't being used and Tilly was whispering, it would no doubt be hard to catch whatever the woman was saying. However, Egan was sure that enough people would have heard even without voice amplification and that within seconds—if it hadn't happened already—news of this would be all over town.

"How did you know about me?" Melinda asked, moving up from the back of the crowd. The question and the movement yanked Tilly's stony glare from Alana and Egan to her.

Tilly dismissed her as if swatting a fly. "Your mother." Her voice was flat now, and even though she wasn't tall enough to actually look down her nose at Melinda, she was obviously trying to do that. "She contacted me about a year ago and tried to tell me a bunch of lies."

Egan had thought the day had already met its quota of bombshells. Apparently not, though.

"My mother?" Melinda questioned. "She told you about me? About Easton?"

"She told me lies," Tilly snarled in a low growling whisper. "Jack might have bedded you out of grief, but that's it. Nothing more happened."

"Sweet merciful heaven," Alana grumbled, and she managed to make it sound like the rawest of profanities.

Alana yanked out her phone from her pocket, and Egan realized she was pulling up a photo. Of a kid. But not just any ordinary kid, he soon noticed when he looked at that little face. That little smile. Those little eyes. Obviously, Jack's DNA had won out big-time in the boy's creation because he was the spitting image of Jack.

"Deny this," Alana snapped, taking on some of Tilly's outrage. "I dare you to deny this."

Everything went silent. Egan wasn't even sure anyone was still breathing. And the only sound that came was a small whimpering gasp from Tilly's throat.

At that moment, the skies opened up, and the storm came with a vengeance.

CHAPTER TWENTY-FIVE

ALANA SAT IN her car and stared down at her lap full of lazy daisies. All waiting to be plucked so they could reveal answers.

But Alana wasn't plucking because she was reasonably sure that any question she could ask would have answers she didn't want. Questions like should she try to call—and she could fill in the blank here—Tilly, Melinda… Egan?

If the daisies said yes, then what good would it do? Tilly probably wouldn't speak to her, and Alana considered that a good thing since she didn't especially want to speak to her, either. Other than to make sure Jack's mother hadn't harmed herself. But Tilly had friends to verify that. Friends to hold her and help her get through this.

And Melinda? Well, if the petals urged Alana to call her, what else was there to say that wouldn't involve conversation about Jack and the woman having had sex? Alana could possibly tell Melinda that Easton was a beautiful child, but Melinda already knew that.

That left Egan. Except in his case, she couldn't ask the all-knowing flower petals if she should call him but rather if she should return his call and "just checking on you" texts.

All six of them.

The call and texts had come over the past twenty-four hours since the melee at the life celebration. He was worried about her, no doubts about that, and she had sent him a short reply to let him know she was okay-ish. But she didn't need a lazy daisy to tell her that both of them needed some time to try to sort through the aftermath of what'd happened.

After the sorting, well… Alana had no idea what would happen, and it was too complex a question to even start with the opinion of wildflowers. Still, she didn't want to let go of the flowers just yet in case she changed her mind. That's why she gathered them back into a bunch when she stepped from her car.

She glanced around to make sure she had the place to herself. She did. There were no other vehicles around, and the volume of mud should keep people away for at least another day or two.

The storm had hit fast and had lasted for hours, and it'd left its mark on the grounds of the park. The cleaning crew obviously hadn't had a chance to come in yet because there were hastily dropped life celebration flyers smushed into the ground, and the rain had turned them into paper-mâché stepping stones. She caught glimpses of still-visible words.

Hero.

Jack.

Life.

A few of the flyers had landed just right for her

to see the photo of Jack's smiling face that had been on the back of the flyer.

The podium was still there, too. More or less. The fabric skirting and awning were gone, probably whipped away by the wind. The food and the paintings were gone, too, but she guessed that Tilly had maybe salvaged the one of Jack in the hero mode. The other might be buried under the mud. But Alana immediately had to rethink that theory when she saw it.

And when she saw the woman.

Tilly was standing beneath the big oak, the mud caking her shoes and even part of her ankles, and she was holding the painting. She looked up, spearing Alana with her gaze. Alana speared her right back, letting her know she wasn't going to take any more of her crap.

Then, both of them sighed.

Apparently, crap-taking was over for both of them, and this seemed to be some kind of truce.

"I saved the other painting," Tilly said. "I told Anton to leave this one here. I thought the storm would destroy it."

Tilly turned the painting so that Alana could see that there hadn't been much destruction at all. There were a few mud splatters on it, but Anton must have coated the canvas with some sort of sealant because there was Jack and Egan.

Double heroes.

Of course, Jack had tarnished his heroic halo somewhat by landing in bed with Melinda. But Egan probably felt the same about the bed landings with her.

"It's a beautiful painting," Alana said, figuring that could cause Tilly to launch into a tirade.

It didn't.

"Yes," the woman murmured. She lifted her eyes from the canvas and looked at Alana. "Melinda offered to let me meet Easton. I'm going to do that. I just thought you should know because people will be talking about it."

Alana shrugged. "They already have so much to talk about that anything additional will have to be worked into the current chatter. You could probably have sex on Main Street with the mayor and only garner a tiny mention."

Tilly didn't smile, and Alana had no idea why she'd attempted any lightheartedness. Not when she had so many more important things to say.

"You should see Jack's son," Alana spelled out. "You should work hard to build a relationship with Melinda. And you should stop thinking of me as Jack's wife. Because I have. I've let go, Tilly."

Alana heard the words and was surprised, and pleased, to know they were true. She didn't need the lazy daisies to tell her that.

"Jack loved you," Tilly said like some kind of accusation.

"Yes, I loved him, and he would have loved his son. I think Jack would want you to tell Easton all about his hero dad. Instead of a life celebration, share the memories of Jack's life with his son."

Tilly didn't say anything for a long time, and then she nodded. She opened her mouth as if she might dole out an apology or something, but then she seemed to change her mind.

"I spoke the truth when I said you'd have regrets about being with Egan," Tilly muttered instead.

With that parting jab, she walked away with the painting, trudging through the mud toward a walking trail that would no doubt take her home.

Alana selected one of the daisies. "Should I go after her and tell her to go to hell in a handbasket?" She plucked and went in a different direction for the next question. "Or should I go see Egan?" She plucked a petal and then heard the footsteps.

Before Alana even turned, she knew it was Egan.

And it was.

Egan, the cowboy, wearing his jeans, boots and Stetson, and once again she wondered if she could offer him up to photographers to do "hot cowboy" calendars. He looked like the perfect Mr. July to her.

"Well?" he asked, tipping his head to the flower. "Did it give you an answer?"

"Not yet. I was going to amend my question to should I go see Egan and verify that Tilly is right about the regrets?"

The corner of his mouth lifted into a smile that could have single-handedly coaxed women into his bed. He went to her, doling out more of that incredibly sexy stuff, and he tore off the rest of the petals in one yank.

"Yes," he verified. "You should see me."

That was the equivalent of a blessing and curse.

So was the kiss he brushed on her mouth. He wanted to see her, but he'd just verified the regrets.

Which, in turn, verified the guilt.

He pulled back from the too-short kiss that still managed to rob her of her breath, and he snapped his fingers. She immediately got the image of Tilly doing the same thing when she used the gesture to let Egan and her know they wouldn't be a "they" for very long at all.

"Tilly was wrong," he insisted. "About so many things. Including this." He snapped his fingers again.

Now, he kissed her. A full-blown Egan kiss that had her melting. Oh, yes. It wasn't a snap. Alana was sure this heat could carry through until old age.

Again, though, a "blessing and a curse" kind of thought.

Because Egan wasn't offering her old age. Heck, he wasn't offering anything but this kiss. And that was on her. She was the one who'd asked for a fling.

Even though the kiss melted her some more, the regret thoughts were still there when he eased back and looked into her eyes. "No," he said out of the blue, causing her to frown.

"No?" she questioned.

"We aren't doing what Melinda and Jack did," Egan stated. "We aren't drowning our grief or sorrow. Maybe it started out that way, but it sure as hell isn't about that now."

Ah, in the blessing-curse battle, the blessing had won this one. Alana smiled. "Really?" she asked, and she gave herself another melting by kissing him. Oh, mercy. It was good to give and get like this.

"Then, what is it?" she risked asking.

He got that sex-warrior smile. "It's love. I'm in love with you, Alana."

Alana smiled, too, though hers had a sighing kind of "I'm drowning in this guy" dreamy edge to it.

"Yes," she answered, expressing that sigh. "Look, even the lazy daisies agree," she said, plucking not just a single petal but an entire handful of them. "See? That proves my point."

Egan lifted an eyebrow in a teasing gesture. "I didn't hear you ask the flowers any question."

"Oh, I asked several. All silent ones." Alana kissed him. "I asked them if this Top Gun cowboy in front of me is the hottest guy around? Yes," she immediately provided. "By the way, that was the unanimous agreement from not only me but every single one of the petals."

"Tell the petals, and yourself, thank you, that I'm flattered," he said notching up the "sexy warrior" look and smile.

She kissed him again and continued with the second question she'd silently asked. "Is it love? Another yes. Not a single no in the bunch. Because these clearly aren't stupid flowers."

Alana kissed him again, and she made this count. It would definitely qualify as a couple of steps past foreplay, and she smiled at that rush. That tingle. Mercy, the man could make her feel so many wonderful things.

"The final question I asked—am I in love with Egan, the real deal kind of love?" Alana continued. "But I didn't need lazy daisy petals to confirm my answer to that. I'm absolutely sure of what I feel for you. It's love," she spelled out. "Messy, wonderful, complicated, perfect love. And it's all for you, Lieutenant Colonel Egan Donnelly."

Alana tossed the flower in the air, the petals raining down on them as she kissed the man she loved. And the Top Gun cowboy who loved her kissed her right back.

* * * * *

Look for the next book in USA TODAY
bestselling author Delores Fossen's
Cowboy Brothers in Arms miniseries
when Always a Maverick *goes on*
sale in April 2024, only from
Canary Street Press!

Do you love romance books?

JOIN

on Facebook by scanning the code below:

A group dedicated to book recommendations, author exclusives, SWOONING and all things romance! A community made for romance readers by romance readers.

Facebook.com/groups/readloverepeat

Get 3 FREE REWARDS!

We'll send you 2 FREE Books plus a FREE Mystery Gift.

FREE Value Over $20

Both the **Romance** and **Suspense** collections feature compelling novels written by many of today's bestselling authors.

YES! Please send me 2 FREE novels from the Essential Romance or Essential Suspense Collection and my FREE gift (gift is worth about $10 retail). After receiving them, if I don't wish to receive any more books, I can return the shipping statement marked "cancel." If I don't cancel, I will receive 4 brand-new novels every month and be billed just $7.49 each in the U.S. or $7.74 each in Canada. That's a savings of at least 17% off the cover price. It's quite a bargain! Shipping and handling is just 50¢ per book in the U.S. and $1.25 per book in Canada.* I understand that accepting the 2 free books and gift places me under no obligation to buy anything. I can always return a shipment and cancel at any time by calling the number below. The free books and gift are mine to keep no matter what I decide.

Choose one:
- ☐ **Essential Romance** (194/394 BPA GRNM)
- ☐ **Essential Suspense** (191/391 BPA GRNM)
- ☐ **Or Try Both!** (194/394 & 191/391 BPA GRQZ)

Name (please print)

Address | Apt. #

City | State/Province | Zip/Postal Code

Email: Please check this box ☐ if you would like to receive newsletters and promotional emails from Harlequin Enterprises ULC and its affiliates. You can unsubscribe anytime.

Mail to the **Harlequin Reader Service:**
IN U.S.A.: P.O. Box 1341, Buffalo, NY 14240-8531
IN CANADA: P.O. Box 603, Fort Erie, Ontario L2A 5X3

Want to try 2 free books from another series! Call 1-800-873-8635 or visit www.ReaderService.com.

*Terms and prices subject to change without notice. Prices do not include sales taxes, which will be charged (if applicable) based on your state or country of residence. Canadian residents will be charged applicable taxes. Offer not valid in Quebec. This offer is limited to one order per household. Books received may not be as shown. Not valid for current subscribers to the Essential Romance or Essential Suspense Collection. All orders subject to approval. Credit or debit balances in a customer's account(s) may be offset by any other outstanding balance owed by or to the customer. Please allow 4 to 6 weeks for delivery. Offer available while quantities last.

Your Privacy—Your information is being collected by Harlequin Enterprises ULC, operating as Harlequin Reader Service. For a complete summary of the information we collect, how we use this information and to whom it is disclosed, please visit our privacy notice located at corporate.harlequin.com/privacy-notice. From time to time we may also exchange your personal information with reputable third parties. If you wish to opt out of this sharing of your personal information, please visit readerservice.com/consumerschoice or call 1-800-873-8635. **Notice to California Residents**—Under California law, you have specific rights to control and access your data. For more information on these rights and how to exercise them, visit corporate.harlequin.com/california-privacy.

STRS23